PROJECTION

"PROJECTION is a crime novel like no other. It's a week in the loony bin; it's a psycho tour de force. Keith Ablow has the expertise and an overachiever's grasp."
—James Ellroy, author of *L. A. Confidential*

"Ablow has become king of the psychological thriller."
—Dennis Lehane, author of *Prayers for Rain*

"This realistic and suspenseful story should please laymen and experts alike." —*Booklist*

"*Projection* . . . isn't for the squeamish . . . Readers of Thomas Harris's gruesome Hannibal Lecter tales . . . would do well to look here." —*Boulder Camera*

"*Projection* is first-rate fiction: smart, tough, and moving."
—Robert B. Parker, author of *Hush Money*

"A trip into the catacombs of the mind . . . Ablow, a forensic psychiatrist, understands the darkest recesses of the human mind." —*Cleveland Plain Dealer*

"A tale lavishly laced with sex and violence."
—*Publishers Weekly*

More . . .

DENIAL

"[DENIAL] could only have been written by a psychiatrist or a psychiatric patient. Keith Ablow is a very fine writer. DENIAL is a stark and terrifying journey into the mind of the criminally insane. An absolutely spellbinding and shocking tale." —Nelson DeMille

"Gripping . . . The forensic details are convincing, and the writing is sharp, making Clevenger's return trip from hell an undeniably uplifting story." —*People* magazine

"Deftly, with driving prose, Ablow portrays the horror and bleakness of damaged lives." —Jonathan Kellerman, bestselling author of *The Clinic*

"Sex, murder, madness, and medicine. What more could any thriller reader want? A disturbing, riveting read, DENIAL is written with insights only a forensic psychiatrist could have, with characters vividly human because they're humanly flawed. Keith Ablow has written the prescription for terror. Readers should fill it only if they are caught up on their sleep." —Michael Palmer, author of *Critical Judgment*

"DENIAL places the reader on the cutting edge of psychiatric thrillers, and in the hands of an author whose expertise as a psychiatrist make this story as authentic as it is compelling. Here is the major start of a career, the future of suspense fiction." —Bestselling true crime writer Jack Olsen

"Wonderful inside detail . . . The psychological thriller has gotten some professional help, and it works." —*Newsday*

"DENIAL, which is a perfect title, is not easy to read, but it is harder to put down. The characters are compelling for all their flaws, the story is tightly told, and the outcome is anything but predictable." —*Cleveland Plain Dealer*

"A first-rate debut thriller involving forensic psychology . . . distinctly unusual hero . . . A novel for the self-destructive in all of us." —*Kirkus Reviews* (starred)

"A convincing, seductively fascinating portrait of a man and a milieu obsessed with sensation and trapped in denial of that obsession." —*Publishers Weekly*

"Every once in a while, a mystery comes along that, while compelling, exciting and satisfying, is more like great literature, than junk food to be gobbled down and immediately forgotten. DENIAL is such a read, a superb, even sublime, novel." —John L. Schwartz, M.D., *Psychiatric Times*

"A powerful first novel by a forensic psychiatrist who plumbs the depths of misery and degradation even better than Patricia Cornwell and as good as Jonathan Kellerman." —*The Register Herald* (Beckley, WV)

"Ablow weaves an intriguing story . . . Only someone with this background could create such real characters in a compelling debut." —*Southbridge* (MA) *Evening News*

Projection

A NOVEL OF TERROR AND REDEMPTION

KEITH ABLOW

St. Martin's Paperbacks

Published by arrangement with Pantheon Books

PROJECTION

Copyright © 1999 by Keith Ablow.

ISBN: 0-312-97574-0

Printed in the United States of America

Pantheon hardcover edition / September 1999
St. Martin's Paperbacks edition / November 2000

St. Martin's Paperbacks are published by St. Martin's Press, 175 Fifth Avenue, New York, N.Y. 10010.

10 9 8 7 6 5 4 3 2

In memory of
Gary Provost and Dr. James Mann,
sculptors of character and plot, in fiction and in life

ACKNOWLEDGMENTS

Pat Hass, Dan Frank, and Sonny Mehta invested my manuscript and my method with their extraordinary talents. I will be eternally grateful.

My deepest thanks also to Beth Vesel, my agent at Sanford Greenburger Associates, who continues to guide my career with firm hand and warm heart.

Finally, I thank my wife Deborah for the miracle of our daughter Devin Blake, born as this story took shape.

One

I watched Josiah King pace in front of the witness stand. His stout, six-foot-two frame, outfitted in a plumcolored, double-breasted suit, dominated the scene. "Dr. Elmonte," he started, "can you give an opinion, with a reasonable degree of medical certainty, whether Dr. Lucas knew right from wrong at the time he took the lives of Sarah Johnston and Monique Peletier?"

Elmonte, a slender and pretty blonde who was a full professor of psychiatry at Yale Medical School, stared at Lucas and nodded once. "I can."

Lucas pulled at his salt-and-pepper hair and whistled from the defense table as though he was heckling a schoolgirl. Three television cameras—two from local networks and one from COURT TV—swung in his direction.

"Dr. Lucas," Judge Barton scolded.

Lucas shoved his heavily casted right arm off the table and slumped forward to lay his head down. He was wearing the scrubs he'd been given at Lynn State Hospital, where, for the past five months, he had been locked up on a unit for dangerous patients. Defendants accused of capital crimes are usually held at the Massachusetts Correctional Institute in Concord, but Lucas had unraveled there, ranting around the clock about the devil. Early one morning he had braced his right arm between the bars of his cell and snapped his radius, ulna and humerus. That was enough to make the transfer to a psychiatric ward happen.

King had been watching Lucas, but now looked back at Elmonte. "I'm sorry. Your opinion, doctor?"

Elmonte turned to the jury. Her blue blazer and gold monogram lapel pin complemented her authoritative tone. I could see why King had chosen her as an expert witness for the defense. "Dr. Lucas lacked the capacity to distinguish right from wrong at the time of Ms. Johnston's and Ms. Peletier's deaths," she said.

King nodded and glanced at Lucas. "Did Dr. Lucas, therefore, lack the ability to conform his behavior to the requirements of the law?"

"He lacked that ability. He could not control himself."

"You would conclude, then, doctor, that Trevor Lucas should not be held legally responsible for the violent acts he committed on the days in question."

Red Donovan, the new district attorney, shot to his feet. "Objection." Mid-forties, with an athlete's build and waves of rust-colored hair, he reminded me of a human torch. The Lucas case was his most publicized trial since taking office just eight months before. "Dr. Elmonte was qualified before the court as a psychiatric expert, not a legal scholar."

"Sustained," Barton said. He looked down at Elmonte. "The jury will decide questions of legal responsibility. Please confine your comments to the patient's state of mind."

"Of course," she said, a touch of arrogance in her tone.

King was still pacing. "You would conclude, Dr. Elmonte, that the accused was insane at the time he killed Ms. Johnston and Ms. Peletier."

"I believe he was insane."

Lucas stood up for the fifth time. "Objection," he barked, staring down at his casted arm. "*I* didn't kill anyone."

"Dr. Lucas," Barton fumed, "sit down and be quiet." His bald head, large even for his massive shoulders, reddened. He waited a few moments after Lucas took his seat, then turned to Josiah King. "Defense counsel has submitted a motion indicating that the defendant's impaired state of mind at the time of the crimes in question shall serve as the mainstay of his defense. Is that still your contention?"

"It is, Your Honor," King said.

"Then I would advise you—and your client— that further outbursts will not be tolerated."

"Understood, Your Honor," King said. He walked

to the defense table and stood by Lucas. "May I continue?"

"Of course."

King took a few moments to refocus. "Dr. Elmonte, would you tell the jury what you have learned about Dr. Lucas that supports your conclusion that he was insane at the time of the two homicides?"

Elmonte turned to the jury again. "Dr. Lucas suffers from bipolar disorder," she said. "Even while functioning brilliantly as a plastic surgeon, he has, at least for the past decade, been subject to severe mood swings. At one moment he is somber, at another elated, without any stimulus intervening. His appetites—for sex, sleep, food—wax and wane unpredictably. He may be voracious today and completely disinterested tomorrow. Most importantly, his thinking often includes paranoid delusions."

I looked over at Emma Hancock, Lynn's Police Commissioner. Monique Peletier, the second victim, had been her niece. She looked back at me and shook her head in disgust. Her lips silently mouthed, "Bullshit."

"Might the symptoms you speak of explain Dr. Lucas' violent acts?" King asked.

"They would. In the weeks prior to the murders, Dr. Lucas developed the fixed and false paranoid belief—the delusion—that he was an agent of

Satan, a pawn in a final struggle between forces of good and evil. As he put it, he was the devil's 'right-hand man.' "

I heard sobbing from the front of the room and noticed Karl Johnston, Sarah's father, bent over in his seat at the end of the second bench, his head in his hands.

"The devil's right-hand man." King looked over at Johnston, pursed his lips and closed his eyes in the necessary display of empathy. His fingers massaged his overgrown eyebrows. "This is very difficult for everyone involved, Dr. Elmonte," he went on, "but I need to ask whether Dr. Lucas' psychiatric symptoms might explain why the victims were disfigured in the way they were."

She nodded. "In the days prior to Ms. Johnston's and Ms. Peletier's deaths, Dr. Lucas had come to believe that his right arm was no longer his own. It was Satan's. The doctor was horrified as he removed the breasts of each woman, even more so as he lacerated the genital area of Ms. Peletier, but he had no control over what his arm did."

"Is there a scientific name for this phenomenon?" King asked.

"*Alien hand.* The condition is well known in the literature. Oliver Sacks even writes of it."

I smiled, in spite of my raw nerves. Before closing my psychotherapy practice and becoming a forensic psychiatrist myself, I had treated more than a thousand patients and had never seen a single case of *alien hand* syndrome. Neither had any psychiatrist I knew.

"We notice that the arm is casted today," King continued. "Could you tell us why?"

"Dr. Lucas fractured the arm in three places using the bars of his cell for leverage. He wanted to be rid of it. Its actions—the arm's—were abhorrent to him."

Donovan popped up, again. "Objection. The doctor qualified before the court as a psychiatrist, not a mind-reader. She can't speak for the—"

"Dr. Lucas hates what the arm did," Elmonte interrupted. "That's why he tried to break it off."

I left for the lobby before King had finished his questioning. The judge had announced there would be a short recess before Red Donovan's cross-examination of Elmonte, but I couldn't sit in the courtroom any longer.

My head was tight with anxiety. A cigarette would have calmed me down, but I didn't feel like freezing in the winter air. I thought of sneaking one in the men's room, but that reminded me too much of the days when I would have rushed into the stalls for a blast of cocaine. And I didn't have enough sober time behind me to risk rekindling old habits. So I just stood there, watching the sculpted metal doors of the courtroom.

Nicotine wouldn't erase the truth anyhow. And

the truth was the thing eating at me: Lucas had pled NGI—not guilty by reason of insanity—but he hadn't actually murdered anyone. Four mutilated bodies had been found in and around the urban squalor of Lynn, not two, and the last victims had been killed after Lucas had turned himself over to the police.

The prevailing theory was that Lucas' crimes had spawned a "copycat" killer. I knew better. One person had claimed all four victims.

Josiah King had to have considered making that argument the focus of Lucas' defense, but it would have been tough to sell to a jury. There were disparities between the first two killings and the last two. Sarah Johnston and Monique Peletier had been Lucas' patients and his lovers. The breast implants he had placed in each woman had been cut out of them. Their genitals had been shaved clean or mangled.

The victims found after Lucas had surrendered were also cut up, but their bodies were discovered in neighboring cities, not Lynn itself. The third victim, Michael Wembley, had been male. The fourth, Rachel Lloyd, had been set afire after her death. And neither Wembley nor Lloyd had been linked romantically to Lucas.

Those differences would go most of the way to supporting the "copycat" theory and pinning the first two killings on Lucas, especially since a jury might relish sending a rich doctor away for life.

No wonder a not guilty by reason of insanity verdict seemed like a deal to him. Five, ten years on a locked psychiatric unit beats life in prison hands down.

The only way Lucas would go free would be if I told what I knew about the four murders. And I couldn't.

Thinking about that started my heart pounding. I stepped into an alcove off the lobby, took a cigarette from my shirt pocket, lighted it and inhaled a third of its length. I turned and blew the smoke in back of me, took another long drag, then ground the butt out with the heel of my boot.

I wondered whether Lucas was fabricating all of his symptoms or whether the stress of his impending trial had actually touched off a break with reality. I had known for a long time that his character was warped, but what he had done to his arm seemed the act of a truly insane man, not simply a sociopath.

The doors to the courtroom opened. King, Donovan and a flood of reporters and spectators poured out. I spotted Emma Hancock right away. She was fifty-five years old, with graying hair, but her powerful build still demanded space in a crowd. I walked over to her. Without a word, we picked up our pace and started toward the concession stand one floor down.

Calvin Sanger, a reporter from the *Lynn Item*,

appeared by Hancock's side and started matching our stride. He was a black man in his early thirties who was persistent and insightful—a good combination for a reporter and a nightmare for the police. He himself had made news every year for the past five, finishing the Boston Marathon near the front of the pack. He raised his pad and pen and started to ask a question.

"No comment," Hancock said.

Sanger slowed his pace, drifted in back of us and reappeared next to me. "He has no comment, either," Hancock bristled.

"Do you agree with Dr. Elmonte's diagnosis?" Sanger persisted.

Hancock stepped in front of us and blocked the way. She glared at Sanger. "Don't make me say it again, Calvin. I've always kept you in the loop, when I could. Right?"

"Right, but . . ."

"But nothing. Don't blow it."

"Give me a break. You haven't said a word about Lucas since he was arrested."

Hancock started to walk away. I jogged a few steps to catch up with her.

"Any progress toward finding the second killer, Commissioner?" Sanger called after us.

My pulse quickened. I glanced at Hancock. "He can go straight to hell," she said.

I bought our coffee at the concession stand. We

sat down on a wooden bench carved with obscenities. The jingle I had learned growing up on Lynn's decrepit streets, empty veins of a city that died with America's industry after World War II, was etched in ball pen next to my thigh.

*Lynn, Lynn, City of Sin, Never Come
Out the Way You Went In.*

"Elmonte's a piece of work," she said. "You can pay a psychiatrist to say anything. Present company, of course, excepted."

"Thanks."

"I didn't mean it as a compliment," she smirked. "I thought you might learn something from her."

Hancock had hired me as a forensic psychiatrist for the Lynn Police Department dozens of times, including the case that ended with Trevor Lucas' arrest. When she had run for mayor of Lynn, I figured I was about to lose my meal ticket, but she'd lost that election, then been promoted from captain to Commissioner. "I thought you valued my independent thinking," I said.

"I'm already paying you two hundred fifty an hour. If I value your independence any more, the department's gonna go broke."

I ran my fingertip back and forth over the word *sin*. "What do you think the jury will do?" I asked.

"Convict. Two counts, murder one."

"If he's found NGI he still goes away a long time."

"Time isn't the point."

"What's the point, then?" I took a gulp of coffee.

"Like the Bible says, 'An eye for an eye.' " Hancock often quoted Scripture. Unmarried and childless, she had focused her love on work and church. She crossed and uncrossed her legs, obviously uncomfortable in the gray flannel skirt she was wearing. Street clothes went with the Commissioner's job, but they didn't go with Hancock's demeanor. "Glad to see you dressed for court. With that ponytail of yours you could do some fine undercover work—as a dealer."

I was wearing jeans, a black turtleneck and black cowboy boots, pretty much what I always wore. "The jeans are only a couple of years old," I joked.

Hancock was looking away and shaking her head.

"It's not like I'm on the stand today." I saw the muscles in her jaw working against each other and realized she was listening to her own thoughts, not me. She started clicking the long, red nails of her thumb and forefinger together. That was a bad sign. "Emma," I said. "You there?"

"I want Lucas in prison, not some cushy hospital."

"What difference does it make, so long as he's off the street?"

She turned and squinted at me. " 'What *difference* does it make?' Obviously, you haven't spent much time in places like Concord."

"I've evaluated prisoners there."

"Sure, in some interview room, with waxed floors and a Mr. Coffee outside the door. I mean the bowels of the place—the filthy, rodent-infested, eight-by-eight cages where they warehouse monsters like Lucas."

"No. I haven't seen those."

"It's hell on earth," she said, toying with the gold cross around her neck. "Terrible things are allowed to go on. Beatings. Rapes. Stabbings."

"Torture."

"Punishment. I want him to suffer for what he did to Monique."

I didn't want to argue social policy with Hancock where her niece's accused killer was involved, but I'd never had much use for the penal system. "I thought we were supposed to be rehabilitating people." I half-smiled.

"Now there's the bleeding heart shrink I know and love. All excited about reclaiming a soul. You think you could heal Lucas, make him all better?"

I shook my head. I had shut down my psychotherapy practice when an adolescent boy I had been treating committed suicide. I wasn't sure any more how much help I could be to anyone. And Lucas, while no killer, was a very sick character.

One of his passions had been hunting for vulnerable women, usually naked dancers, and bartering cosmetic surgery for sex. They had to pay him back with the sadomasochistic games he liked, whenever he liked. The games could get pretty ugly. "I couldn't heal him," I said, "but maybe somebody. I don't know."

"Well, I *do*. Evil only comprehends raw force." She finished her coffee and tossed the cup in the garbage. "Anyhow, it's too late for Lucas. If he needed help, he should have gone and gotten it before he butchered two good people."

I knew Monique's death had left Hancock in that cold space between grief and rage. "I can't begin to think what it's like for you sitting in that courtroom," I said, hoping she would open up.

She steered clear of the invitation. "King has no chance with the NGI plea," she said, shaking her head. "He would have been better off working the *'They've got the wrong man'* angle. Sanger can be a pain in the ass, but he's sharp. We don't have a single decent lead on the copycat killer, and he knows it. So does that jury, if they read the *Item*. All it takes to gum up the works is one good citizen who's watched too many *Perry Mason* reruns."

My guilty conscience spoke: "You think there's a chance they'll acquit Lucas based on reasonable doubt even without King raising the issue?"

"No way. King would have had to put the single-killer argument front and center, then stand his ground like a great oak. And it still would have been a hundred-to-one shot." She shook her head. "Lucas is going down. Premeditated murder, with extreme atrocity and cruelty. Life in prison, no possibility of parole. I just wish we had the death penalty back on the books. I'd pull the switch myself."

I didn't respond. Half a minute passed in silence.

"You seem a little out of it today," Hancock said. "Any news on Kathy?"

My skin turned to goose flesh. I'd been living with Kathy during the murders. "Still no sign of her. Just the one-way airline reservation to London. She could have gone anywhere from there."

"I don't get that. She just up and left?"

"Once we called it quits, there wasn't a lot to stick around for. She was completely estranged from her family."

"Still, one day she's the star obstetrician at Stonehill Hospital, the next she throws it all away and takes off for another country."

"She was unpredictable."

"So were you, Francis—with your intentions. Not that it's any of my business."

"My intentions?"

"Did you expect her to live in sin forever? She's a Catholic." She paused. "Not to mention your 'extracurricular' activities. You never made a secret of your wandering eye."

I had even less desire to talk sex and religion with Hancock than I did social policy. "Maybe she'll be back someday," I said dismissively.

"Anything's possible," Hancock said. "People will surprise you, usually when you least expect it."

Red Donovan stood at the prosecution table and buried the fingers of one hand in his hair. He blew out a long breath. "Let's see if I followed everything you had to say, doctor," he started. His voice was a street-fighter's rasp. "The defendant believes his right arm has a will of its own. Is that about the long and short of it?"

"Not exactly," Elmonte said flatly.

"No?"

"Dr. Lucas is unshakably convinced the arm is not only beyond his control, but that it does not belong to him. It is Satan's arm."

I heard Hancock clear her throat. She had taken a seat in the middle of the front row, just behind the defense table. I was on the aisle, near the door.

Donovan held up his hands. "My mistake." He walked around to the front of the table. "The defendant believes his right arm is owned and operated by the devil."

"You could put it that way."

"Kind of like a franchise."

A few jurors chuckled.

"Objection," Josiah King said, rising out of his seat.

"Sustained," Barton said. He looked at Donovan. "You are welcome in my courtroom—as an attorney. If you've decided to become a comic, you'll need to find another stage."

Donovan nodded. "Pardon me." He paused. "Are you aware, Dr. Elmonte, of Dr. Lucas' activities on the days that Sarah Johnston and Monique Peletier were murdered?"

"I'm aware of some of his activities."

"Are you aware he performed surgery on three patients on each of those days?"

Elmonte straightened up in her seat. As the fabric of her blouse shifted, I noticed it was unbuttoned lower than courtroom etiquette would dictate, showing the top of her white lace bra. "I was not aware of the number of surgeries, but . . ."

Donovan walked back to the table and picked up a folder. He turned to Elmonte. "In fact," he said, reading from the folder, "he removed a basal cell carcinoma from one patient's nose, performed two blepharoplasties—what are those?"

"Blepharoplasty involves excision of superfluous tissue from the eyelids."

"OK. Two lid jobs." He smiled. "A rhinoplasty. I know that one: it's a nose job. And two liposuctions—that would be sucking fat from thighs and tummies and what have you." He tossed the folder back on the table. "Is Dr. Lucas right-handed or left-handed?"

"He's right-handed."

"And that's the hand owned and operated by Satan."

Another chuckle from a juror.

"Mr. Donovan," Barton deadpanned. "Careful."

Donovan nodded. He was playing with fire, and he knew it. Robert "Buzz" Barton, also known as the "Rock," was one of the smartest and toughest Superior Court judges in the country.

Barton looked down at Elmonte. "Answer the question, doctor," he said.

"The right hand is the one afflicted," Elmonte said.

"Well then, Dr. Elmonte, how do we understand Dr. Lucas performing complicated surgical procedures with that hand on the days in question?"

"The fact that Dr. Lucas suffers with *alien hand* does not necessarily prevent him from performing some behaviors he has mastered. Technical work like surgery can become quite automatic."

"Is it possible Dr. Lucas believed that Satan conducted those surgeries?"

"I would assume that is exactly what he believed."

"You would assume."

"To a reasonable degree of medical certainty," she deadpanned.

"You didn't ask him directly?"

"No."

"Why not?"

"I didn't need to. *Alien hand* is a major mental illness. It doesn't come and go like a headache."

"Why didn't he sign Satan's name to the invoices?"

"Objection!" King shouted.

"In fact, he signed bills under his own name totaling thirty-two thousand dollars for those procedures on those very days," Donovan went on. "With his right hand."

"That's irrelevant," King said. "Dr. Lucas' income and billing practices are not—"

"The objection is . . . ," Barton started.

"Your honor," Donovan argued, "those billings go directly to the defendant's mental state on the days of the murders. He had the self-control to perform delicate surgeries and even the presence of mind to oversee the bookkeeping. But we're being asked to believe his hand was possessed by the devil."

"As I was about to say, Mr. Donovan, the objection is overruled. But I'm warning you: the court does not appreciate your tone."

"Understood. Thank you." Donovan walked toward Elmonte. He stopped about six feet from her. "Isn't it possible, doctor, that the defendant is fabricating his symptoms?"

"There is almost no possibility," Elmonte said.

"Why do you say that?"

"The psychological testing we administered to Dr. Lucas, including both the Minnesota Multiphasic Personality Inventory and the Rorschach, showed him to be minimizing his symptoms. He was trying to appear less sick than he is, not more sick."

"But the defendant is a pretty smart guy, isn't he?"

"Dr. Lucas scores in the extremely gifted range," she said. "Under more ideal testing conditions, he would certainly reach the genius level." She smirked. "He's a 'pretty smart guy.' "

"Truly." Donovan paused. "You admire him."

"Objection," King said.

"Could that affect the test results?" Donovan pressed.

"Sustained," Barton said. He glared at Donovan. "Last chance."

"Wouldn't such a *gifted* man," Donovan continued, "be able to figure out what answers to give on a standardized test, so as to appear one way versus another? Say, ill versus depraved?"

"The tests are very sensitive. They generally detect when someone is lying."

"Generally."

"Almost always."

"Isn't it the case that the tests are less reliable when administered to individuals who are legally sane, but have severe character pathology—psychopaths and sociopaths?"

"It is correct that the tests are somewhat—"

I heard a shriek from the front of the courtroom. I jumped up and saw the stenographer cover her mouth, her eyes wide with terror.

Lucas was clutching Josiah King's gold fountain pen in his fist, high above his head. He drove his fist down to the table.

Several jurors turned away. Others gasped and leaned forward for a better view. An elderly woman in the first row broke down in tears. The television cameras panned the courtroom like hungry aliens, their lenses spinning into focus here, then there, feasting on the turmoil.

King lunged to restrain Lucas, but couldn't stop the pen from rising and falling a second, then a third time. Blood sprayed from the pen as it arced up and down.

"Security!" Barton shouted.

The guard rushed to help. Together they managed to force Lucas into a headlock, with his arms in the air. I saw that the center of his hand was punctured in three places. Blood streamed down his arm.

Barton hammered away with his gavel. "Remove the defendant!" he seethed.

Another guard had rushed in from the lobby. Each of them wrestled control of one of Lucas' arms and one of his legs and started to carry him out.

My eyes met Lucas' as he passed by. "Clevenger!" he screamed. He threw his head back to keep looking at me.

My stomach fell. I felt a wave of nausea coming. I slipped out of the courtroom amid the chaos and climbed into my Ram truck—a silver '89 I'd taken in trade for a '94 Range Rover I'd fallen behind on. I lighted another cigarette and filled my lungs with smoke, holding my breath as long as I could. I did that again, then started the car and headed past the boarded storefronts of Union Street and onto the Lynnway, toward Boston. As the road curved past the Schooner Pub I pictured the bar, stocked with single malt scotches. A few ounces, and I'd be rid of the churning in my gut. I could almost taste the bronze-colored liquid, the aroma blanketing me, the warmth spreading down my throat. I gritted my teeth and accelerated past the place, frightened by how much I wanted to turn in.

TWO

Darkness captures Boston by 5:00 P.M. during winter. I was happy for it. The intensity of the guilt I felt dropped each day with the sun, as if the eye of the universe had closed, and my lie was lost in the blackness blanketing the whole city.

I walked into my Chelsea loft and hit the PLAY-BACK button on my answering machine.

"Eleven new messages," the woman on the computer chip said. "Message one. Received today at 9:40 A.M."

"Dr. Clevenger, this is Dr. Roger Drake at McLean Hospital. I've been seeing a woman in the outpatient department here. She's in her fifties. A very serious major depression that isn't responding to treatment. I've tried her on a number of antidepressants and mood stabilizers. If anything, her condition is worsening. A colleague of mine tells me he referred a complicated patient of his to you for psychotherapy a few years back with rather spectacular results. I heard the same from a friend over at Mass. General. They both say when all else fails, you're the man to call—"

I hit the STOP button. "The man to call," I repeated out loud. Not anymore.

I picked up the receiver and dialed the Executive Sweet escort service. Clamping down on my other addictions had intensified my appetite for sex. I had called Executive about once a week during the three months I'd lived in the apartment, always swearing to myself it would be the last time.

"Yes," a gruff voice said.

"I wondered who might be available tonight."

"Where are you?"

"Chelsea."

"Hotel Stanley?"

"I'm at home."

"Where's that?"

"One Winnisimmet Street. Eighth floor."

"Name?"

"Clevenger."

"Number?"

"884-1804."

"Call you right back."

I knew the guy was dialing directory assistance to make sure I was for real, not just getting my jollies by having him send a girl to some vacant building in my line of sight. The phone rang in thirty seconds. I picked up. "Clevenger," I said.

"You alone, or with friends?" the man asked.

"Alone."

"It's one hundred eighty the hour, cash, two

hundred fifty on a major credit card. I can have a girl there in twenty minutes."

"Who's available?"

"I have a twenty-nine-year-old Japanese. Big chest. I've got a black girl, very young, maybe nineteen."

I'd met both of them. "Who else?"

"If you can wait about an hour I've got a twenty-three-year-old blonde. Not huge upstairs, but very pretty. Built like a greyhound. You know, she could model. That type."

"I'll take the blonde."

The standard disclaimer was next. "You understand this is a nonsexual service."

"Of course."

"She'll be there in one hour."

I hung up. I would have predicted that coming face-to-face with the immorality of hiring troubled women to get me off would make me want to stop. But what actually made me want to stop was the way the girls treated me—with a mechanical politeness that left me feeling the full weight of my solitude. Maybe I had myself to blame for that; I always chose a different girl, lest I become attached to any one of them.

I walked to the wall of floor-to-ceiling windows and looked out at Chelsea's countless rowhouses, triple deckers, factories, the occasional smokestack. My eyes traveled the length of the Tobin Bridge as it arched into Boston, its steel

skeleton still choked with commuters, their head-
lights a centipede against the charcoal sky. Rachel
Lloyd, the fourth and last murder victim, the only
woman I had ever truly loved, had had the same
view out her windows, two buildings away. I
wondered whether the silent procession of lights
was one of the things she had cherished about this
tiny, fierce city.

I knew some of the other reasons she had chosen Chelsea as her home. It was a cheap enough
place to live, but that wasn't part of it; working as
a stripper had given her enough money to hide out
in a quiet suburb had she wanted to. She relished
the nakedness of the place, the fact that Chelsea's
two square miles churned with the unbridled ener-
gies of people on the edge, ravenous people desperate for more than what they had. It is a city in
which English has been a second language since
1848 when the Irish, speaking Gaelic, arrived to
work themselves and drink themselves near death
in factories owned by the Protestant gentry. Russ-
ian Jews escaping anti-Semitism were next,
speaking Yiddish. Italians followed. Then Poles.
Then Puerto Ricans and Vietnamese and Cambo-
dians and El Salvadorans and Guatemalans and so
on and so on and so on, all the way to Serbs fleeing Bosnia. It is a city that has burned nearly to the
ground twice—first in 1908, then in 1973. The
streets are incendiary. The people wear their pain
on their sleeves and in their faces. And Rachel

trusted pain much more than she trusted pleasure. It felt more honest and familiar to her, because she had been in so much pain herself.

I had never bared my soul to a woman before, certainly not to Kathy (who I happened to be living with at the time), but Rachel's suffering and the fact that she was in touch with it had made me feel safe telling her anything. I felt a little better once I moved to Chelsea, close to the memory of her.

It was a full hour before I heard a knock on the iron door. The excitement of a prostitute on my threshold was even less intense than the anticipation of having her there. Regret seized me. I said nothing.

"Hey. Anyone home?" The voice was young. A few moments passed. "Jesus." A heavy sigh. Then, a little louder and a little desperate: "Hello?"

I figured she was probably a single mother with a heroin habit to feed. The fact that she sounded upset being stood up by a john saddened me and made me feel connected to her. I shook my head. "Coming," I said.

"Already?"

The joke instantly dissolved my maiden-in-distress fantasy. But I kept walking toward the door. Because I needed the sex. Like I needed the dark. It could help cover up the anguish I had seen in Trevor Lucas' face as he cried out my name. I reached into my pocket to feel for my roll of twenties, flipped open the latch and slid the door a foot along its track.

She looked her age, which meant she looked half of mine. She was about five feet five, with light brown (not blonde) shoulder-length hair and chestnut eyes—eyes that reminded me of Rachel's. Her white wool coat, soiled along the seams and the collar, was wrapped tightly around her. "I'm Ginger," she smiled. Her teeth were perfect, which surprised me. Every other girl from the service had had something crooked or broken.

"Call me Clove," I said. "Might as well both use aliases."

"We're all set, then?"

The deal with Executive included the right to call everything off before anything started. I stepped aside, and she squeezed past me.

I closed the door, walked to the couch and took the twenties out of my pocket. I counted ten of them into a fan pattern on the seat cushion. Giving her the money wasn't allowed because a cop would use that hand-to-hand exchange as evidence of solicitation. I sat down next to the cash and watched as she took off her coat and started to walk around. She was dressed in blue jeans and a black stretch top that showed off her tight body. I knew I could see it anytime I wanted to, feel it on demand, move inside it at my leisure. My pulse quickened. Control over such intimacies—petty, bought and paid for though they are—is intoxicating to a man who, like me, felt unloved and unsafe as a boy.

"This place is huge," she said. "What was it before?"

"A pasta factory."

"You don't keep much in here."

The couch was the only piece of furniture in the loft other than my bed. "I just moved myself in."

"A lot of guys have big houses in Brookline or Marblehead for the family and then a place where they go for . . . dates."

I had sold my Victorian overlooking Preston beach in Marblehead to pay back taxes and gambling debts and stop pretending to be more substantial than I felt inside. My only family was a mother who had written me off as a hopeless addict. "I don't have any other place," I said.

"Oh." She looked confused.

"What?"

"Are you a struggling actor or a model or something?"

That was the first direct question about my life an escort had asked me. I wasn't ready to be direct myself. "Just struggling," I said.

She walked over to a framed quote I'd hung on the wall. "Beat means rawness of the nerves," she read. "It is a state of mind from which all unessentials have been stripped. To be beat is to be at the bottom of your personality, looking up." She turned to me. "You feel beat?"

"Pretty much."

"It's going around."

"You want to talk about it?"

"No thanks."

"Fair enough. We don't have to talk at all."

My beeper went off. I recognized the number as the *Lynn Daily Evening Item*. There'd been a time I had paid a couple reporters there to page me with breaking news on a serial rape case I was working. But that was over a year ago. I figured Calvin Sanger was at his desk late and had a few more questions for me. "No comment," I muttered.

"Huh?" Ginger said.

"Nothing."

"You have to get that?"

"No."

She shrugged. "I heard about a dancer from the Lynx Club who lived in one of these places."

My throat tightened.

"She got killed."

I didn't want to talk about Rachel, especially her murder. I wanted to be with her, to hold her and touch her hair. "Why don't you come over here?" I said.

"I don't do anything anal," she said in that mechanical tone I hated. "Light spanking is allowed, but nothing that can leave marks. No going down on me. No water sports. And we'll be using my condoms."

"Great." I could be mechanical, too. "Take off your clothes, starting with your top," I told her. "Slowly."

She nodded at the windows behind her. "Wouldn't you rather use the bed?"

"No. I wouldn't."

She tensed up, which told me she wasn't as used to the business as her monologue on ground rules had suggested. That excited me. She laid her coat down, then slowly took off her top and her bra. Her nipples were erect. I felt myself getting hard.

"It's cold in here," she said.

I pointed at her pants.

She looked down and away from herself as she took off her shoes, unbuttoned and unzipped her jeans and stepped out of them. She was wearing white panties.

I stayed silent.

"You don't want to go to the bed?"

"No."

"You're only my fourth customer ever, believe it or not." She bent over slightly as she slid the panties down her legs and off. When she stood up she crossed her forearms and laced her fingers together in front of her groin. She shrugged. "What now?"

Part of me wanted *what now* to be her lying on

her back in front of me, touching herself until she came, then turning around so I could spank her. But I thought I saw her eyes start to fill up. Rachel's eyes. My throat felt even tighter. "Let's get into bed so I can hold you," I managed. "That's it. That's all I want."

I followed her to the bed, an antique four-poster made of mahogany. It was the only piece of furniture from Marblehead I hadn't sold. She lay down on the olive green, velvet comforter, watching me with wide eyes as I sat on the edge of the mattress, facing her. I ran my fingers lightly down her cheek, along her neck, between her breasts and over the firm rises and falls of her abdomen. Waves of nearly invisible, soft hairs stood on end, then faded back into place. She closed her eyes as my fingers kissed the warm, wet skin between her legs and glided down her thigh to her knee. Then she hooked one finger inside the waist of my jeans, which was enough to make me sigh. I lay on my back next to her. Without a word, she rolled flush to me and rested her head on my chest. And then I closed my eyes.

The phone woke me. I glanced at my watch and saw we had slept through more than half the hour I had paid for. I eased away from Ginger and grabbed the cordless off the floor. "Clove," I said.

Ginger laughed.

"*Who?* I'm calling for Frank Clevenger," Emma Hancock half-shouted.

Sirens blared in the background. I propped myself on one arm. "It's me, Emma."

"Sorry. I didn't hear you right. I need you to meet me at Lynn State Hospital," she said. "Right away."

"What happened?"

"Lucas went berserk. He's taken hostages."

I had to concentrate to breathe. "Hostages? How the hell . . . ?"

More sirens. "I'll fill you in when you get here." She hung up.

I jumped up and started to pull on my boots. "I've got to go," I said.

Ginger reached for the blanket at the foot of the bed and drew it over herself. She sat against the headboard. "What was that about hostages?"

I grabbed my coat off the couch.

"Are you a cop?" she asked.

"No." I wanted to leave it at that, but she hadn't moved to get dressed. I picked her jeans and panties off the floor. "I'm a psychiatrist," I said. "I work with the police."

"A psychiatrist?"

I brought her clothes to the bed and held them out. "I have to get going." Even with my mind rushing through images of Lucas barricaded on the locked unit, I noticed how soft her panties felt in my hand.

She took the clothes from me. "Can I wait here for you?"

"Probably not a good idea."

She stood up, still wrapped in the blanket. "Probably not. I don't think I've had a good idea yet."

I started toward the door, but turned around. I cannot keep my distance from troubled people. "Don't you have other appointments?" I asked.

"Look, it was a stupid thing for me to ask. If you want to find me again, I'm staying at the Lynn Y. My name's Cynthia. Cynthia Baxter."

"Frank Clevenger." I had a dozen more questions, but no time to ask them and nothing much in the apartment worth stealing. I looked into her eyes, searching for danger. I didn't sense any—not that I had been even a fair judge of danger in the past. And I couldn't know what my miscalculation would cost me this time. "Stay, if you want," I told her. "Sounds like we're both due for a good idea."

I sped down Route 16 to the Lynnway, took a right on to Union Street and followed it through the decay of Lynn until it dead-ended into Jessup Road, almost at the Saugus line. Halfway to the state hospital, I stopped at a roadblock of wooden horses. A state trooper in black leather boots laced to the knee was standing in front of them. Three TV vans and a few other cars were lined up on the side of the road. I noticed Calvin Sanger from the

Item talking with Josh Resnek, an investigative reporter for the *Boston Globe*. Sanger noticed me, too, and nodded.

The trooper lumbered to my window and passed the beam of his flashlight over my face. "Only official vehicles past this point," he said. "Trouble at the hospital."

"I heard. That's where I'm headed." I pointed at my Forensic Examiner's badge on the dash.

He aimed the light at it and squinted doubtfully. "I don't think they're looking for more local people," he said. "We've got experts from the state up there."

I glanced at my watch. 8:50 P.M. "Stop busting my balls," I said.

"Huh?" He planted his hands on his hips.

"I said, 'Stop busting my balls.' I've got to meet Emma Hancock, and you're wasting my fucking time."

"Get out of the car."

The thought of Lucas killing somebody at the hospital when I was the one responsible for him being locked up there overshadowed everything else. "You want me out, drag me out. My friends over there in the press will eat it up. You'll be patrolling skating rinks and public bathrooms. Tomorrow."

He didn't flinch. His hand moved to his baton.

"Look," I said, trying another tack, "Hancock

told me to get my ass up there. If I'm late, she'll come down on me like a ton of bricks."

"Cunt."

H' venom took me by surprise. I knew I should try to keep pace with it, but didn't have any hatred toward Hancock to draw on. "Give a woman a little power," I managed, "and she thinks she's actually supposed to use it."

"Somebody ought to give that bitch what she really needs." He patted the handle of his baton.

I reached back to my college football locker room days. "The high hard one."

He slammed his fist into his palm three times. "Right up the ass." He walked to the horses and dragged them out of the way. As I accelerated past him, he gave me a thumbs-up sign.

A convoy of ambulances and fire trucks lined the last fifty yards leading to the hospital. A dozen cruisers, lights flashing, were parked haphazardly on the green out front. Two SWAT vans were nose-to-nose in the semicircular driveway. A huge spotlight illuminated the facade of the building, its seven stories of brick a monolith against the darkness.

I spotted Emma Hancock's red Jeep Cherokee in the center of the chaos. She was standing beside the car, talking with a willowy man in a trench coat. I parked and started toward them.

Hancock saw me, waved and walked to meet me on the green.

"What the hell is going on here?" I asked her. "It's like World War—"

She held up a hand. "I'll bring you up to speed." She let out a long breath. "Lucas took control of Ward Five. We don't know how, but he got hold of a knife. A couple of other maniacs up there have knives, too."

"Did somebody hit a panic button? How did you find out?"

"Lucas sent one of the orderlies down to the station with an ultimatum."

"What did he say he wants?"

"Cardinal Bernard Law, for starters. He wants a private consultation with him."

"Is Law in town?"

"Who knows? We're certainly not getting the Boston diocese mixed up in this."

"What else does he want?"

"A helicopter."

"What did he say would happen if his demands aren't met?"

"He didn't. We've evacuated the rest of the building, but there are three nurses, two social workers and a dietitian up there on the unit." She shook her head. "One of the nurses is pregnant."

"Jesus."

"The orderly said there was also a visitor."

"Any idea who?"

"The description fits Elmonte, and nobody's

been able to locate her. That makes seven people at risk up there." She paused. "Actually, eight. The unborn child."

"Not to mention the patients."

"Yeah, right, the 'patients.' Like Gary Kaminsky, the lowlife who kidnapped and raped that little girl on Elm Street, then claimed voices made him do it. And he's not the worst of them, Frank. Peter Zweig is up there."

Zweig was a nineteen-year-old black man who had killed his mother and father, then brought their remains to a local church to offer them as sacrifices. "He's very sick," I said.

"My heart bleeds for him," she scoffed. "He's as guilty of multiple homicide as Lucas."

I shuddered at that truth. "You could be right."

"I know I'm right. If it weren't for the staff and Elmonte, I'd seal off the building and come back next spring for proper burials."

"That's very Christian of you."

"It's a lot more Christian than letting demons walk the earth."

The man in the trench coat walked up to us. He wore a black goatee and was carrying a bullhorn. He looked about forty-five years old. "Dr. Lawrence Winston," he said, staring into my eyes.

We shook hands. "Frank Clevenger."

"Dr. Winston is a psychologist working with the State Police," Hancock said. She glanced at me and rolled her eyes. "We have additional resources because the hospital is a state facility."

"Glad for the help," I told him.

"The majority of my time is spent teaching at Harvard," Winston offered. "But fieldwork is still fascinating to me. I understand you work in the community full-time."

I glanced at his tie—shiny red silk with embroidered Harvard crests. "That's right." I winked. "I'm a full-time field hand."

"I always tell my students how important it is to have the perspective of a local psychologist."

I heard *local* loud and clear. "Psychiatrist," I countered. "I went the medical school route." I paused. "Do you have an M.D. supervising you? Maybe I know him."

His face fell. "You might not. He spends most of his time at Harvard, too."

"Try me."

"Abraham Hodges."

Hodges and I had closed a few bars in Cambridge together. He was book smart and street smart, a rare combination. "Abe's a good man," I said. "You're lucky. You can learn a lot from him."

Winston cleared his throat. "Commissioner Hancock and I were discussing Dr. Lucas' character structure before you arrived."

"Dr. Winston feels that giving in to Lucas' demands would be the wrong move," Hancock said. "It plays into his narcissism."

"If we stand firm, Lucas will fold his hand," Winston smiled. "No pun intended. *Alien hand*, what a crock." He turned serious again. "The only way people are going to get hurt is if we let ourselves be manipulated."

I thought about that. It didn't make sense. "Your theory would be correct if we were dealing with a pure sociopath," I said, "but I'm not sure Lucas is in control of his behavior anymore. I think he may truly be psychotic. You can win a game of tug-of-war with somebody insane and end up with a rope around your neck."

"Are you familiar with the latest study on hostage situations in the *American Journal of Forensic Psychology*? Grovner and Waznoff et al.?"

Quoting scientific literature is a warning sign of an expert with no intuition. "I don't read the journals a lot," I said.

"I won't bore you with the details. I found the study design a bit cumbersome myself. But the conclusion was illuminating. In nineteen hostage crises involving barricade, eighty-four percent were resolved to the satisfaction of law enforcement authorities when a strategy of rigid noncooperation was employed."

"I think law enforcement was pretty satisfied with Waco and Ruby Ridge."

Hancock stiffened.

"The helicopter might reassure him he has a way out," I went on.

"I'd rather convince him he doesn't," Winston shot back. "Then he'll realize from the beginning that he has nothing to gain by violence."

"He nearly tore his arm off trying to escape from the last place he was locked up. He didn't stand to gain much from doing that."

"And he didn't accomplish anything other than hurting himself. I suggest we be as immovable as the bars of his cell." His eyes lit up, and his gaze flicked from me, to Hancock, then back, as if he expected congratulations for the simile.

I was about to suggest he check out his idea with Abe Hodges when shouts erupted from the front of the green. I turned and saw two firefighters and a cop looking up at a naked, obese woman who was leaning out the fifth-floor window at the far corner of the building. They ran toward her.

"No one say a word," Winston yelled at the men on the ground. He took off after them.

I walked, not that it mattered what I did. The poor woman would be spooked whether four shadowy figures raced toward her or five. Before any of us were halfway there, she shrieked once and dove from the window. Complete silence descended as she plunged toward the ground. I heard her skull crack against the sidewalk. For a few moments, everyone stood still, staring at her body on the cement. Then we all ran the rest of the way toward her. When we reached her, we fell silent again as we stood over her twisted body. Her long, white hair lay in a pool of blood. Her neck, breasts and stomach were carved up.

"Lord God," Winston whispered.

Sweat had blanketed me. I started to shiver in the cold night air.

The firefighters knelt down beside her. The older one listened for breathing. "Nothing," he said. He felt for a pulse and shook his head. They started CPR.

Even with reflected light bathing the woman's body, it took me a minute to figure out that the bloody lines cut into her weren't haphazard. They looked like letters, upside down. I moved to her feet, but the two men kept leaning over her, then backing off, so I couldn't manage to get a good view.

"No go," the younger firefighter said. "We should shock her." He ran toward the ambulance for a defibrillator.

Hancock knelt down. She squinted at the hospital identification bracelet around the woman's wrist. "Grace Cummings," she said. "Birth date, September 11, 1929. She was sixty-eight."

"Grace Cummings. Sounds familiar," Winston said.

"She was the one who drove her car into the group of kids waiting for a bus on Glover Street in Saugus," Hancock said. "One of them ended up paralyzed. It got a lot of press. She was awaiting trial for assault with intent to murder."

Blood flowed from the letters carved into her. I

couldn't make them out. "Why would they kill her?"

Winston shook his head. "Nobody necessarily forced her out the window. What's to say she didn't slash herself up and jump?"

I knelt down next to Hancock and started to blot the wounds with my sleeve.

"What are you doing?" she asked. She tried to pull my hand away from the body, but I kept at it. After a few seconds, she stopped tugging at me, settled back on her heels and stared at the body.

The letters were starting to ooze again, but the words were legible.

SWEET BOY

"What the hell is that supposed to mean?" Hancock asked.

My pulse moved to my throat. "I don't know," I said. "But I think Lucas will see to it we find out."

"Trevor Lucas, this is Dr. Winston," the bullhorn blared.

I turned and saw Winston walking toward the front of the green, holding the bullhorn to his lips. "Make him stop," I told Hancock.

"I'm a psychologist with the state," Winston went on.

"I don't have clear authority here, Frank," Hancock said. "He does." She pointed at a black Caprice just pulling into the hospital lot.

"Who's that?"

"Jack Rice. He's a State Police captain. Winston reports to him."

"Come out and meet me, one-on-one," Winston said. "Whatever has angered you cannot be changed through violence."

"We better get to Rice." I jogged to his car. Hancock followed.

When Rice stepped out of the passenger side I was surprised to see that he was only about five feet tall and pudgy, almost swollen-looking. His hair was light brown and baby-fine. He wore a tailored gray suit, blue pin-striped button-down and red paisley tie that made him look like an oversized display item from a Brooks Brothers window. He greeted Hancock, who introduced me.

"Your man Winston is going to screw things up if you let him bully Lucas," I said immediately.

Hancock tried to be diplomatic. "Dr. Clevenger appreciates Dr. Winston's training in these matters, but we've had experience with Lucas. He's an extraordinary . . ."

Rice glanced over my shoulder at Winston.

"We just had a death," Hancock said. "A woman jumped from the fifth floor. She'd been cut up, badly."

"I got the report on my way over. Who was she?"

"Grace Cummings. Sixty-eight years old."

"A nurse?"

"No. A prisoner."

"Thank God."

Winston's electric monotone filled the hospital grounds. "I want you to tell me your concerns, face-to-face. Manto-man."

I hung my head in despair.

"What's your problem, doctor?" Rice asked me.

"The language is too threatening for someone paranoid," I said. "To Lucas, being called out like this can seem like a test of his manhood. We don't want that. We want him to feel safe, at least for now. That's why telling him we'll get him in touch with Cardinal Law, or get him that helicopter . . ."

Rice shook his head. "Absolutely not. I've already made my position on that clear to Commissioner Hancock. We don't make deals with kidnappers."

"I'm not talking about a deal. I'm talking about a strategy," I said. "Bullying Lucas isn't going to work. He's capable of anything."

"That doesn't put me in the mood to give in to him."

"Winston's approach won't work."

"No?" He grinned and nodded over my shoulder.

I had the feeling I might be talking to someone crazy. "No," I said.

He nodded again. "Take a look."

I turned around and saw Lucas standing inside the glass doors to the hospital lobby. He was still wearing his scrubs and his cast. Several other figures were behind him, but the panes of glass adjacent to the door were fogged up, and I couldn't quite make them out. Lucas took a step forward, and the door slid open. He barely poked his head out to look left and right, then stepped back inside.

"You have nothing to be afraid of," Winston blared.

A moment later, Lucas and four others walked out the door. He was in the middle of the first row of three, arm in arm with two nurses dressed in white who looked petrified. Each woman's outside arm was held aloft by a man behind her, and each had a large knife at her throat. The five of them looked like a bizarre bird with steel fangs.

Winston let his bullhorn drop to his side and took a step back.

"Come talk with me," Lucas called to him.

Winston backed up another step.

I heard Rice's police radio crackle. "No clear shot," a voice said.

"Damn," Rice said.

"I don't recognize the big one in back on the left," Hancock said, "but the one on the right, the black man, is Zweig."

"One doctor to another, like you said," Lucas baited Winston. "Face-to-face."

Winston turned and looked at the three of us watching him.

"We have nothing to fear from one another," Lucas said. "We're both men of honor."

"Don't do it," I said, just loud enough, I hoped, for Winston alone to hear.

Maybe it was my telling him what to do, or not to do, that made Winston take the chance. I can't say. Maybe I could have helped him more by staying silent, giving him a little quiet time to remember data from some obscure journal article that would justify a retreat in the name of science. As it happened, he looked back at us once more, then walked slowly toward Lucas.

The two men stood about ten yards from the front door of the hospital, only a few feet apart, staring at one another. Winston said something I couldn't make out. Then Lucas smiled, and I saw his mouth form a single word: *Harpy.*

I knew from a college course in Greek mythology that a Harpy was a voracious monster with the head and trunk of a woman and the tail, wings and talons of a bird. "Get out of there!" I yelled to Winston.

Winston took a step back. The bird advanced on him. He turned to run, but its two wings—each fashioned of a man and a woman—closed around him. He fell to the ground with the bird on him. I heard his muffled screams and saw his fingers scraping the frozen earth as he struggled, in vain, to crawl away.

Rice fumbled for his radio. "Nail that fucker," he sputtered into it.

"Still no shot," a voice answered.

"Nothing clear and clean," another voice responded.

"No go," a third barked.

Winston's screams died out in ten, fifteen seconds that passed like an hour, and Lucas and the others stood up, striking the same strange pose as they had before. Winston lay in a fetal position, motionless. The two knives dripped blood—Winston's blood, I was sure—down the necks of the two women hostages.

Lucas' face was blank, but his eyes were wild. They locked on mine. "My life!" he screamed. "Give me my life!" Trickles of blood ran from the corners of his mouth, down his chin. His face went blank again. He and the four others slowly backed up toward the hospital, the doors opened for them, and they were gone.

Three

Rice exploded toward Winston like a missile on tiny legs and was the first to reach him, just ahead of Hancock and me. He crouched down and rolled Winston onto his back, then shot immediately to his feet again. We all stood there, transfixed with horror. Twenty or more stab wounds to Winston's neck, chest and stomach oozed blood. One eye was punctured, the other wide open, staring at the sky. A hunk of his lower lip was missing. Blood streamed down his chin and neck and fed a crooked rivulet running on the pavement.

Two paramedics—one female and one male—arrived, but stood a respectful distance behind Rice.

Hancock made the sign of the cross and started whispering a prayer. Just as she did, a pink bubble formed at Winston's nostril, then disappeared. We watched it happen two more times. Then nothing.

"My God, he was breathing," Rice said. He shook his head, no doubt thinking the same thing I was—that Winston was most of the way on his journey out of this world and better off finishing the trip. "We have to try," he said quietly. He knelt down and listened at Winston's nose for breathing.

Apparently hearing none, he gently tilted Winston's head back, then grabbed his chin and pulled his lower jaw down to open his mouth and start resuscitation. As soon as he did, blood poured from the corners of Winston's mouth. The rivulet on the pavement swelled to a puddle. Rice's hand started to tremble. "His tongue's gone," he said.

I saw another pink bubble advance and recede. I was certain Hancock and Rice saw it, too, but none of us mentioned it.

"Get a stretcher," Rice shouted up at the paramedics.

The male paramedic ran toward the ambulance.

"Go help him," Rice ordered the woman.

She looked confused. "It's right near the door, not buried under anything," she said.

"Go!" Rice barked.

She turned and jogged away.

Rice moved his hand, which I now noticed was too big for his body—a mitt of a hand—and covered Winston's nose and mouth, sealing his fate. Hancock and I exchanged glances, but didn't try to stop him. He kept his hand there until the paramedics had almost reached us with the stretcher. When he stood up there wasn't a hint of breath left in Winston. "Bring him over to Stonehill Hospital," he told the two of them. "No rush." He walked away.

I waited until after 2 A.M. to start the drive back to Chelsea. I felt the same strange rootedness to the spot where Winston had died as a murderer might to the scene of his crime. Or perhaps what I felt was closer to the connection of a general to a battlefield. I had held fast to my principles, or what I thought them to be, which meant holding back certain facts about the killings. My heart had told me it was the right thing to do, the only thing to do, and now two more people were dead. I didn't want to leave Lynn State at all, but Hancock suggested I go home to rest and keep my beeper on in case she needed me. I worried she would wonder why I couldn't break away. I knew in my head she couldn't guess I felt responsible for what had happened, but I was so full of guilt I imagined anyone could sense it surging through me.

I rolled down both front windows and let the cold morning air whip across my face. I tried to convince myself I was justified letting Lucas sit in prison and be tried for crimes he had not committed. His hands were far from clean, after all. He had known who was responsible for the murders long before I had, yet had done nothing to stop the carnage. On the contrary, he had relished his connection to the violence, violence that had ultimately taken Rachel from me.

At least I had put a stop to the killing.

The trouble was I didn't believe I had the right to condemn anyone, not even Lucas. I remembered feeling revolted during the murder investigation when he suggested the two of us were alike. Now, with the deaths of Grace Cummings and Lawrence Winston, my hands were bloodied, too.

The Schooner Pub rose up on the left-hand side of the road. You need a drink, I told myself. That's how it starts. *You need.* And the need was real, always is, real enough for me to stop the car and wait for the red arrow to turn green and make the U-turn back to the Schooner lot. Because I did need something—not a drink, even my brain could register that much. I needed the courage to face what I had to do next. And I didn't have it. The booze makes you forget that you're a coward, for a while, until a while runs out, and whatever you needed to face has grown claws and become a monster you don't ever want to meet. And then the monster starts pissing out the booze faster than you can pour it in, and then you *need* something else, like cocaine or speed or, God help you, heroin, first up your nose, then in your lungs, then into your veins, to scramble your neurotransmitters enough to keep the beast off balance.

I didn't turn the engine off. I sat in the Schooner lot seized by a memory of myself lying in bed with Kathy not a year before, my nasal passages caked with dried blood, my left arm numb to the elbow, wondering whether I would make it through the night or die, then remembering another stash of coke in the armoire, stealing out of bed and feeling for it between folded towels and blankets in the dark, reassured that my fingers could still twist off the wire tie around the tiny Baggie, then inhaling the powder in short, sweet blasts that made my heart quicken and my chest tighten and my mind freeze mercifully between thoughts. And that image, frightful because it was not only revolting, but strangely seductive, got me screeching back on to the Lynnway.

"You're completely alone," I whispered, hearing the words half as an indictment of my lifestyle, half as a comfort. I had no family to check in with. There would be no message on my machine from someone making sure I hadn't gone off the deep end once and for all. My friends were bartenders and bookies and cops and the city coroner. Good people, every last one of them. And I loved them, but I didn't know whether that was because we were close or because they knew enough (or had been through enough hell themselves) to keep their distance. Maybe a light touch and the gift of space are the greatest things you can give a man like me, cornered too many times by a father raging through the night, a bottle in one hand, a belt in the other.

I had let Rachel in close. Then I had lost her.

I saw the round tower of West Lynn Creamery coming up, across from Webster Avenue, which starts with a boarded-up Pizza Palace and ends with the Lynn Y. I swerved to make the hard right on to Webster, guessing that Cynthia would have headed back to her place when I hadn't come home within a few hours.

I stayed in my truck a minute or two deciding whether to go inside. What was I there for, after all? If it was sex, I could have it delivered. A different girl every time. If I was trying to bury my grief over Rachel's death or escape my guilt over the deaths of Grace Cummings and Lawrence Winston, then I was just drugging myself again.

I ground the heels of my hands into my eyes. I was thinking too much—my chief defense against feeling too much. I wanted to see Cynthia. I got out of the truck.

The Y had been a Comfort Inn for about a year in the early 90s, until whoever had been betting on Lynn's revitalization realized the city wasn't coming back from the grave, and donated the building for a tax credit. Over the years that followed, the place became a way station for schizophrenics, addicts and prostitutes coming from someplace worse or going someplace worse, but together enough for the time being to turn their welfare checks into $380-a-month or $22-a-day rent, instead of drink, dope or lottery tickets.

The staff's attempt to keep up the lobby had resulted in a surreal combination of Paine furniture and pained people. On my way to the reception desk I passed a crumpled man and woman, past middle age, seated on separate love seats in front of a knotty pine false fireplace. The love seats faced one another, but the man and woman made no eye contact. He stared up at the mirror over the mantel, she, into the empty hollow where a fire would burn. I couldn't tell whether or not they were a couple, whether or not they were on their way up in life or down, whether this was a pit stop or their last stop. But even in my burnt-out state, those questions were enough to make me want to plant myself in one of the armchairs near them and burrow into their story. The impulse was no surprise to me. I have always felt an undertow of humanity pulling me into desperate lives, probably because I grew up in desperation myself.

The desk clerk, a young man who suffered what looked like cerebral palsy, informed me there were no visitors allowed after midnight, then rang Cynthia's room after I slipped him ten bucks. She told him to send me up.

I took the stairs to the third floor. The door to room 305 opened with one knock, and Cynthia stood there in a white T-shirt that barely reached her thighs. She tilted her head, and her straight, light brown hair cascaded to one side of her face. "I waited a while, then left," she said. "I figured something bad must have happened at the hospital."

I swallowed hard. "Things went wrong."

She held out her hand. I took it and followed

her into the room. The only light came from a set of sconces on either side of the bed. Only half the bulbs worked, but they showed what I expected— an economy hotel room part of the way to disrepair, with stained wall-to-wall carpeting and faded, floor-to-ceiling floral draperies. I was surprised to see what looked like a pretty competent oil painting of a winged woman in a flowing violet robe hanging over the bed.

"Two people were killed," I said, not knowing why I was confiding in her.

Cynthia turned around. She had the rare ability to say nothing. And she had those eyes that seemed to understand everything. Rachel's eyes.

I let go of her hand and just stood there in front of her. I looked out the windows into the darkness. "One of them was a patient. A woman close to seventy. The other one was a psychologist who was there trying to help."

"How did they die?"

"Do you follow the papers?"

"Not much."

"There's a doctor named Trevor . . ."

"Well, everyone follows *that*," she said.

"Right." I sometimes forgot how much media attention the case had generated. "Trevor Lucas took over the psychiatric unit where he's been locked up during the trial. It looks like he threw the woman out a fifth-story window. She'd been cut up badly. The psychologist was killed—stabbed to death—trying to negotiate with Lucas face-to-face."

She sat down on the edge of the bed. "You watched all that?"

I sat down next to her. The horror of what I had seen Lucas do hours before and what I had done to him months ago gripped me all at once. I closed my eyes and buried my head in my hands. The image of Winston struggling for his life came to me. I pictured his fingers clawing the ground as he tried to free himself from the bizarre beast Lucas had created. The muscles in my hands, arms and chest contracted involuntarily. Breathing was an effort.

"Are you OK?" she asked. She rested her hand lightly on the nape of my neck.

I didn't answer.

She traced the arc of my ear with one fingertip. "Do you want to get some sleep?"

I needed something much more than rest—to be rid of my isolation, to tell someone the truth. I had the habit, then, of seeing people as I wanted to see them. And I saw her as pure and trustworthy, a river to carry my sins away. Some people go to church and talk to a priest. Others choose a psychiatrist as their confessor. My religion has no name, but three clear tenets: that people are connected to each other in mystical, immeasurable ways, that we have the power to heal one another and that truth often precipitates out of our society and settles at the bottom. It felt good and right to choose a hooker in a motel-turned-rooming house as a repository for my soul. But it was a terrible mistake.

"He didn't do it." I said. My scalp tingled with the gravity of what I had revealed.

"What do you mean?" Cynthia asked.

I raked my fingers down my face as I sat up and stared at the ceiling. I took a deep breath, let it out. "Trevor Lucas. He didn't commit the murders he's on trial for."

"Why do you think that?"

I looked her in the eyes. I couldn't control the flow of my truth. "Because I know who the real killer is."

She nodded tentatively, becoming visibly tense. She glanced at the door.

I realized she might be worried I was about to confess to the murders myself. "I haven't seen her in over five months. I helped hide her, right after Lucas was arrested."

"Her?"

"The killer."

She squinted at me like she was trying to figure out if I was leveling with her. How could she be sure, after all, that I wasn't a compulsive liar, a nut case writing myself into the news of the day? That, or something worse. My apartment certainly didn't look like a doctor would live there. I didn't look like a doctor, to begin with. "She killed two people. Why would you help her get away?"

"She was sick," I said. "She couldn't stop herself."

"Then she'd have been found not guilty."

"No, she wouldn't. She would have spent the rest of her life in prison. These days juries convict no matter what mental state the defendant was in at the time of the crimes. Jeffrey Dahmer ate seventeen people, and he was found sane enough to die in prison."

"But it's not up to you to . . ." Cynthia stared into my eyes a few seconds. "Who was this woman? How well did you know her?"

I finally, too late, held back. "A friend. I thought we were close, but we weren't."

"So you let Trevor Lucas stand trial for something he didn't do. To save her."

"I figured Lucas would get the right lawyer and beat the case. But he ended up pleading insanity himself." I paused. "He seems to have actually gone insane. I think being locked up drove him over the edge."

"Where is the woman?"

"Somewhere she can get help—somewhere she can't leave."

Cynthia looked away several seconds, then stared directly into my eyes. "Why are you telling me all this?"

"I had to tell someone. My instincts told me I could trust you." I glanced up at the painting of the angel over her bed.

"So what do your instincts tell you to do now?" Cynthia asked.

I thought about that. The picture my mind painted wasn't of the violence I had just witnessed, but of Lucas being carried out of the courtroom the morning before. "Help him," I said automatically.

"Lucas?"

"Yes."

"How?"

"I don't know."

She touched my face. "You'll find a way."

"What makes you so sure?"

"Because I know you."

I wanted to believe that. I wanted to believe that, even after losing Rachel, I could find another angel.

"You're a shaman, Frank. A healer," Cynthia was saying. "It's the reason you suffer so much. You feel your own pain, and everyone else's—including Dr. Lucas."

"Well, I didn't feel anything but contempt for him before, and now . . ."

"And now you know you're human." She put a finger to my lips before I could answer. "You don't need to say anything else. I understand." She

stood up, slowly pulled her T-shirt over her head
and let it drop to the ground. "I can feel other people's pain, too."

I was still lost in the beginnings of a day overshadowed by nightmares of bloodletting. I took
hold of Cynthia's hips, so smooth and firm and far
from death, and pulled her to me.

I stumbled through three broken hours of sleep,
awakened at least a dozen times by screams—
sometimes Winston's, sometimes Lucas', sometimes my own—that evaporated as soon as my
eyes found the lighted billboard for Camel ciga-
rettes outside Rachel's window. I rode the camel
back into my uneasy slumber, the way Spider-
Man had carried me there when I was a boy, when
my night terrors were of my father chasing me up
the stairs of the triple decker we lived in, shouting
obscenities.

At 6:20 I woke up for good. The morning light
was starting to drown out the spotlights over the
billboard. Cynthia's hand was resting on mine. I
lifted it gently and set it down on the hospital-
style, woven white blankets that covered us. She
swallowed once and took a single, deep breath,
but her eyes stayed closed. I unclipped my pager
from the bed frame where I'd left it and carried it
with me to the bathroom, hoping a shower would
make me feel like I'd slept the night.

I wasn't three minutes under the spray when the

mustard-colored, plastic curtain slid open, and Cynthia stepped in next to me. She pushed me against the tile wall behind the shower head, then knelt in front of me. The water fell on her face and shoulders as she took my penis in her mouth. The room had fogged up, so that even with my eyes open, looking down at her, I could imagine Rachel there. I took her hair in my hands as she took me inside her again and again. The pleasure started crashing deep in my groin and brain at the same time. I had to lean hard against the wall to stay on my feet. She held me tight. My body crested in spasms, then relaxed like an outgoing tide, the way your arms float away after being pressed against the sides of a doorway. I knelt down, the hot water showering both of us, and kissed her ears and neck, the curves of her shoulders, her breasts.

My pager started chirping. I wanted to stay right where I was.

"Better check," Cynthia whispered.

I groaned in protest, but helped her to her feet and stepped out of the shower.

The number on the pager was for Emma Hancock's cellular. I tied a towel around my waist and walked into the bedroom. There was no phone there. I stepped back into the bathroom to tell Cynthia I'd be getting dressed and leaving to make a call.

"There's a cellular in my bag," she said.

My face must have registered surprise.

She shrugged. "Tool of the trade."

I spotted her black leather handbag—styled like a pouch, with a drawstring—on the seat cushion of a wicker armchair near the window. I picked it up and pulled it open. Something about poking around in it made me feel like a little boy, but I didn't see anything that reminded me of my mother's purse. I had to reach through rolling papers, Trojan and MAGNUM condoms, and a canister of mace to find the phone. I dialed Hancock.

"Frank?" she answered.

"Yup." I noticed Cynthia's driver's license face-up in her bag. I focused on it just long enough to read her full name, Cynthia J. Baxter. The license had been issued by the state of Maryland.

"Where are you?"

"The Y."

"What are you doing there?"

"I didn't feel like driving back to Chelsea. I took a room here and slept a little."

"The Y. Very swank. Why didn't you just bunk at the Lynn shelter? It's even cheaper."

"Didn't think of it. Next time."

"I keep hoping there won't be a next time." She paused. "I needed to give you an update. Lucas just issued another ultimatum."

"I'll say it again: We should land that helicopter right in the hospital parking lot. Drain the gas, if that makes Rice happy. At least Lucas could literally see a way out."

"Lucas didn't mention the helicopter this time. Or Cardinal Law."

"No? Who does he want now? The Pope?"

"Not quite. You."

The room suddenly felt claustrophobic. My heart started to pound. I wondered if Lucas had told what he knew about the killings. What I knew.

"Still there?" Hancock said.

"Yeah."

"What do you figure he wants with you? I'm the one who arrested him."

She was also the one who had arranged to have the life nearly beaten out of him while he was being held at the Lynn jail. But what I had done to him was much worse. "Your guess is as good as mine," I said. I looked out the window.

"You sound nervous. Nobody's suggesting you hurl yourself into any volcano. I just thought you might come up with a way to use his demand to stall him."

I cleared my throat. "What exactly is he demanding?"

"He says he wants to meet with you. On the unit. He promised to set two of the hostages—the two social workers—free at the same time he takes you inside."

Out of the corner of my eye I saw Cynthia walk

into the room, but my gaze stayed focused out-side. "And if I don't go?"

"He says he'll kill them. Actually, he said 'the Harpy will devour them.'"

My skin turned to gooseflesh. "He wrote all this in a note?"

"No. Laura Elmonte delivered the ultimatum by phone. She didn't sound anything like the smooth talker she was yesterday on the witness stand. She kept gasping for air, struggling to get her words out. Somebody was doing something to her. I don't want to think what."

"How long did he give me to decide?"

"Twelve hours. What he doesn't know is that Sir Rice here is planning to storm the unit at four P.M."

"He can't do that. Lucas is too smart and too paranoid. They'll end up carrying everyone out in body bags."

"I'm not in favor of it, either. But Rice doesn't need my OK on state property."

I looked at my watch. 6:50. "So I really only have about eight hours to decide."

"Decide what?"

"Whether I'll meet with Lucas on the locked unit." I saw Cynthia turn around. I looked over at her. My mind was mostly frozen on a memory of the five-person beast Lucas called a Harpy, but I could see the fear in her face. She sat down on the edge of the bed, watching me.

"Let me save you time and trouble," Hancock

said. "There is no chance, *absolutely no chance,* I would authorize you going onto that unit. If you want to commit suicide, you're not going to do it on my time."

I remembered Lucas' crazed eyes locked on mine as he stood over Winston's body. "He's sick," I said, more to myself than Hancock.

"Great. Why don't you go down to the morgue and have a chat with Winston about how well the good doctor responds to therapy?"

"Winston challenged him. I'd be surrendering to him. At least at the beginning."

"And we could etch that on your tombstone. *He surrendered to a serial killer.*"

"What inscription would you suggest for the hostages? How about for the baby?"

"Look, I know you somehow get through to people, people no one else can reach. You have a gift. That's why you're worth what you charge. But it's not just Lucas, Frank. You've got Zweig and Kaminsky up there. We also I.D.'d the tall white man who came out with Lucas and Zweig to kill Winston. It was Craig Bishop."

I closed my eyes and hung my head. "I thought he got transferred back to prison to await trial."

"The Bishop family has a few bucks, I guess— enough anyhow to hire a scumbag lawyer to get the transfer reversed. They argued his mental illness was too complex to be adequately treated in a prison environment. Personally I don't see anything complicated about it: Beheading your victims isn't a lot different than shooting them, when you come right down to it."

"Lucas would have to release the two social workers first," I said.

"He'd never agree to . . . ," she started, then caught herself. "I can't believe we're actually wasting our breath on this insanity. I called you to figure out how to bluff our way into more time, not so we could spin our wheels thinking about a kamikaze mission that's never going to happen."

"Let's work Rice on the Cardinal and the helicopter, then."

"I'm not about to propose that the Catholic Church . . ."

"What about the helicopter?"

"You really think that could change things?"

I thought it would keep Hancock busy. "As a sign of good faith it could go a long way. Meanwhile, tell Lucas I'm thinking about his offer. Tell him I'd probably go for it if he released three hostages—the pregnant nurse first, within four hours from now, and two more when I go in."

"As a bluff. Period. Right?"

"You're the one calling the shots."

"You're not planning to go behind my back and do something stupid."

I figured whatever I ended up doing would happen right in front of her. "You have my word."

"Good. I'll bring up the chopper issue again with Rice."

"I'll be over to talk with him myself soon. Page me if you need me." I hung up. I stood there, looking out the window at everything, but nothing in particular, knowing at some level that the next chapter in my life would be the darkest.

"Are you going to meet with him? On the unit?" Cynthia asked from the bed.

I turned to her. "I don't know."

"You look like you do." Her voice was part kindness, part protest.

I am no stranger and no friend to denial. I took a few seconds to rid myself of it. "If I get out of there alive," I said, "I'll come find you."

Four

I left the Y at about 7:15 A.M. Cynthia walked me to my truck. The morning was even colder than I had expected. With the wind chill, it had to be five below—more than a match for my motorcycle jacket, worn through on the right elbow from a spill I'd taken one rainy night en route to Sturgis, South Dakota, for a Harley rally. We kissed, our breath mingling and turning white in the winter air.

As I watched Cynthia walk away, a red Cutlass Supreme, probably about a '90, pulled up.

Calvin Sanger took the cigarette from his lips, leaned across the front seat and rolled down the passenger-side window. "You're a little ways from home," he said. He had on the same clothes he'd been wearing at Lynn State Hospital—beige, wide-wale corduroys, a red flannel shirt and a brown leather bomber jacket. Everything hung loosely on his six-foot, rope-thin frame. From what I'd heard about his habits when he was working a big story, he'd probably caught an hour's sleep at his desk at the *Item*. But he didn't look tired.

"I ran out of steam on the Lynnway," I said. "I stopped here for the night."

He looked over at the building. "I hope you didn't pay more than fifty bucks."

"The rooms only run about twenty."

"I know that," he said, flicking ash out his window and blowing smoke. "I also know her."

That comment made me wonder about being Cynthia's "fourth customer ever." "I guess it's your job to know things," I said.

"As much as I can." He smiled the wide smile captured every year, front-page on the *Item*, as he finished the Boston Marathon. He wasn't thirty-five yet, but his face was dominated by a prominent forehead, strong cheekbones and a square jaw that would probably keep him looking about the way he did right into his sixties. His black skin made his pale blue eyes seem translucent.

"Nothing wrong with that," I said. I was getting cold and I wasn't about to answer any questions. "See you up at the hospital." I turned to open my door.

"One question," he called out. "If you have a second."

I turned back to him. "Like Hancock said, I can't comment on the trial, or the hostage situation."

"Of course not. That's understood. I'm trying to get my head around something else."

I didn't respond.

"This copycat case," he went on.

My jaw tightened.

"The idea is that Trevor Lucas cut up the first two victims—Sarah Johnston and Monique Peletier—and that some other butcher did the last two—Michael Wembley and the dancer."

I didn't like Rachel going nameless. "Michael Wembley and Rachel Lloyd."

"Yeah, the stripper."

"Go ahead."

"What I don't quite get is why Hancock dismisses the fact that *all four* victims knew Lucas."

"She doesn't dismiss it. She investigated it. So did the D.A.'s office." I shrugged. "They were obviously more impressed by the fact that the last two victims were killed after Lucas turned himself over to police."

"Sure. And that does seem impressive, until you really let yourself wonder whether the good doctor did any of them. The killer could have been connected to all four victims *and* Lucas."

I thought Sanger was studying me for my reaction. Or maybe my guilt was making me paranoid. "There were differences," I said. "The first two bodies were found in Lynn. They were both female. Lucas' prints were all over the place. They were patients of his. They were also his lovers."

"That doesn't mean he killed them."

"That's why there's a jury."

"Yeah, but Lucas' plea is insanity, not that he didn't do it."

"You might want to take a cue from that."

"Even though he's ranting about not killing anybody."

" 'Ranting' may be the operative word there. But you're the journalist."

"What do *you* think? I mean, doesn't it seem possible this copycat killer is actually the original?"

"Me?" I bent over and rested my hands on the door frame. "I think I'm a shrink, Calvin, and you're a reporter, and Emma Hancock's a seasoned cop. The best I've met. I think we know what she wants us to know. Nothing more. And you gotta believe that if she thought there was a chance somebody other than Trevor Lucas cut up her niece, she'd be digging so deep in the streets the whole city would shake." My fingers had gone numb. "That's what I think."

He took a long drag on his cigarette and swallowed the smoke, letting it out through his nose. "Probably true."

I felt as if I had shown more emotion than I ought to have. I turned to open the door to my truck, then turned back. "Anyone ever mention those things can kill you."

"Nobody who's watched me run." He winked. "See you at the hospital."

"Sure." I climbed into my truck as he drove off.

I started the engine, lighted my own cigarette, then snaked my way through side streets to the Lynnway, checking my rearview mirror to make sure Sanger hadn't doubled back to follow me.

By 7:40 I was headed north on Route 95. The sun was blinding. A light drizzle kept icing my windshield.

After forty-three years on the planet there was only one person I had to see before stepping to the edge. I picked up the phone and dialed Matt Hollander at the Austin Grate Clinic twenty miles north in Rowley.

Hollander and I had trained together in psychiatry at Tufts. He had been a year ahead of me and was assigned as my mentor when I started the residency. It was a good match. I had a stronger tendency then toward arrogance (a synonym for low self-esteem), but Hollander's remarkable ability to understand even the most bizarre emotions and behaviors convinced me immediately that I had a lot to learn about human nature and that I was in the right place to learn it. I started to talk less and listen more, a way of being that American Indians and Buddhists may come to naturally, but the rest of us have to strive for. Woody Allen once said that 90 percent of life is about showing up. Ninety percent of healing people in psychological pain is shutting up—at least long enough to let them bleed the truth. That sounds easy, but it isn't.

Since residency, while I'd opened and closed my psychotherapy practice and started chasing forensic cases, Hollander had used his family fortune to acquire a string of premier psychiatric hospitals.

Neither of us could have predicted when we met at Tufts that, fifteen years later, I would have asked him for a favor that had put us both at odds with our professional ethics and with the law.

The attendant answered. I gave my name, asked for Hollander and waited.

"It's been a long time," Hollander said.

"I wondered whether I could come by."

"Where can I meet you? How about the Agawam? Right down the street from here, on 1A."

I figured he might not want me on hospital grounds, not after what we'd done together. "I know the place. I'll be there in twenty-five minutes."

"No rush." He hung up.

The Agawam is a diner in the old tradition, with acceptable food, loud help and a mystical resonance that draws customers two and three deep at the counter. Hollander was already waiting for me in a six-man booth toward the back. He waved me over.

I sat down. A half-finished plate of corned beef

hash and boiled potatoes was still steaming in front of him. "I'm glad to see you, Matt," I said. "You look . . ."

"I look big." He shrugged his meaty shoulders and smiled, swallowing my hand in both of his. He was dressed in an oversized white button-down shirt and khakis, but I could tell he was all of the three hundred pounds he'd been the last time I'd seen him, about six months before. His hair, prematurely gray, was wet and combed neatly back. His sapphire blue eyes gleamed. "I keep getting bigger and bigger, and I feel better and better."

I nodded. During residency Hollander had shared with me his theory that fat molecules grease the "wheels" of the mind. He had defended it by citing examples of great large men, like Ben Franklin, Winston Churchill, "Minnesota Fats," H. L. Mencken and Luciano Pavarotti. Bums, thieves and killers, he had argued, are almost always thin as a rail. "I needed to touch base."

"You could have gotten in contact sooner. I think I told you to let things cool down for a month or so."

"I figured the longer the better."

"Why?"

"Just safer."

He dug into his hash, swallowed a forkful, then nodded. "I can buy that—if you mean emotionally."

"Huh?"

"You didn't want to go near your feelings."

"C'mon. Save it for the paying clients."

"You weren't scared of the police. You were scared of your heart."

I leaned toward him and dropped my voice. "Matt, what we did could get us twenty to life. That's what I was afraid of. I didn't want my heart—and the rest of me—locked up at MCI Concord."

"Bullshit." He flagged down the waitress.

"I don't need to eat."

"I do."

I looked and saw that most of the hash was gone.

"You were afraid of facing the facts of your life: You lived with someone over a year. You thought you loved her. Part of you—a very dark part— probably did. And you say you didn't know her from Adam."

"Fine. Maybe you're right. But that's not why I'm here."

He pointed his fork at me. "Don't 'maybe' me, or I'll take a chunk out of your cheek." He soaked up some grease with a piece of bread that disappeared, as if by magic, into his mouth and down his throat. "You've got work to do figuring out why you'd rather live with a stranger."

"After living with my parents, I guess I thought it was safer."

"Well, now you know better. Or you should.

Strangers don't necessarily have fewer demons. They just haven't introduced you to them."

I thought about how much I had confided in Cynthia. I stayed silent.

Hollander patted his mouth with a napkin. "The real issue here is that you don't have the balls to get introduced to yourself."

"Huh?"

"You're a beaten little boy, Frank. All that helplessness and rage is still inside you. The need for vengeance. You didn't pick up booze and cocaine for no reason. And you didn't pick a killer to live with by accident."

"You're saying I chose her *because* she was violent?"

"Yes. I am." A forkful of potato and another piece of bread disappeared. "Because, unconsciously, my friend, violence reaches to the core of your being like nothing else. And it always will—until you open yourself up and take the risk of letting someone get close enough to hurt you, who loves you, instead."

The waitress, a fiftyish woman with a man's build and voice, stepped to our table. "Hit you again, doc?"

Hollander pointed at his plate. His eyes stayed on me.

"I guess that's a 'yes.' What'll you have, honey?"

"Coffee, that's all."

"Cream and sugar?"

"Neither."

"Mutt and Jeff," she chuckled, then left.

"I know none of this is easy, Frank. I'm just getting around to embracing my own fragile, foolish, miserable, magnificent soul."

"Congratulations."

"It's been one long, wretched courtship. And it's not over by a long shot. But it's well worth the effort." He winked. "So tell me: Why did you pick today to call?"

"I may not be around here for a while."

"Where you headed?"

"I've got to get some things straightened out with my family. I don't know if I ever told you about the trouble my aunt ..." I stopped. I couldn't lie to him. "I'm going onto the locked unit to negotiate with Trevor Lucas."

Hollander's lip curled. "Don't be a goddamn fool. If you go in there, you may never come out."

"He's got seven hostages. Two other people are already dead."

"And you want to be the third?"

"One of the hostages is a nurse who's pregnant."

He kept staring at me. The anger slowly left his face. "I heard everything on the tube," he said. "All three networks ran it as the lead story. I worried you'd blame yourself."

"I let Lucas sit in jail. I let him go to trial, even

though I knew the truth. Why wouldn't I blame myself?"

"I don't know, Frank. I'm not in the business of assessing blame. Neither were you, last I remember." He glanced over my shoulder to make sure he couldn't be overheard, then stared directly into my eyes. His voice grew kind. "Unless I was hallucinating, you snuck a murderess into my home in the middle of the night six months ago, almost to the day, and begged me to hide her on my Secure Care Unit. You were horrified by the idea that a woman who became a killer because she was tortured as a child, ruined before she had a chance, would end up behind bars for life, never mind electrocuted by the state. And I'm dead certain you told me that your Rachel—who may just have been what you really needed in a woman—would have wanted her killer treated, not destroyed. I remember I was struck by that. I thought it spoke volumes about her."

My throat tightened.

The waitress stepped to our table with my coffee and Hollander's second helping of hash.

"Thanks," I managed.

She looked at me with sympathy as she put the cup and plate down. She probably thought I was one of Hollander's patients. "I won't bother the two of you. Just wave me down if you need more coffee." She headed back behind the counter.

Hollander leaned toward me, absorbing four,

five inches of the table into his gut. "Maybe you ought to give yourself a break, instead of a death sentence at Lucas' hands. You didn't ask to get caught up in all this, and nobody could have predicted things going the way they did. We both figured some shyster lawyer would spring Lucas in a heartbeat."

"It didn't happen that way."

"No. It didn't. And the police didn't solve the case after one victim. And Lucas didn't stop the killings after the second victim—which he could have. And, twenty years ago, nobody protected an eleven-year-old girl whose father was raping her and her kid sister. And nobody ever got that girl any help, until now, which is exactly four bodies too late in the game. Five, if you count the life she should have had herself." He shoveled in a forkful of hash. "The world isn't very predictable, pal, which means you can't control it. Putting your life on the line may fool everyone else into thinking you're a saint, but don't look for me to be singing any praises at your wake."

"The last thing I want at my wake," I said, "is you breaking into song."

Hollander smiled, in spite of himself. He attacked his hash, then grew serious again. "So you had hopes of seeing her," he said.

My heart began to race. "I didn't say that."

"Right. You said you needed to touch base with me, out of the blue, just before laying your life on the line." He tapped his forehead. "Don't forget I grease and oil this rocket ship every day. You want to touch base with what we did and the person we did it for. You need to know whether you were a fool."

"I'm not sure I want to know that."

"And you'd be better off letting it go."

Several seconds passed with nothing but the clinking of Hollander's fork to fill the time.

"Is she still on the unit?" I asked. "Did you move her to another hospital?"

He pressed his lips together. Deep furrows appeared across his brow. "For your own good, I should probably lie to you."

"If you believed that, you'd be in a different business."

He looked out the window. "Before Lucas' trial started I thought about sending her to my facility in the Virgin Islands. That may have been the right thing to do." His eyes shifted back to meet mine. "But I didn't do it."

"Why not?"

"She kept begging me to set up a visit with you first. Part of me must have wanted to see it happen." He shook his head. "I may be crazier than you."

"Doubtful."

He reached for my coffee and took a swig. "If I arrange for you to see her, you'll have to be discreet. You can't use her real name or your own. I admitted her as Nancy Matheson. I've worked hard to keep her under wraps. I've even held on to staff I might otherwise have fired, in order to limit turnover and expose her to as few people as possible."

"Thank you. I knew how much I was asking when I brought her to you."

"Don't mention it. Just don't blow it."

"Does anyone suspect the truth?"

"I don't think so. At the beginning—the first few weeks of her stay—she kept insisting she was a doctor herself, that she'd been drugged and brought to the unit illegally. I dealt with that reality by helping the staff diagnose paranoid schizophrenia and then ordering very high doses of Haldol and Ativan for sedation. Once she gave me the chance to sit with her for long enough, she seemed to understand it was in her best interest to be in the hospital, rather than behind bars. She hasn't mentioned the doctor thing since." He finished off his hash. "Still, you never know; there is one counselor—a very kind young man named Scott Trembley—who took a special interest in her from the word go. I'm told they still talk privately every day."

"But this Trembley hasn't brought anything up."

"Not to me."

"You're not being very reassuring."

"Sorry. I didn't know it was my job to make you feel better."

I glanced out the window, at nothing in particular. "Have you been able to reach her? Do you think she's making progress?"

"Hard to say. I've only had six months. I don't have to tell you we're talking about pathology that could take many years to address."

"So she's not *any* better?"

He shrugged. "Baby steps, my boy. She seems a little more willing to talk about her childhood, maybe a bit more open to the idea that her own early trauma might have fueled her rage as an adult. I see her on the unit, though, not in the community. She may still be taking the path of least resistance, telling me what she thinks I want to hear."

"She has an extraordinary capacity to deceive."

"Most serial killers do."

I followed Hollander's Suburban Silverado down Route 97 East to a simple wooden arrow nailed to a tree and painted with the letters *AGC*. The road curved through miles of farmhouses and woods before ending at a set of stone pillars at the entrance to the Austin Grate Clinic. We parked in the semicircular drive of Hollander's majestic residence.

Hollander was at my door before I was halfway out of the car. I remembered his size had always seemed inversely proportional to his speed. "I've called ahead to the chief of nursing, so everything will be set for the visit," he said. "I told her you're a psychiatrist consulting on the case."

We walked to the main building, built in 1809 as a prominent merchant's mansion, then converted to a school and a nursing home before being turned into a psychiatric hospital by the prior owner. Hollander had stripped away layers of wall-to-wall carpet, linoleum and Formica and restored every inch of wide-pine flooring, wainscoting and chair rail. Walking through the lobby and corridors gave no hint of the building's earlier—or current—uses. It reminded me a little of the admissions offices of the half-dozen Ivy League colleges that had rejected me, which might be one reason I had never taken up Hollander on his offers of a job at Austin Grate. Elegance leaves me feeling unsettled, dangling too high above the uglier reality of things. The doors and walls of the elevator we took were overlaid with raised mahogany panels. The brass controls gleamed. Graffiti would have reassured me, but there wasn't a single obscenity scrawled anywhere. Hollander pressed the button for the fourth floor. "We had to renovate the Secure Care Unit in compliance with more rigid state standards," he said. "You won't miss the difference."

As the doors glided open, the incandescent lighting of the elevator was flooded out by fluorescent ceiling fixtures. The floors were covered with high-gloss green and black vinyl squares. The walls were cinder block painted white. Everything gleamed, but nothing caught the eye. "Beautiful wood underneath all this concrete and plastic, just like downstairs," Hollander said, shaking his head. "Damn shame. I would have left it exposed if the decision were mine. When you build a fortress, people act like they belong in one."

At the entrance to the unit two iron doors with chicken-wire windows were separated by a guard station behind half-inch plate glass. The guard flipped a switch to unlock the first door for us. Hollander paused before instructing him to let us through the second one. "Fifteen minutes, max," he said. "And if Ms. Matheson seems to be losing control or beginning to voice her delusions about being a physician, you'll need to leave immediately. Understood?"

I nodded.

Hollander signaled the guard. The lock clicked. We walked inside.

The main hallway of the unit was barren, save for an occasional art poster under Plexiglas bolted to the wall. Nurses ferried medications here and there. I saw just three patients in the Day Room, each with a staff member within arm's length. "Low census?" I asked.

"Actually we're full. Nine men. Nine women,"

Hollander said. "Every patient here is on a fifty/ten program. Fifty minutes in your room, ten minutes out, other than scheduled therapy sessions. We rotate the schedules so a maximum of three patients are in common areas at any one time."

"Very efficient," I said.

"It's simple arithmetic," he said, winking at me. "If you get no structure as a kid—and you know as well as I that there isn't a single person in here who's known anything but chaos and cruelty—the world ends up jamming all the structure you missed, plus interest, down your throat in a single dose. Locked doors, room programs, jail cells."

"I guess it's necessary."

"Of course it's necessary. These are dangerous people. But it's also a tragedy. That's what the criminal justice system doesn't understand. You can't punish the evil out of anyone."

I thought of Trevor Lucas, but said nothing.

"You know what Gerry Spence said."

"No."

"The desire to be a judge should disqualify one from serving."

Hollander escorted me to Interview C, a room about ten by twelve feet, with faint pink walls, a small, natural wood coffee table and two upholstered armchairs facing one another. Another chicken-wire window looked onto the ward's main corridor. "I hope you get what you came for," he said. He walked out.

I sat down in one of the armchairs. I tried to move it for a better view out the window, but it wouldn't budge. I looked down and saw that the legs were bracketed to the floor. I checked out the coffee table and found the same thing.

A few minutes later the random footsteps I heard in the hallway distilled into two sets headed my way. I stood up. My heart began to race. The emotional momentum that had carried me back to Austin Grate evaporated. What had I really hoped to get out of seeing her, after all? What did it mean that I wanted to see her? I thought of turning her away and hitting the road.

The door opened. Kathy stood there in jeans and a white T-shirt, Hollander by her side. Her blonde hair, perfect build and green eyes were no different than when I'd left her with him six months before, no different than when we'd lived together in Marblehead. On the face of it, we'd made a pretty picture: a psychiatrist and an obstetrician in a Victorian by the beach. No one would have guessed it the backdrop for murderous jealousy.

Kathy had been sleeping with Trevor Lucas and me at the same time, brimming over with rage toward our other sexual partners. There had been four. Staring at her, I felt the same strange mixture of hatred, pity and grief I had felt the night I carried her into Hollander's house, knowing she had killed three of Lucas' lovers (one of them male) and my only real love, Rachel.

"Will you be seeing Ms. Matheson alone?" Hollander asked.

Kathy glanced at him, then at me.

I hesitated. I could still call the whole thing off. But I knew that would leave me in more turmoil, not less.

"You'd like me to stay with you?" Hollander asked.

"No," I blurted out. I tried to collect myself, remembering how important it was that my inter- action with Kathy appear professional. "Let me know when our fifteen minutes have passed."

Hollander led Kathy to the armchair opposite mine. "Find me at the house when you're through," he told me, then left the room.

My mind was frozen with anxiety. I slowly took my seat. Neither of us said a word. A ticking sound filled the room. I looked up and noticed a clock mounted behind an iron grid over the chicken-wire window.

"Why are you here?" Kathy said finally, her voice emotionless.

"I can't say exactly why." I hadn't missed Kathy, wasn't glad to see her, didn't feel anything like longing. But I still felt connected to her. Maybe it was not only violence, but pain that joined us. Though Kathy hadn't confessed her traumatic past to me until after the killings, both of us had been in harm's way as children. Both of us had sought mastery over our suffering by becoming doctors, trying to relieve the suffering of others.

A few seconds passed. She smiled faintly. "Are you OK?"

"Getting by."

"I was hoping one of us was doing better than that."

I nodded.

"Have you been able to stay away from the drugs? Are you getting stronger?"

I thought of Hollander's words at breakfast, but I could not bear her reaching out to me. "Have they been kind to you here?" I asked.

Her face lost every hint of amiability. "That must feel good. Finally being in total control."

"It's not about that."

"Oh," she mocked. "It's so easy to get confused. You're free to go. I'm locked up. Your friend Matt can pump me full of Haldol or Thorazine anytime he feels like it. I can be strip-searched if they think I stole a pencil or a plastic spoon. If I were to threaten you, I'd land in the 'quiet room' or in restraints." Her eyes moved to my crotch. "It just *seemed* like you were on top."

I instinctively moved my forearm to cover myself. "This is going wrong. Can we kind of start again?"

"Does having that much power get you hard,

Frank? Did you fantasize about me coming in here in a little johnny, open at the back?" She spread her knees apart and ran a finger up one thigh, then over the denim seam between her legs. "Does it make you want to spank me?" She caught her lower lip between her teeth like a shy schoolgirl. "Does it make you want to fuck me?"

My stomach churned. "It makes me sad," I managed. "It makes me wish I could help you."

"You want to help me," she chuckled, leaning forward and squinting incredulously. "That's what putting me in this hell was all about?"

"I wanted you in a hospital instead of in prison."

"Because this is your domain."

"Because you're ill." Because I thought I loved you.

"Ah, yes. Sick little Kathy. Wind her up, and she thanks the all-powerful shrink for sparing her. What about *your* sickness?" She settled back into her chair. "I could have sworn you were torturing me for killing your little whore Rachel."

I took those words like a roundhouse kick to my gut. "Don't," I said.

"Look at you," she said, rolling her eyes. "You're still obsessed with her."

If I had let myself go I would have leapt at Kathy and beaten her with my fists for soiling Rachel's name. But I reminded myself that it was her illness speaking. My visit had ignited her primitive jealousy and rage. I had to keep my composure—to think and act like a psychiatrist. "And you still hate her," I managed, "even though she's dead. Do you have any idea why? Has Hollander helped you figure it out?"

"It's Psych 101, really. He thinks my dad raping me, then blowing me off in favor of my little sister when I reached puberty has a lot to do with it. He thinks I've been confused and angry ever since. Very angry."

"What do you think?"

She stared blankly at me. Her voice became mechanical. "I feel like I can express my emotions more openly. I'm sure I wouldn't hurt anyone again."

I wanted to tap into Kathy's grief over what had happened to her. "Have *you* started to hurt?"

"You really are getting off on this little power trip, aren't you?"

"I'm not looking for power. I brought you here to get well."

"You might be able to fool your friend Matt into believing that crap, but you and I should start being honest with each other, Frank. You figured out a way to lock me *and* Trevor up, even though he didn't do anything wrong."

"He knew." My teeth ground against each other. "He let you go on killing."

"As if anyone could have stopped me." She sounded proud and defiant. "All he did was let me love him. That's what really eats at you. You'd never let anyone close enough for that to happen." She shook her head. "You almost got the system to straitjacket both of us forever. But I guess Trevor's a lot harder to handle than you figured. Lock *him* in a loony bin, and he ends up running the place."

My heart began to race. I had no idea she had heard about Lynn State.

"The morning paper comes here, too, sweetheart. They like us to stay in touch with reality."

"I didn't want any of that to happen."

"But you made it happen."

My skin turned to gooseflesh.

She got to her feet and took a step toward me. "I'd do anything to save Trevor." She unbuttoned her jeans. "Let me go to Lynn State to see him. He needs me."

Just the thought of Kathy joining forces with Trevor on the locked unit frightened me to my marrow.

"Please. I could help that pregnant woman and her baby."

With the headlines obviously reaching Kathy so reliably, I hated to think how she would respond to hearing I had gone onto the locked unit myself. I felt desperate to leave. I got up and started toward the door.

Kathy blocked my path. She unzipped her fly. "They won't let me use a razor here, so I can't shave it the way Trevor likes, but it's still pretty. It still belongs to him."

I caught the eye of one of the nurses down the hall and motioned for her.

Kathy grabbed my other wrist and brought my hand to the perfect slopes of her abdomen, flesh I had caressed hungrily just six months before. "Put it down my pants," she said. "Take what you want. Just let me be with him for a little while."

I jerked my hand away just before the nurse made it to the room. She opened the door. "Finished so soon?"

Kathy turned to face the wall. "So soon?" she mimicked in a sickly sweet singsong.

I rushed out and headed toward the locked door.

"Doctor," Kathy called after me.

I didn't look back.

"Will I be seeing you again? You remind me so much of my father."

I wanted to get away from Kathy and Austin Grate as fast as I could, but I knew Hollander was waiting for me. I started over to his house, steeling myself against the emotional hurricane inside me. At his door I slammed down the bulbous brass knocker three or four times. Several seconds passed before I felt the floor of the verandah start to vibrate with his footsteps. He opened the door and looked into my eyes. He pressed his lips

together. "I warned you," he said. "Follow me."
He turned around and led me into his study.

Flames raged in the fireplace, occasionally
jumping to lick the pair of griffins carved into the
sides of the marble mantel. Hollander poured himself into a huge tapestried armchair. I took a seat
on the couch. I was shaking slightly and embarrassed for it. "Take a moment to relax," he said.

I held my legs still, but the rest of me kept
trembling.

He patted the air with his palms.

I looked away from him.

"A few deep breaths."

My fists were tight in my lap. "Don't fucking
play therapist with me, Matt." I tried to settle
myself down, but couldn't keep myself from saying what was on my mind. "Why in God's name
would you think she's any better? I don't see any
progress whatsoever."

"No. You look like you saw something mon-
strous," Hollander deadpanned. His piercing eyes
were unblinking.

"She's as lost in her infatuation with Trevor
Lucas as the day I dragged her here. She begged
me to get her to Lynn State, onto the locked unit."
I stared at him. "And I don't think she feels a bit of
remorse for murdering four people. I think she's
more venomous toward her victims now than she
was six months ago."

"I'm not sure you're thinking at all," he said evenly. "I would have expected more from you."

That cut me to the quick. Having been beaten down as a boy by my father, I had taken my nurturance as a man where I could find it. And I had found a fair measure in Hollander.

His features softened. Maybe he saw the hurt in my face. He leaned forward in his chair. His tone became gentle. "Let's gather the few facts at hand. How did Kathy make you feel?"

"Angry."

"That certainly comes through . . ."

"Sad."

He nodded, waiting me out.

"Helpless." Putting that word to the havoc in my gut made me start to relax. "Completely helpless."

"Never stop listening with the third ear, Frank."

The third ear. I settled back into the worn leather cushions of the couch. Everything became clearer. I was so personally involved in Kathy's drama that I'd failed to monitor my emotions for clues to hers. The way she had made me feel was likely a mirror of her own internal state.

"What could it mean that you feel utterly without power after sitting with Kathy?"

"She feels that way," I said immediately, remembering her protests about my putting her on the Secure Care Unit—what she called my "domain."

"I'd guess she feels it times a hundred." He held

his hands up to frame the moment at hand. "The two of you lived together. On equal footing. Now you're visiting her on a psychiatric ward. No matter what's come before, now she's a mental patient, and you're a psychiatrist. That leaves her exquisitely vulnerable."

"And very angry." I thought more about my talk with her. My scalp tightened as I remembered her last words. "She told me I reminded her of her father," I said.

Hollander closed his eyes. When he opened them he looked exhilarated, yet peaceful. "That sounds like progress to me."

We sat in silence a little while, as if noting the presence of a force more powerful than either of us. Psychiatrists call it empathy, but most people know it as God.

"The helplessness you made her feel is only a hint of how it must feel to be raped again and again and again by your father when you're nine and ten and eleven," Hollander went on. "She can't bear to face that horror, so she projects it. She makes you experience a measure of her grief and rage and helplessness—as gifts of soul, if you'll accept them. And then she tells you where it all really came from—if you'll listen."

"She projected her 'soul' on other people more than on me. I'm still walking around."

"Her violence is the most powerful data of all. You know as well as I that leaving mutilated bod-

ies to be found by the police means she was mutilated, at least psychologically. Only people who
have been spiritually murdered end up as killers.
Charlie Manson let us in on that. He yelled it out
to Bugliosi in the courtroom the moment he was
sentenced to death. 'You can't kill me, I'm already
dead.' People thought he was ranting, but he was
telling us his truth."

"You don't think there's any murderer whose
acts are inexplicable. Primary evil. Out of the
womb."

"No."

"No exception."

"None." He smiled warmly. "These are rhetori-
cal questions, Frank. You believe the same as I do.
What is it you really need to know?"

"Did I do the right thing bringing her here?"

"As opposed to what?"

"Should I have turned her over to the police?"

His eyes narrowed. "And turned over your
humanity? Knowing what you knew about how
she came to kill, having taken an oath to heal and
do no harm, how could you let her be locked in a
cage like an animal for the rest of her life?" He
leaned forward. "She's *violently ill*. You did what
every parent or sister or brother or lover of a person sick with violence would do given the chance.
Given the courage. You got her help."

"But look what's happened."

"Remember one of the primary laws of physics:

Every force begets an equal and opposite force. You bucked the system, my friend. You performed an act of grace. When you do that, it's like throwing down the gauntlet to Satan. All kinds of hell can come looking for you."

I sat silently for several seconds, remembering Lucas screaming about Satan in the courtroom. I thought about the fact that he had asked first for the Cardinal, then for me. Maybe vengeance had little to do with him calling me onto the locked unit. Maybe, whether he knew it consciously or not, he was ready to confront the hell inside him.

"What are you thinking?" Hollander asked.

"The night I carried Kathy in here I told you I didn't think I could bring myself to help a man like Trevor Lucas, not after he'd stood by and let all the killing go on. Not after what he let happen to Rachel."

"And . . ."

"Now I don't think anything will be right for me until I do help him."

Hollander looked into the flames, obviously deep in thought, then looked back at me. "Lucas may have layer upon layer of defenses keeping him from his inner truth. If that truth is as grim as we think, projecting it in your direction could make you feel things you've never experienced before. Very ugly things. And if you're wildly successful and actually get past Lucas' defenses to the core of his pathology, he may have to kill you

just because you've seen it. He may not even realize why."

"But there's a chance my seeing it and feeling it
would defuse it."

"That's the power of empathy." He shook his
head. "I wouldn't be betting on you."

"It's not like the hostages are looking at great
odds right now."

He took a deep breath, let it out. "There's a
chance. A sliver of a chance."

"Then I've got to take it."

We sat for a while without saying a word. Hollander broke the silence. "What I said before—
about expecting more from you . . . ," he started.

I nodded.

"No one could."

Five

I started racing back toward Lynn just before 11:00 A.M. Within a few miles my mind was turning on itself like a hung jury. Was Hollander right? Had bringing Kathy to Austin Grate been an act of grace? Or was Kathy's verdict closer to the truth—that I only paid lip service to believing that Trevor would get a lawyer and go free, that I was fooling myself into thinking I was getting her help, that I unconsciously wanted to put *both* of them away?

I thought back to the night I had pried Kathy's confession from her twisted mind. I had convinced her to meet me at Walton's Ocean Front, a secluded inn on Plum Island, a crooked finger of land off Newburyport, most of the way to New Hampshire from Boston. Under the influence of a dose of sodium amytal, she had confessed not only to the four murders but also to setting the house fire that had killed her little sister. She had been consumed by jealousy and hate when her father began having sex with the younger girl, just as she was consumed by those raw emotions when Trevor and I took other lovers.

I had thought of killing Kathy that night, of avenging Rachel's death. I had beaten back the impulse. I knew then as I did now, without any doubt, that no child asks to be broken psychologically, that no human decides to become a killer. Kathy had tried to run away from her pathology, becoming an obstetrician, delivering new life into the world, living in a fine home with perfect furnishings. But the past is a tireless adversary. The race from one's truth is an endless, unwinnable folly.

Under cover of that night's black rain, I had carried Kathy, a woman I had lived with and had thought that I loved, to Hollander's door.

"No," I said aloud. I had not contrived to destroy her or Lucas. I had done what I thought was right. I had done it despite society's rules, for which I have a great deal of respect and what I consider a healthy measure of contempt. There had been horrific consequences. Now being a man, being a healer, meant facing them head on.

My pager beeped again. I didn't recognize the number on the display, but when I dialed it on my car phone Emma Hancock answered. "Where are you?" I asked her.

"Carlos' place. I'm glad you don't know the number," she said. "In the old days you might have."

"Who the hell is Carlos?"

"Lynn's finest. A Dominican entrepreneur on

Union Street. We just raided his humble abode on a tip from a very frightened fourteen-year-old who got caught snorting cocaine in the boy's room at the Caldwell Middle School. Turns out Carlos gave it to him as a gift for running some packages to his other customers. We found an ounce, maybe an ounce and a half stashed everywhere from the radiators to the toilet tank over here." She paused. "I paged you because it sounds like Lucas is taking the bait. He asked for an extra hour before releasing the first of the three hostages we demanded in exchange for you and the chopper."

"Why? Why did he want the hour?"

"I don't know. Lucky he did, though. It gives us more breathing room."

I doubted Lucas was helping us out, but didn't see any reason to guess with Hancock at the bizarre plans he might be making. "Did Rice give in on the helicopter idea?" I asked.

"It landed in front of Lynn State about five minutes ago. The question is where we ultimately go with all this. If Lucas actually comes through on his end of the bargain he'll be pretty upset when we don't deliver. We need a plan to stall him— maybe even get a few more people out of there before Rice moves in with the troops at four o'clock. He's already got three armored assault vehicles and twenty ambulances lined up on Jessup Road. And I hear the chopper is decked out for combat."

"When could you meet me at the hospital?"

"I should be out of here in a little over half an hour. Where are you, anyway? Could we hook up at, say, eleven forty-five?"

I looked at my watch. 11:07. "No problem. I'll be there," I said. I was no more than twenty minutes from Lynn State, but sped up, knowing I needed all the time at the hospital I could get before Hancock showed up.

Calvin Sanger, possibly the last person I wanted to see, was sitting on the hood of his Cutlass at the head of Jessup Road, smoking a cigarette. I would have flown right by him, but he spotted my truck and jogged into the middle of the street. I stopped a few yards from him. He walked to my window. As the car in back of me passed, he nodded at the driver. I worried he'd had me tailed.

"Nothing's changed," he said. "Lucas is still running the show."

"I'd better get up there."

"Right." He looked up the road, then back at me. "Listen, Frank. I'm the little guy in this thing," he said, the arrogance in his voice suggesting he thought a great deal more of himself. "I'm at the *Lynn Daily Evening Item*. Circulation twenty-five thousand. It's nowhere."

"It's where they sign your checks."

"All three hundred eighty-five a week. The girls

you and I know at the Y probably do better." He took a last drag off his cigarette, dropped the butt and ground it out with his foot. "I'd just love to beat the big boys to the punch here. If you give me the inside story on what's being planned up there, it could really launch me. I could land at the *Boston Globe*."

"I don't have it to give."

"I have friends on the force in Revere and Salem. I could get you cases out of both stations."

"Calvin, I can't . . ."

His eye twitched. "Won't." His tone turned bitter. "What about Hancock? She must have more info on the copycat than she's letting on. Tell me what you know, and I'll see to it you come out looking like a hero. Make me work for it, all bets are off."

"Meaning?"

"There are winners and losers in every story, heroes and villains in every city. If I set my mind to it, you won't get a case in Lynn, never mind Revere or Salem."

I generally respond poorly to threats. I looked through my windshield. Without warning, I threw open my door. It caught Sanger flush in the chest. He stumbled back, falling to one knee. I got out of the truck and walked over to him. He was gasping for air. I grabbed his collar and yanked his face up toward mine. "Write whatever twenty-dollar story

you can come up with," I said. "You'll be the first
to know if I take it personally." I got back in the
truck and drove the rest of the way down Jessup.

The grounds of Lynn State looked like a Desert
Storm salvage yard. A Huey helicopter, complete
with .50-caliber machine guns tucked inside the
doors, sat in the middle of the grass out front, surrounded by police cruisers. A white canopy tent
sheltered a giant PA system and stacks of wooden
crates. The parking area was dominated by the
three assault vehicles—hulking, olive green
armored trucks perched atop twenty-four-inch
tires. In back of them stood an aluminum-walled
"temporary structure" stenciled with STATE
POLICE. Rice's black Caprice was angled along
one side. I parked next to it and jogged up a set of
makeshift wooden steps into the trailer.

Rice was seated at his desk meeting with one of
his troopers. He looked past him, at me. "Speak of
the devil," he said. He stood up, which made most
of his tiny torso disappear behind the desk. "Dr.
Clevenger, I was just talking about you with Lieutenant Patterson."

Patterson stood up, too. He was at least a few
inches over six feet tall, with defensive end shoulders and a barrel chest. He was dressed in midnight blue fatigues and a ribbed, midnight blue
turtleneck sweater. His blond hair was shaved
closed to his scalp. He swallowed my hand in his
and pumped it twice, too forcefully.

"I think we've got the good Dr. Lucas focused on his whirlybird and his plans to meet with you," Rice smiled. "Lieutenant Patterson feels we should move the assault up to twelve-thirty P.M. We can keep Lucas occupied with planning for the big swap a little while after he releases the first prisoner, but he's gonna get antsy pretty quick."

"What's the plan, exactly?"

"I'll let the lieutenant explain."

Patterson took a deep breath and let it out through his nose, like he was about to bench press twice his weight. "We proceed as if you're going to enter the building," he said. "That way we have a chance of snatching the two hostages Lucas thinks he'll be trading for you. At the last moment, we'll launch the assault."

"What sort of assault?" I asked him.

"We have multiple waves of attack. At twelve twenty-eight a team of six scales the back wall of the hospital and prepares to blast through the rear fifth-floor windows. At exactly twelve-thirty, the chopper goes airborne, and the PA system set up in the tent warns everybody on the unit to hit the floor. Thirty seconds later the chopper blasts away through the windows to cut down anything still standing. That paves the way for the troopers on the back wall to strike, just as the assault vehicles crash through the front doors to inject additional troops." His eyes lit up. "We achieve complete domination of the site within four minutes."

"What do you estimate the body count at?"

"If we get lucky, zero," Rice broke in.

"You've got psychotic patients up there who hear voices without a PA system blaring at them."

"Psychotic *killers*," Patterson said. "They've probably all thrown in with Lucas by now."

"One of them got thrown out the window by Lucas," I said.

Patterson shrugged. "All they have to do is lie down when they're told."

"They're paranoid. They're not going to lie down just because you tell them to."

"They'll end up lying down one way or . . . ," Patterson started.

Rice held up his mitt of a hand. My mind flashed back to him covering Winston's bloodied nose and mouth. I felt a reluctant respect for him. "Do you have an idea what might protect them?" he asked. "What sort of warning or message might get through?"

"I can get through," I said.

"You won't be available. We've got to use you to fake the hostage exchange. There's no time for you to be jawing on the PA."

"I mean I can get through in person—by actually going onto the locked unit. I think we should go forward with the swap."

"Come again?" Rice said, squinting at me.

"I think I can talk Lucas into surrendering."

"I must be missing something. Didn't we both

watch Dr. Winston butchered not thirty yards from here?"

I nodded. "Winston went up against Lucas like a character out of a John Wayne western. He baited him. I'm going in because Lucas asked for me. I'm complying with his wishes."

"And what in God's name would you do once you're in there?" Patterson said.

In God's name. I didn't miss the reference. I paused. "I'd listen," I answered.

"You'd listen. That's gonna be very fucking effective."

Rice looked as if he was trying to understand. He sat down Indian style on his desk chair and leaned forward, his head balanced on his fists. "Listen . . . to what?"

"To *him.* To Lucas." I shook my head, trying to come up with words to match what I believed in my heart. "If all he wanted to do was kill me he could have asked to meet me, instead of Winston, in front of the hospital. He needs something else from me—enough to be willing to give up three of his hostages before he even gets close to it."

"What's he need? Psychoanalysis?" Patterson joked.

I had to keep my cool. "Of a kind," I told him. "Maybe Lucas needs me to help him figure a way to release the hostages without feeling as if he's been conquered."

"Who gives a shit what he feels?"

"I think the families of the hostages would. I think the father of that baby up there would."

Rice's eyes stayed fastened on mine. He let out a long breath. "Why do you believe you could pull that off, doctor? Why do you think Lucas would let you get close enough to help him do the right thing?"

Patterson stormed out.

"I don't know why," I answered Rice. "But I'm willing to find out. And that's a pretty remarkable achievement on Lucas' part in and of itself. I don't think we should ignore it."

He studied me a little while. "There would have to be steady progress—hostages being released right along," he deadpanned. "If another murder takes place, whether it's yours or anyone else's, we jump-start Patterson's strategy."

"Fair enough," I said.

Several seconds passed. "Let me ask you something," Rice said. "Why did you think I would go for something like this to begin with? I'm not even sure myself why I'm signing on with it."

"I saw what you did with Winston. Anyone who has the courage to help someone end his life knows something about how precious life is."

He looked away.

"Where did you learn?"

"Vietnam." He met my eyes again. He pressed his lips together, remembering. "I was a tunnel rat."

I knew tunnel rats had the unenviable responsibility for exploring the underground maze the North Vietnamese had dug nearly from one end of their country to the other. I waited for Rice to go on.

"You wouldn't believe the things in those tunnels," he said, smiling faintly. "In some places they were barely wide enough to drag yourself through on your belly. In other places whole medical clinics had been set up. And shelters for families." His face turned somber. "Sometimes we only found out exactly what was in a tunnel after we'd filled it full of grenades." He paused. "I've seen enough killing in my life to last me the next three, doctor . . . Frank. If you can prevent some here I'd be eternally grateful to you. But once you're inside that locked unit, there's nothing I can do to help you."

I nodded. "You already have."

I didn't feel good about having gone to Rice without telling Emma Hancock. Three years before she had given me a rare second chance to get started in forensics again, after I had become persona non grata with her predecessor at the Lynn Police Department, in the wake of the Marcus Prescott fiasco.

Prescott was a thirty-two-year-old attorney who had raped a Lynn Classical High cheerleader. When he had pleaded insanity, claiming he had no memory of the attack, I had testified for the defense that his symptoms were consistent with multiple personality disorder. The jury had found him innocent and committed him to Bridgewater State Hospital. Not a week after the team there had released him, he tracked the girl down at Brown University, raped her again and strangled her.

I'd been ready to throw in the towel on my career when Hancock had called. Since that day we had been through hell together, back way beyond the killings that got Lucas arrested, to dozens of other ugly cases. That probably explained why I had reached out to Rice alone; I was convinced our friendship meant she would never sanction putting my head in the jaws of the beast.

Rice and I were standing outside the State Police trailer when I saw Hancock's red Jeep Cherokee drive onto the hospital grounds at 11:50. We'd gotten a message through to Lucas that we wanted the trading to take place all at once, at 12:30—the pregnant nurse and two social workers in exchange for me. He had agreed, demanding only that we meet on the very spot Winston had been killed. I could have heard that as a homicidal threat, but I chose to understand it as Lucas desperately trying to maintain a position of power while under siege.

Hancock parked next to my Ram and walked up to us. "Sorry I'm late. Where are we on planning?" she asked. She buttoned her coat, a plain gray wool that seemed conservative even for a fifty-five-year-old civil servant. "We should cut the heat to the building, for starters."

Neither Rice nor I said anything right away. After a few seconds, he glanced at me, then turned to Hancock. "We have a definitive plan that we . . ."

I saw her cheek quiver slightly on the second *we*. Her nails clicked just once. I held up a hand. "It was my idea."

She guessed immediately which idea I was talking about. "I already told you there's no chance I'd go along with that," she said. Her voice had defeat built into it. Rice had final say on what went down, and she knew it. She tried to keep authority in her tone, but concern overwhelmed it. "It's suicide, Frank. Forget about it. Understand?" She looked from Rice to me, then back at him.

"What's your problem, exactly?" Rice asked.

"Nothing that won't go away if you tell me how the doctor's safety is reasonably assured."

"He's not looking for any assurance."

Her jaws worked against each other. "I could go to Governor Cellucci on this. You're using a private citizen like a Navy Seal."

"You could go to Cellucci," he said. "It wouldn't change the plan, but you could. Meanwhile, I'm gonna go sweat the details so our sharpshooters have a chance to pick off Lucas if he tries anything." He walked up the wooden steps into the trailer.

Hancock looked down at the ground.

"He was going to storm the unit at twelve-thirty," I said. "He's got a lunatic lieutenant named Patterson who thinks he can pull off another raid at Entebbe."

"I know Patterson. He's bad news." She looked at me. "Why are you doing this?"

I felt as if she were looking through me. "It's the right thing to do. It's the right thing for me."

Her lips pursed. "Why? Why do you want to get yourself killed here?"

"I don't want to die, Emma. I'm not planning on it."

"You've lost all objectivity. You're *in* this thing, instead of outside it."

I could feel Hancock burrowing toward the truth— that I bore a good deal of the responsibility for getting us all into this mess, including Lucas. Part of me wished I could tell her everything. About Lucas being innocent of the murder of her niece. About Kathy. "I have a feeling in my gut," was all I did tell her. "You once told me I should always go with it."

"That's what I'm driving at. What's in your gut? What are you feeling?" She shook her head. "Listen to me. I sound like a shrink myself."

"You should probably avoid that. I doubt it would go over big at the station."

She smirked. "Tell me, anyhow."

"I feel like I can turn things around."

"Even if you're the only one who sees it that way."

"I think Lucas feels it, too. That's why he's asking for me. And Rice warmed up to the idea, even after Patterson had him ready to launch the assault."

"Lucas also feels his arm is Satan's. I'm not putting a lot of stock in his view of things," Hancock said. "As for Rice, he has nothing to lose." She averted her eyes. "I do."

I knew Hancock still dreamed of being mayor one day. I figured she was referring to the bad press she would net if I botched things. "If I screw up, call a press conference. Tell the reporters you disagreed with the strategy from the word 'go.' They know the State Police are the ones calling the shots. You'll come off looking OK."

Her eyes fastened back on mine. "I don't care how I come off looking," she said. "I care about . . ." She caught herself. "You know what? I'm not going to waste my breath."

I didn't need more than a fragment of a sentence to hear a whole volume about the distance toward one another Hancock and I had traveled since we'd started working together. "You gambled on me when no one else would," I told her. "I'll never forget that. You sure you can't bet on me one more time?"

She studied me three, four long seconds. "I hope you beat the odds, Frank. You always seem to," she said. "But this time I can't stomach them." She turned and walked away.

12:28. Rice and I braced against the raw winter air as we watched the entrance to the hospital, the last seconds of my freedom melting away like drops off an icicle, falling to the blood-stained grass at our feet. Winston's blood. "Remember," he said, "if you think things are going wrong, bolt to your right. Dive, if you have to. Patterson has enough firepower trained on this spot to vaporize anyone following you. And we'll do our best for the hostages."

I nodded. Hearing Patterson's name connected with my survival didn't reassure me. Not that anything could have. I knew if I didn't die in the next few minutes, I would face another kind of hell on the locked unit.

"Just over a minute to go. How do you feel?"

I wasn't certain what to answer. I wasn't terrified. Nor was I feeling courageous. I would have said "numb," but that wasn't quite right, either. I felt as if my whole life, every single action and emotion up to that instant, had led me to stand where I stood, waiting for Lucas. "I'm . . . all set," I said finally, then shrugged.

Rice pressed his lips together, nodded. "My commanding officer used to ask me how I felt before I dropped into one of those tunnels. I could never come up with the right words, either. 'All set' comes as close as anything." He glanced at his watch, then extended his hand. I took it. "Sorry you have to take this trip alone," he said.

Alone. A familiar word in my life. I winked. "Me, too."

We shook hands. I watched him walk away.

"See you on the other side," he called over his shoulder.

Maybe stress had distorted my perspective, but I swear that in that instant, against the backdrop of military vehicles, lofty pines and a crystalline winter sky, Rice looked tall to me. Giant. I had a memory of my father walking out of my bedroom after taking his belt to me, leaving me in tears on the floor. He had towered over me, but I had never thought of him as anything but unsteady—a circus clown on rickety stilts. Shivers spread through me as I smiled at the power of the heart to see the truth. Then, without another thought, I turned back toward the hospital and saw Lucas standing dead center inside the sliding glass doors. The sun's glare made it hard to see his face, but I could tell he was still wearing scrubs. He took a few steps backward into the lobby, then marched through the doors, arm in arm with the same entourage that had accompanied him before— Peter Zweig, Craig Bishop and the two nurses. The Harpy. Zweig and Bishop, in white orderly's outfits, held knives to the women's necks, just like they had before Winston had been killed.

My certainty about the moment fractured. Part of me wanted to run. I wondered whether Hancock had been on the right track; maybe what I was really looking for was a chance to do myself in under cover of heroics. Maybe guilt over letting Lucas stand trial for murder was driving me to serve myself up as his next victim. I tried comforting myself by recalling that every moment of insight I had achieved with patients had been preceded by an impulse in me to back off. The truth always felt like a barracuda on the line, at once beckoning and demanding to be cut loose. Finally I had cut everyone loose, closing down my practice, then myself.

What truth, I wondered, would be told now—something about Lucas' suffering or my own self-destructiveness? I felt my chances of escape dwindle with each of the Harpy's steps forward. The beast closed to ten yards. I noticed red spots appearing on Bishop's white pant leg. At five I could see the ruby droplets falling through the air. I squinted at the knives held to the nurses' throats, but saw no trace of blood. Four yards, then three, and the Harpy stopped. I looked at Lucas' face. His jaws were clenched. His pupils were tiny black dots. Pinpoints. I noticed that the blood dripped from between him and Bishop, but the two men stood flush against one another, and I couldn't see exactly where it was coming from. I buried my fear by focusing on the details of the exchange we had planned. "You agreed to release three hostages," I said.

Lucas swallowed hard. He was sweating. "You doubt my word?" He closed his eyes, as if overwhelmed with pain, then fastened them on mine again. "Lies are your domain."

"I took you at your word. That's why I'm standing here."

"Unless you're a fool. Or a madman driven to your own demise." He leaned slightly forward and thrust his neck out. His eyes grew wider. I focused on his lips and glistening white teeth, my heart pounding as every cue told me he was about to call out the word that had tripped the explosive assault on Winston. I glanced at the hospital roof and saw sharpshooters kneeling at each corner. But it was too late for me to run. Too late even to dive. Lucas raised his face skyward. The muscles in his throat stood out like iron struts. "Satan must be vanquished!" he shouted, his voice echoing off the building, then trailing off in a pneumonic gasp.

Sweat dripped down my own brow. "Three hostages," I repeated, clinging to the words as an anchor to keep me from drifting into sheer panic.

Lucas stared at me, his face blank. "One, two, three."

The Harpy advanced another few feet. Its arms lifted skyward. Zweig and Bishop bared their teeth like Rottweilers.

At that instant I was convinced I would die. I had a single thought, really more a vision, of Rachel. She wasn't propped on fluffy clouds or draped in flowing white robes. She was naked, standing before me on a stretch of jet black, steaming asphalt that did not burn her feet. Her arms were outstretched, palms up, and I could see that the scars from when she had slashed her wrist as a girl were gone. Her skin was pristine again. She said nothing, but her eyes told me she was at peace. And as my throat tightened with wonder at that healing I realized that more than a few seconds had gone by. Rachel disappeared. I was still standing before the Harpy. I looked at Lucas, then past him at three figures—two black men and an old woman—advancing from the sliding glass doors to the hospital. Each was dressed in a hospital gown. They were patients.

"Three for one," Lucas said flatly. The Harpy's arms relaxed. " 'You're a valuable commodity."

"You agreed to release the pregnant—"

"Three lives," Lucas sputtered, grimacing in pain. "Can we count any one more than any other? Is anyone expendable? Human refuse?"

I heard the question as a reference to my letting Lucas stand trial in place of Kathy. Or perhaps another person had brokered Lucas' life before I had. I wanted to know, hungered to know. The barracuda beckoned. "Let's go inside," I said.

"Come closer."

I took a few steps.

"Here. Closer."

A few more steps. I was within a yard of Lucas, literally in his shadow. I noticed that the red droplets were pooling on the hard ground now, instead of being absorbed by Bishop's pant leg. I looked up to find their source and lost my breath. I took a step back. My legs were weak. I had to concentrate to avoid stumbling and triggering Patterson's arsenal.

"Don't let this bother you," Lucas said. He held his right arm straight out. It had been severed midway up the forearm, then sutured with at least two hundred haphazard blue nylon stitches. Parts of the wound still oozed blood. "Not what I would call an elegant job, nothing to rival Halsted or DeBakey, but given that I was forced to use my left hand . . ." He regarded the wound with detachment, then let the stump fall back to his side. "If thine arm offends thee, cut it off."

The ghastliness of what Lucas had done chased away my fear. Resonating with the suffering of others has always, for better or worse, steadied me. "I wish it were that easy," I said.

"If what were easy?" Lucas bristled.

"To be rid of your demons." I paused, unsure how hard to press him. "They weren't in your arm."

"*Satan's* arm!" Lucas glared. "I have proof."

"Show me."

"In there." He threw his head back at the hospital.

"Show me."

Lucas chuckled. Sweat dripped off his chin. "My pleasure." I held my breath as the Harpy closed in on me. I could feel Lucas' breath on my face. I gritted my teeth as the monster embraced me. The sun disappeared. I felt us moving together toward the hospital and—I knew in my heart—nearly unspeakable horrors.

Six

With the Harpy still surrounding me, I walked in silence through the lobby and down a long corridor. Zweig, Kaminsky, Lucas and the nurses were positioned in a way that made it hard to see where we were going, but I had visited Lynn State before and remembered the basic layout of the place. We were headed toward the service elevator at the back of the building. I remembered the odor, too—a cocktail of institutional antiseptics that never quite covered up the mustiness. A building can absorb only so much desperation before it starts to reek of it. Too much sweat in the mattresses. Too much urine in the grout. Drywall stained by leaks and cracked by time, full of screams. We turned, then stopped. Elevator doors clamored open. We moved inside. A bell chimed at each floor en route to the fifth. The doors opened again. We marched out, then down a short hallway. I heard dead bolts sliding and got a glimpse of the thick iron door to Ward 5B. It swung open for us. As we took our first steps onto the unit, a few drops of Lucas' blood landed on my arm and ran down to my fist, tight with fear. I

instinctively opened my hand and tried to flick the
blood away, but more drops were feeding the
stream. It flowed onto my palm and between my
fingers. I wiped the blood onto my pant leg. Just
then, Zweig and Bishop broke off from the Harpy,
taking the two nurses with them. I was alone with
Lucas. I couldn't help staring at his severed arm.

He pointed down the hallway with his stump,
dragging my gaze with it. "The battlefield."

I forced myself to look around. I had expected
chaos on the unit. The order I saw was more terrifying. The Day Room, about twenty by thirty feet,
had been emptied of furniture. Two rows of a
dozen male and female patients, all of them
dressed in white orderly's uniforms, knelt in the
middle of the floor, their backs to me, their faces
tilted up toward the grated windows. They were
chanting, but I couldn't tell what they were saying. When I had visited Lucas in his jail cell after
his arrest on murder charges, he'd been chanting
the same way. I closed my eyes to focus and
barely made out their words.

I have no life. I have no death.

"The Samurai warrior's prayer," Lucas said.
"Readying the spirit for combat."

I glanced at him, then looked down the hallway
in front of us. Ward 5B was a twenty-bed unit, ten
rooms on either side. Patients were standing at

attention at the doorways to several of them. The quiet room—a euphemism for a padded cell—was at the end of the hallway. The door was ajar. A large ring of keys hung from the lock.

I turned to see into the nurses' station. My chest tightened. A young woman sat perfectly still in one of the chairs overlooking the Day Room, her eyes vacant. She was naked and gagged. Her hospital identification badge was clipped to the skin just above her left breast. Her wrists were bound behind her.

"Satan in the uterus," Lucas said. "She was bleeding, yet insists it isn't her time of the month."

I took a few steps toward her, focusing on her swollen abdomen. I heard my own breathing over the constant chant coming from the Day Room. I turned and looked directly into Lucas' eyes. "She's pregnant," I said as calmly as I could. "If she was bleeding she needs help right away."

"Of course she needs help. She's infested."

"She needs an obstetrician."

"She needs to be purified before God!" he shouted. "Satan chews at her womb!"

I didn't respond.

Lucas seemed shaken by the surge of madness in him. He struggled to regain composure. "You'll see. You'll see what pure evil can do." He started down the hallway.

I followed him, but stopped at the first room to the left. It was empty except for a conference table and a set of stainless steel shelves designed to hold plastic food trays. The table and the floor were streaked with blood. Puddles had collected in places, some of them congealed to mounds of ruby-black jelly.

"My OR," Lucas called back to me from further down the hall. "I had to make do."

I noticed a few of the food trays had been pulled halfway out of their metal sleeves. They held an assortment of perfectly aligned hypodermic syringes, sutures and bloodied razor blades. My heart was pounding. I glanced back at the door to the unit, instinctively checking whether escape was possible. The door was bolted shut. I recognized Craig Bishop standing against the wall next to it, peering out through the plate glass window, crowing his neck now and then to make sure no one was trying to approach the unit. Despite my terror I was taken aback by that. Lucas had recruited a cold-blooded killer, a man who had beheaded his victims, as a security guard. I wondered how he had won Bishop's confidence.

"Frank," Lucas shouted. "Come here."

I was light-headed. The buzz of fluorescent lights combined with the constant chant from the Day Room made me want to cover my ears. When I joined Lucas outside the fourth room on the right, the rest of my strength drained out of me. I broke into a cold sweat.

A woman was lying naked in four-point

restraints atop a soiled bedsheet. Her head was shaved. A fresh line of what had to be hundreds of perfectly placed sutures ran from her chin, down her neck, between her breasts, along the line of her abdomen and between her legs. Her eyes were closed, but she was breathing. An IV ran into each arm. A large man in his forties with a hospital identification bracelet on his wrist sat next to the bed holding a clipboard.

"Pulse?" Lucas asked him.

The man didn't answer.

"Gabriel!" Lucas clapped his hands. "Her vitals."

"Yes, doctor," the man said in an emotionless baritone. "Pulse sixty-two. Pressure ninety over sixty." His eyes were unblinking, and his pupils, in contrast to Lucas', were huge.

"Increase the drip." Lucas glanced at me. "Gabriel was a health aide before he lost his way."

That reference helped me remember Gabriel's case. His full name was Gabriel Vernon, and he was awaiting trial for dismembering his gay lover.

Gabriel struggled out of his seat. He stood at least six foot four and had to weigh 275 pounds. With shaking hands he adjusted the little plastic clips that controlled the rate of flow of the IVs. I wondered if his weakness and tremor were side effects of antipsychotic medication. In high doses the medicines can cause a syndrome that mimics Parkinson's disease.

"She looks rough," Lucas said, "but she'll recover."

"Who is she?"

"You don't know?"

I shook my head.

"Doctor Laura. Not the famous one."

I didn't catch on. I guess I didn't want to.

"The one who testified before God that I was psychotic. A lunatic."

I squinted at her face and finally recognized Laura Elmonte's features. The walls undulated. I grabbed hold of the door frame. "What have you done to her?"

"Incision and drainage."

"Incision and drainage? Of what?"

"Black bile."

"She was helping you."

"She was helping Satan to me!" he seethed. "She was stuffed full of Lucifer's lies. All that gibberish about *'alien hand'* while the dark one snaked up my arm." He started marching down the hall.

There was nothing for me to do but follow him. I wondered whether that was what Craig Bishop, Peter Zweig, Gabriel Vernon and the others felt. Psychotic patients—even psychotic killers—need something or someone to steady them against the chaos in their minds. Who better than a physician from their own ranks? I took a deep breath and managed to walk the rest of the corridor staring straight ahead, reminded by low moans and weak cries that a gallery of terrors lay in the rooms to either side of me. I hadn't seen the two social workers or the dietitian on the unit yet. And I knew from what had happened to Grace Cummings that Lucas' violence could engulf patients as well as staff.

Lucas stopped in front of the next-to-the-last room on the right. Two patients—one male and one female—stood at the doorway. They bowed slightly in deference to him. Lucas gestured for me to join him inside. I assumed he meant the room to be mine. When I reached it, however, I saw a pale, naked man face-down on the bed in four-point restraints. His head was shaved like Elmonte's and marked with a black upside-down *V* running ear to ear, the point of the *V* at the crown of his head. I wondered whether he might be one of the social workers. Lucas walked to the side of his bed. "I'll need you to scrub in with me on this one," he said, stroking the man's scalp.

The man struggled to move his head away, but Lucas' fingers stayed with him.

"Lord knows I've tried everything. Haldol. Thorazine. The quiet room. Even shock therapy."

"Shock therapy," I said, more to myself than to Lucas.

He nodded at the electroconvulsive therapy machine in the corner of the room. As a medical student I'd been amazed how small the machines were, not much bigger than boom boxes on legs. I figured something that throws a man into epileptic fits ought to look ominous—a wall of blackened steel and chrome dials. "We got seizures of respectable length, too," Lucas said. "Fifteen seconds or more. A dozen times. But he's not responding."

A kind of desperation, a distant cousin to courage and a much closer one to panic, grabbed hold of me. "What are you trying to help him with?" I asked, taking a step closer.

"Evil, like the rest. He killed his own son," Lucas said. "Can you imagine such a thing? A boy just eight years old. And he won't pray for his own salvation." He leaned next to the man's ear. *"He refuses to renounce the demons in his skull."*

I took another step toward the two of them. "Maybe you haven't reached the little boy in him," I said reflexively, a boxer fighting on instinct.

Lucas seemed not to have heard me. He straightened up but stayed focused on the man's head. "Luckily I rotated through three months of neurosurgery before I settled on plastics," he said. "Together you and I will get where we need to go."

"Where is that?" I asked.

"The amygdala."

The amygdala is a tiny structure that looks like an almond buried deep beneath the cerebral hemispheres, near the center of the brain. Neuroscientists consider it a critical processing center for emotions and behavior, including anger and violence. "What do you mean, get there?" I asked.

"Surgically. It must be removed."

I could feel my pulse in my temples. "You can't . . ."

"I know I don't have the benefit of CT guidance, or my right hand for that matter," Lucas went on. "But we'll manage."

"You'll never get at his disease with a scalpel," I said. "Or Haldol. Or shock treatments."

Lucas glared at me.

Something inside me drove me past any hint of safety. Maybe I wanted to absorb Lucas' rage myself. I'd done it countless times for my mother, standing in as a punching bag when my father was drunk and swinging. I'd done it for my patients until my own sanity had started to wear thin. Or maybe it was the gambler in me, throwing down the truth the way I used to throw down my last couple grand—my mortgage-drug-car-bar money—on a single hand of blackjack, as if the Fates would hesitate to clean me out. "You can't cut out his disease any more than you can rid yourself of evil by chopping off your arm," I said.

His face flushed and his lip curled. "You need time to think," he said, barely containing himself. "We have a job to do here before I can leave." He turned on his heels. "Come along."

I followed Lucas across the hall to the last room on the left, next to the quiet room. He pulled open the door and swept his stump over the threshold. His lip still quivered with rage. "Your room, sir."

I looked in. A bare mattress lay between raised bed rails. Leather wrist and ankle restraints were buckled to each corner.

"Too bad Rachel's gone," he said, with a twisted grin. "The two of you could have had quite a time in a place like this."

If I needed a reminder of the malignant character layered beneath Lucas' insanity, that did the trick. I remembered the day he had boasted to me about the humiliation he had heaped on women, including Emma Hancock's niece. And I remembered that he had let Kathy go on killing and killing, until Rachel was dead.

The nearest patient was at least ten feet away. Against Lucas' one arm I could easily maneuver him into a choke hold. I could probably snap his neck before any of his Haldol zombies made it over to us. I was farther from the chanting in the Day Room, but it suddenly echoed louder in my ears.

I have no life. I have no death.

"I remember watching her dance at the Lynx Club," Lucas went on. "She had that nice ass. A very nice little ass."

I fantasized how it would feel to overcome the last of Lucas' life force with the quick twist that would sever his spinal cord. I heard—almost felt—his vertebrae cracking against my arm. Maybe Lieutenant Patterson had been right, maybe that was the best treatment for a beast. Take him off the planet. God's work here on earth. I looked at Lucas. Some of what I was feeling must have been in my eyes because he took a step back. He nearly cowered. And all of a sudden, and only for an instant, he looked less a monster and more a frightened, disfigured man. A sick man. I remembered how Hollander had warned me to inspect my own emotions to make certain they weren't projections from Lucas' psyche. And that helped me convince myself, barely, that I was feeling his murderous rage, that I didn't own it unless— until—I acted on it. To triumph over his madness, I had to refuse madness. If Satan is anything, he is a master of temptation, a drug pusher selling the potential darkness inside every one of us.

I closed my eyes to keep from seeing the way I could kill him. "I was wrong to let you stay locked up in prison," I said. "I wanted to see you suffer. I didn't know how ill you were already."

I felt a blaze of pain across my left cheek, then a kick to my gut that knocked the wind out of me. I stumbled back into the room and fell hard onto the linoleum floor, gasping for air.

Lucas stood at the door, a scalpel in his hand. "I am waging a war against the darkest force in the universe," he declared. "I have lost my own arm to the enemy. You can be of tremendous help. You can be a soldier for Almighty God. But you have to be willing and pure of heart." He stepped back. The door swung shut, and the dead bolt slid home.

I lay on my side catching my breath. A dull ache spread through my gut. I watched drops of blood from my cheek feed a little pool that had started to form at the border of one green linoleum square and one gray linoleum square. I blindly traced the length of my wound with my fingertip, guessing it ran about four inches, knowing it ran deep. I struggled to a kneeling position. I took in as much air as my pain would allow and used the bed rails to pull myself to my feet. I walked to the sink and looked in the mirror mounted above it. I figured I needed about ten, fifteen stitches. I turned on the faucet and doused my face with cold water, but the blood kept coming. I pressed my cheek to my shoulder to tamponade the vessels. As I did, I heard footsteps outside my door, then Lucas' voice.

"You're certain that's twenty milligrams," he said. "Don't underdose. Never underdose."

"Exactly twenty," Gabriel Vernon answered in his baritone.

Twenty of Haldol would drop a racehorse.

"Get it into him. Do whatever you need to."

The door swung open. Gabriel Vernon stepped into the room. He was so broad that the entire door frame disappeared behind him. I immediately looked for a syringe in his hand, but saw that he was holding a tiny paper cup. "Medicine for you," he said flatly. His sunken eyes were unblinking. "Take it." He walked within a couple of feet of me and held out the cup.

I looked and saw an orange liquid. I had hoped for pills. Pills can be "cheeked," then spit out. I'd written my share of "mouth check" orders on violent inpatients who could stash four, five different medicines with the flick of a tongue.

"Take it," Vernon repeated.

I knew if I didn't drink it, he'd force me to. Or he'd come back with an injection. But, even so, I didn't reach for the cup. Twenty milligrams of Haldol wasn't a lethal dose, but it would put me out, probably through the entire day and night. And anything could happen in that long a time.

"Please. You got to take it. I got to make you take it."

Did he not want to hurt me, I wondered? Or didn't he want to be bothered with the hassle of hurting me? I reached for the cup. He handed it to me carefully. I noticed he had stopped shaking. I brought the cup to my lips and sipped the liquid. A sickly sweet orange flavoring almost covered up the bitterness. I'd tasted that combination of fruit and chemical before. It wasn't Haldol. It was methadone, the opiate used to get people off heroin. I'd stolen a few sips from the Atlantic Hos-

pital inpatient unit once when I was out of cocaine
and out of cash and needed to settle my nerves.
Suddenly, Lucas' tiny pupils made sense to me;
methadone causes pupils to constrict. I looked at
the orange liquid and shook my head. The road
back from addiction had been the toughest journey of my life.

Vernon started toward me, his hands outstretched. As his fingers closed around my shoulders I fired down the twenty milligrams. He
stopped, took a couple steps back and watched
me. I felt the liquid coat my throat, then warm my
stomach. The enemy was inside. "You take this
poison yourself, Gabriel?" I asked.

"It's medicine." He studied me. "I took mine
before you took yours."

That probably explained why his hands had
been trembling minutes ago, but no longer. He'd
been withdrawing and needed a dose. I noticed
that his pupils had shrunk down to nothing. "Who
gives it to you?"

"The doctor."

It is physiologically impossible to become
addicted to methadone in twenty-four hours.
Somehow the patients had gotten access to the
drug before taking over the unit. "How long have
you been on it? Is everyone here using it?"

He took a few steps back. "Case conference in
two hours," he said. "In the Day Room." He
turned and walked out.

I sat down on the bed. I was starting to feel light-headed. I'd swallowed as much methadone as a thirty-bags-a-day addict—a serious junkie— would need to steady himself. Without a habit, the opiate receptors in my brain were wide-open territory and would be deluged in minutes. I fell back onto the mattress. My heart told me I should have fought against Vernon, that being beaten into using a drug would somehow have vaccinated me against falling in love with it. Regret welled up in me for an instant, then was gone. Opiates are like grease for the superego. They keep you rolling through the times and places in your life where conscience should slow you down or grind you to a halt. Psychic pain, that gift from God that can warn us we are lost, is quelled. I closed my eyes. Even more quickly than I guessed it would, my body seemed to get heavy, sinking deeper into the mattress. My mind grew lighter than air. And not unpleasantly, the two parted company.

Vernon shook me awake and pulled me to my feet. His face, never a reassuring sight, seemed to undulate grotesquely now. The room was spinning. Warm blood from my cheek had soaked the shoulder of my shirt and started to trickle down my arm. Yet my heart didn't race. My breathing was even. My fear called to me with a faint scream, very far off, nothing to be done about it. Vernon handed me another paper cup. I winked and tossed it at him. The orange liquid splattered his hospital scrub shirt. Without a word, he turned and walked out of the room. I collapsed onto the mattress and fell back asleep.

Ten, fifteen minutes or an hour or two passed before I woke up in a panic, short of breath. Vernon was straddling my chest. His knees crushed into my biceps, pinning my arms to the mattress. I struggled with everything I had. He barely moved. I threw all my weight to my right side and managed to sink my teeth into his thigh, but he knocked me to the mattress with a backhand to my mouth that made me taste blood. He reached down to the floor. I tried frantically to free myself, kicking wildly. It was hopeless. I tracked his hand with my eyes, expecting a blade, remembering he had castrated a man, but another paper cup appeared. I should have made him wrench my jaws apart. I didn't. I opened my mouth, still in some measure a willing victim, and he poured more orange bitters into me. There was less to swallow than the first time; I guessed I was getting another ten milligrams. As soon as the job was done, he lumbered off me. "Case conference," he said. "Now." He pulled me to a seated position on the mattress. "Let's go."

We started down the corridor. I tried to chart a straight course by focusing on the locked door at the end of the unit, but after drifting several feet I slammed into the cinder block wall. I would have landed face-down on the floor, but Vernon grabbed my arm and held me up. Firmly, almost kindly, he guided me the rest of the way to the Day Room.

The dozen patients who had been chanting now knelt with their backs against the far wall, silently mouthing their words. The grated windows behind them cast a collage of checkerboard shadows over an eight-foot table that had been placed in the middle of the room. Lucas sat at the head of the table, Peter Zweig and Gary Kaminsky to either side. Craig Bishop was taking his place a few seats down. An emaciated woman about sixty who I didn't recognize was already seated next to him. She was holding herself to keep from shivering. I looked into the nurses' station and saw the pregnant woman slumped forward toward the counter, still bound. From the movement in her shoulders I could tell she was breathing. The clock behind her read 3:45.

Lucas stood. "Dr. Clevenger." A single nod. "We've reserved a place of honor for you." He pointed to a chair at the far end of the table. He waited for Vernon to help me into my seat, then told him to wait by the door. His eyes never left me as he sat back down. "I believe you have met everyone here, with the exception of Ms. Gladstone," he said.

I knew *of* Cecelia Gladstone. She was a Boston socialite who had poisoned her husband, president of the Beacon Street Bank, two months earlier.

After her arrest she claimed he had beaten her for years, making murder her only recourse. She had been admitted to Lynn State for a psychiatric evaluation prior to trial. I squinted to bring her into focus and saw that her pupils were almost dime-sized. Her skin was clammy gooseflesh. She was in full-blown opiate withdrawal.

She stared blankly at me.

"Now that we're all acquainted, let me summarize the case at hand," Lucas went on. He turned to Kaminsky. "Listen carefully. You're expected to present Nurse Vawn's case on your own tomorrow." He looked past me, into the nurses' station. "Provided the Lord sustains her through the night."

"Yes, sir."

The notion of a kidnapper and rapist presenting a pregnant woman's "case" made my stomach turn.

"You must pay attention to form," Lucas prodded him.

Kaminsky folded his hands and abruptly leaned forward to listen. Watching him, I lost my own center of gravity and swayed in my seat. I grabbed hold of the table.

"Choppy seas," Lucas said, with a wink. "Stay with us." He waited several seconds, then began his presentation. "Today's patient is Lindsey Simons. Ms. Simons is a twenty-two-year-old single white female from Brookline. She is one of two children born to affluent parents—an attorney and an accountant. She has no children of her own. She has no known medical illnesses and no known drug allergies. She insists none of her first-degree relatives suffers a mental illness. As to employment, we know Ms. Simons has most recently served as a social worker here on the unit. She has worked previously as a clothing store clerk and as a substitute teacher. The symptoms of her present illness consist chiefly of compulsive lying. Without provocation she has attempted to deceive us and our families, promulgating destructive falsehoods about our mental capacities and our characters." He paused, glanced suspiciously at his left arm—his good arm. He looked at me, then quickly away. "Of course we do not hold Ms. Simons directly responsible for her actions. We know Satan can take any form, even one as seemingly innocent as hers." He snapped his fingers and immediately had Gabriel Vernon's attention. "Get the patient," he said flatly.

A minute later Vernon marched a naked woman into the room. She stood about five-feet-seven. Her expression was somber. Her face was pale and angular, with a prominent nose and jaw. Yet she was by no means ugly. Her features, framed by curly black hair to her shoulders, balanced each other well enough to create a profile that, even held hostage, suggested strength. Her nipples were dark and erect. I found myself thinking how closely fear mimicked excitement at the sexual nerve endings.

Vernon escorted the young woman into the space between the windows and the table, the row of kneeling patients behind her. I saw that her back and buttocks were covered with red welts. I had the feeling that Lucas had inflicted the punishment. I wondered whether he had forced himself on her. I pictured him doing it.

"Kneel," Lucas shouted.

Simons' eyes darted around the table, searching, it seemed, for an ally. They settled on mine. For a very brief time we anchored each other amidst the chaos.

"Kneel!" Lucas demanded again.

She sunk slowly to her knees and hung her head.

The patients behind her continued mouthing their prayer.

"Does anyone at the table have a question for Ms. Simons?" Lucas asked.

Peter Zweig, the nineteen-year-old who had killed his parents, cleared his throat. I looked over at him. His hand was moving up and down over his crotch. "Does she hear voices?"

"Ask the patient," Lucas said.

Zweig looked shyly at Simons. "Do you hear voices?"

She looked straight at him and shook her head.

"See visions?" Zweig asked. He dropped his hand into his scrub pants and started stroking himself.

"No."

"Day, date and time," Gary Kaminsky demanded.

"Wednesday, January 15, 1999," she said, making eye contact with him. "Four P.M." She glanced up at the clock. "4:02."

"Who's the . . . President of the United States?" Zweig added, his breathing erratic.

I realized the two of them were spewing random questions from the standardized mental status examination. Psychiatrists use the battery of questions to assess clarity of thought and the presence or absence of hallucinations. Zweig and Kaminsky had obviously been given the exam enough times to memorize parts of it.

"Clinton," Simons answered.

"Do you think about killing yourself?" Craig Bishop half-shouted.

"I've thought about it in the last day," Simons said. "Not before."

"How would you do it?" Bishop asked. "Would you hang yourself?"

'Would you slash your wrists and bleed to death?" Bishop went on. "Would you jump out the window like Grace Cummings?"

I felt as if I were on a carousel, with the room rushing by in blurry snapshots. My forehead was damp with sweat.

She hesitated. "Pills."

Gary Kaminsky started rocking back and forth in his seat. "You have sex dreams?"

She didn't respond. Her eyes fell.

"Do you have dreams where you're getting fucked?"

Cecelia Gladstone grimaced and looked out the windows.

"Where you've got a stiff cock in your pussy and a dildo—"

"Enough!" Lucas shouted, holding up his stump. My whirling consciousness slowed against the force of his voice. He glared at Zweig. "Get out. Now. Go to your room."

I was amazed to see Zweig rise sheepishly out of his seat and walk slowly out. Lucas seemed to have achieved complete control of him and the others.

"Do you have any questions for the patient?" he asked Cecelia Gladstone.

She shook her head. "I need more medicine," she said. "I'm sick."

"Are you a physician?"

She didn't answer.

"Cecelia?"

"No."

"Correct," Lucas said. "Trust that you'll get

what you need when you need it." He angled his chair in Simons' direction. "Are you willing to get well so that you can leave the unit?" he asked her.

"Yes," she said, looking up at him.

"Never look at me." He paused as she hung her head, again. "You feel you can accept treatment?"

She stayed silent.

"Do you want treatment?" Lucas persisted.

She started to cry, then whispered, "Yes." She began to shake uncontrollably.

"Don't be sad. The Lord helps those who help themselves."

"What treatment?" I managed to ask. "What is it she wants?"

Lucas regarded me with a mixture of pleasure and contempt. "To be rid of her lies. To be free and true. Ready for discharge." He reached into the back pocket of his scrubs. A scalpel appeared in his hand. "To be rid of that tongue."

My heart fell. "You can't," was all I could say.

"But I must. No surgeon worthy of his oath would let disease spread through the body when a clean excision could save it."

I collected the little that was left of my energy and concentration. "Let me treat her."

Kaminsky and Bishop began to laugh. "She is a treat," Bishop grinned. "Simons says, 'Cut out her tongue.' " His hand moved to his groin.

Lucas put the scalpel down. "You want to treat her. By all means. That's why you're on the team, doctor." He slid the scalpel the full length of the table. It came to rest just within my reach.

"I wouldn't cut her."

"No? What would you suggest?"

I wanted to harness Lucas' connection, pathologic or not, to prayer. "We should pray," I said automatically. "We should pray for her soul." I nodded at the patients kneeling behind Simons. "Them and us." I paused, wiped away the sweat running into my eyes. "That is, if you really believe she's possessed."

Lucas stared at me silently for several seconds. "Does the group feel this treatment is an option?"

No one spoke.

"Could we have a show of hands?"

At the door, Gabriel Vernon lifted his hand just past his waist.

Lucas glanced at him. "We're very democratic here on the unit," he said after a few moments. "Every one has a voice. Even Gabriel." He paused. "The treatment of choice is the scalpel."

I didn't make a move.

"Use it, and she leaves. Cured. Otherwise, I'm inclined to let Mr. Zweig do his best to treat her."

The room fell utterly silent. I stared at the scalpel.

Simons was the first to speak. "I want you to do it," she said evenly.

I looked over at her. Tears streamed down her face.

"I don't want to die here."

"Mr. Zweig is perfectly qualified to help you," Lucas said.

"No. Please," she sobbed.

"Well, doctor?" Lucas said, looking at me.

I didn't respond.

Lucas turned to Gabriel Vernon. "Bring Ms. Simons to Mr. Zweig's room. And bring him the scalpel."

"I'm begging you," Simons pleaded with me.

My heart raced, despite the methadone coursing through my bloodstream. I knew I could inflict the wound more kindly than Lucas, certainly more kindly than Zweig. But would that not be a devil's bargain? A capitulation to evil? I could feel the projection from Lucas' psyche weighing on mine. I held fast to a single principle: I was on the unit to cure him, not become him. I had to meet his darkness with equally intense light. It was the only way into his psyche and out of this hell. My whole body trembled at the thought of what I was about to say. I barely managed to get the words out. "Take mine, instead." Out of the corner of my eye, I saw Kaminsky and Bishop exchange puzzled glances.

Lucas' lip curled. "She's begging you," he said.

"My lies are greater than hers. Take my tongue and let her go."

Lucas' face reddened. His gaze skipped from patient to patient, as if assessing whether I was reaching any of them. "Trickery!" he spewed. "You're speaking her evil. She's infecting you."

I felt like I had cornered a rabid dog, which is very much what it feels like to touch extreme psychopathology. Showing fear could be the end of me. I had to press on. I slid the scalpel back down the table. It came to rest within inches of Lucas. "You see Satan everywhere because you can't bear to look into your own darkness."

Lucas snatched up the scalpel and started around the table.

I was resolved to fight if I had to, but I didn't want to make a move until I knew for certain Lucas was going to lash out. I sat bolt upright and met his wild eyes with a steady gaze.

Three steps from me, he raised the scalpel.

I stood, poised to lunge for his wrist, but he suddenly veered off toward Simons.

The patients behind her began chanting aloud again. She closed her eyes and opened her mouth.

"No!" I shouted.

A grotesque moan of pain and a chorus of applause filled the room.

Seven

"Satan be damned!" Lucas cried out.

I looked down at Lindsey Simons, lying in the fetal position, holding her mouth as blood poured out of it.

Lucas walked over to me. He tossed the scalpel on the table. "Why don't you take her to your room? Keep her for yourself," he said. "She certainly won't talk back."

The combination of methadone and adrenaline coursing through my system left me feeling dizzy and wired. I glanced at Simons, then at the pregnant nurse bound at her station, then at the scalpel. I took deep breaths, fighting the impulse to grab the blade and drive it into Lucas.

"Why don't we carve her up some more and have her jump like Cummings?" Craig Bishop smirked.

I turned to face him too fast, and the room started to spin.

"C'mon, c'mon, c'mon," he singsonged, like some crazed eight-year-old.

I felt my terror and revulsion flipping into rage. It steadied me, as it does all violent people.

"Cut her. C'mon, c'mon . . ."

Every charged emotion in my being leapt in his direction like lightning to a steel rod. I grabbed the scalpel with one hand and took hold of his hair with the other. I dragged him out of his seat, falling to one knee and bringing his neck across my thigh.

Gabriel Vernon started toward me from the door, but Lucas waved him off.

I placed the tip of the scalpel where I could see the pulsation of Bishop's carotid artery. "What would you carve into her?" I asked him through clenched teeth.

He didn't answer.

"Tell me how you would cut her," I insisted. "*Say it.* What would you carve into her?" I pressed down just hard enough to compress the artery without puncturing it. A millimeter deeper, and his life would start draining out of him.

"Whore," he whispered. Then, more boldly: "Whore. Whore . . ." He kept repeating the slur, louder and louder. "Whore, whore, whore . . ."

I thought of Bishop beheading his victims. I etched the first stroke of the *W* over his carotid, barely cutting the skin. The track of the blade turned white for an instant, then red. A horrific feeling of power surged in me. I etched the second stroke.

Bishop looked directly into my eyes. "Fuck you," he said flatly. He grabbed hold of my wrist and pulled the scalpel hard across his neck. His carotid pumped blood over both of us.

The patients who had been lined up on their knees behind us scattered to the far corners of the room, cowering, wailing, cheering. Cecelia Gladstone buried her face between her knees.

"Christ!" I yelled. I tried to tamponade the severed vessel with my free hand. But before I could put any real pressure on it, Bishop drew the scalpel across his neck again, cutting the carotid that ran up the other side. I struggled to break away, crawling a few feet toward Lucas. Bishop's grip on my wrist was too strong. He slashed himself again and again until, too late, I managed to think clearly enough to relax my fingers and let the scalpel drop to the floor. By that time, his neck was carved up beyond anything I guessed Lucas could repair—especially with his left hand.

My heart pounded painfully as I watched his body try to cling to life. His eyes bulged, as if desperate to hold on to a view of this world. His mouth opened wide and his chest heaved, struggling in vain to get oxygen to vital organs cut off from the circulatory system. I wanted to look away, but I was transfixed. Ten seconds later he lay perfectly still.

The patients fell silent.

"Murderer!" a deep voice bellowed. I looked up. A dark, muscular man about fifty, his head shaved, his arms and neck covered with spider web tattoos, was pointing menacingly in my direction. He started toward me.

The dark power surged in me again. I picked up the scalpel and sprang to my feet. I felt the saliva running thick in my mouth. Sweat poured off me. I wasn't ready just to defend myself. I was ready to kill.

Lucas moved in front of him. "Go to your room," he demanded. He didn't wait for a response. He looked past him at the other patients. "Everyone. Thirty minutes in your rooms."

The man started to walk around him.

I took a step forward.

"Another inch, Mr. Kashoor, and you'll spend the night in the quiet room," Lucas went on. "And I can assure you you'll be praying for light of day."

Kashoor stopped, weighing options. His eyes told me he wanted to get at me very nearly as much as he wanted to avoid whatever punishment he might receive.

"Gabriel," Lucas said, "Mr. Kashoor needs an escort."

Kashoor waited until Gabriel was within a few feet, then turned around and followed the rest of the patients, including Cecelia Gladstone, out of the Day Room.

Gabriel and Gary Kaminsky stood together, looking down at Craig Bishop's body.

"Make certain the others do as they were told," Lucas instructed the two of them. "Medicate anyone in distress."

They hurried to the task.

Lucas walked over to the body. He placed the tip of his shoe on Bishop's forehead, applying enough pressure to tilt his head back and expose the severed carotid arteries. "He's been suicidal for some time," he said, a note of pleasure audible in what sounded like manufactured grief. "I suppose you couldn't have known."

My legs went even more rubbery than before. I shook my head, not wanting to believe I had pushed Bishop over the edge. I felt like a vice had been clamped to my temples.

"Rumor had it you stopped seeing patients after a young man's suicide," Lucas went on. He nodded at the scalpel in my hand. "I guess you really are done with talk therapy. You were hot to put Mr. Kashoor away, too."

Tears choked me. I thought again of Hollander's warning about the emotions Lucas would project onto me. Whose demons were taking possession of me? Lucas'—or my own?

Lindsey Simons began moaning behind me.

I turned toward her and lost my balance, nearly falling. Lucas grabbed me with his one hand, his fingers wrapping tightly around my upper arm. I managed to stay on my feet. Simons was still lying in the fetal position. Without planning to or wanting to I focused on her naked bottom.

"What to do with Miss Society?" he said. "That's the question." He paused. "Why not take her to your room?"

I thought of the four-point restraints buckled to the corners of my bed. Then, God help me, I thought of *her* in the restraints—open, supremely vulnerable. I ground my fists into my eyes, trying to stuff the images back inside my skull. "She's cured," I managed. "We have to let her go." *We.*

"Through the door or the window? What's your pleasure, partner?"

I moved away from him, but he kept his hand locked on my arm.

"Mr. Bishop's idea wasn't entirely without merit," Lucas went on, "except for the fact that he ended up dead over it."

"Satan was in her tongue. She's cured," I repeated.

He took his hand off me, glanced at it suspiciously. "One never knows."

I realized Lucas wasn't even certain amputation had exorcised Satan from his own body. And I wanted desperately to convince him to let Simons go free, partly to prove to myself that there had been some purpose to the blood I had spilled. I decided to try another tack. I remembered Jack Rice from the State Police telling me that hostages would have to be released soon after I entered the locked unit in order to hold off Lieutenant Patterson's assault on the building. "If we don't release someone soon they're going to send SWAT teams up the walls. They didn't give me much time."

He looked at me, still considering.

"Let her go home," I said simply.

"Home," he said with disgust. He paused. "Can I count on your help on the next case?"

"The next case . . ."

"The neurosurgery. The amygdala."

I needed to buy time. Or did I? I could tell Lucas I'd have no part of his insanity. I could try to stand firm against Satan, no matter the consequences.

"Shall we let her go, move on together?" Lucas asked.

I looked at Simons. I was no longer certain whether I was fighting darkness or whether it had consumed me, but I was certain of her suffering and of my ability at that moment to relieve it. I grabbed onto that. "I'll scrub in," I said.

Lucas walked to the door of the Day Room and called for Gabriel Vernon. He got no response. He started down the hallway shouting his name.

I scanned the floor for the chunk of Simons' tongue. I saw it under the conference table. Keeping an eye on the door I crawled underneath the table and picked it up. It felt lighter and less solid than I would have imagined—a little like gelatin, but still warm. I hurried back to Simons, trying not to look at Bishop's corpse. I helped her sit up. Her face was blank, her skin gray and damp. I showed her what was in my hand. She turned in horror. I caught hold of her wrist and held her firmly as she tried to wriggle away.

"Open your mouth," I whispered.

She glanced at me. Her jaws were clenched. Tears began streaming down her face again.

"They might be able to reattach if after you leave. Open your mouth."

She shook her head.

"Now," I said sternly. My head was swimming. "Do it."

She didn't so much open her mouth as relax her jaws.

I pulled down on her chin. Blood poured onto her neck and dripped over her breasts and abdomen. I placed the piece of flesh behind her lower teeth, then pushed up on her chin to close her jaws again. As I did, I noticed she was looking up with new panic in her face.

Gabriel Vernon was standing halfway across the room. He had to have seen what I had just done. He walked toward us, stopping just a few feet away.

I looked into his eyes. I was going to plead with him to keep quiet. "Gabriel . . . ," I started.

"The doctor saves all the specimens," he broke in. He bent down and picked up the scalpel I had dropped.

"Where?" I asked. "For what?"

He didn't respond. "I need another specimen."

Simons pedaled frantically against the linoleum until she had run out of floor and was backed against the wall under the windows. She held her knees and began rocking like a child.

I stood up. "Let her alone. She's no more possessed by Satan than you are."

For a split second his features softened to a kind of confusion. Then his affect went flat again.

I was rifling my mind for a psychological route past Gabriel's devotion to Lucas when he stepped over to Bishop's body, crouched down and sliced a three-inch piece of Bishop's tongue off. He inspected it with no more emotion than I imagined he had displayed harvesting the genitals of the man he had castrated. Then he flicked it under the conference table. He stood up. "Time for you to go," he said to Simons.

I couldn't tell whether Gabriel had willfully disobeyed Lucas in order to help Simons or whether he was demonstrating the concrete thinking typical of schizophrenic patients. Did he care about Simons or did he consider one tongue specimen as good as the next?

Simons seemed too terrified to move.

Gabriel walked over to her, put one hand under each of her arms and lifted her to her feet. Then he bent down and picked her up in his arms. He carried her from the room.

I followed them, pausing at the conference table

and then at the doorjamb to keep from falling myself. I leaned to look down the hallway and saw Gabriel, Lucas and Kaminsky talking at the locked door. I couldn't make out what they were saying. Several seconds later Kaminsky opened the door briefly to let Gabriel and Simons out, then slammed it shut.

I walked back to the windows and waited for something to happen. A minute or two passed before I saw commotion on the green, with police taking shelter behind their cruisers, rifles ready. Jack Rice, Lieutenant Patterson and Emma Hancock emerged from the State Police trailer. Patterson was screaming into what looked like a walkie-talkie. Then I saw Lindsey Simons stagger onto the grass. She was alone. Several officers in black jumpsuits, carrying plastic shields rushed to her and whisked her behind a black SWAT van.

"I'm a man of my word," Lucas called to me.

I turned and saw him at the door to the Day Room.

"How about you? Ready to scrub in?"

"I'll never be ready to butcher anyone."

"You didn't seem to have much of a problem ten minutes ago." He nodded at Bishop's corpse. "I've told you before that we're a lot alike."

I closed my eyes. Nietzsche's words came to me.

Whoever fights monsters should see to it that in the process he does not become a monster.

*And when you look long into an abyss, the
abyss also looks into you.*

How different, really, was what I had done to
Craig Bishop from what Lucas had done to Grace
Cummings? He had carved a sentence into her
body and made her jump five stories. I had carved
the beginning of a word into him and driven him
to cut his own throat.

"Maybe you'd like a little methadone before we
start," Lucas said. "I could use some myself. Or
better yet, I found a vial of pharmaceutical-grade
cocaine."

If I was going to be any good to anyone on the
unit, I needed to be more alert. Cocaine could
bring my nervous system back from the cloud of
opiate intoxication. It would also bring it closer to
ultimate collapse. "The vial might do the trick," I
said.

He smiled. "Done."

I followed Lucas to the medication room midway down the hall. He made certain no one was
nearby, then covered the combination lock as he
punched in a four-digit code. I assumed he was the
only one who had access, which gave him exclusive control over who got which drugs on the
unit—and when. During my years in practice I
had seen my share of heroin addicts in opiate
withdrawal. Six hours without the drug and without methadone, and muscles and joints begin to

tighten up like a diver's with the bends. The stomach heaves mercilessly. Skin turns to clammy goose-flesh. Blood pressure, pulse and body temperature skyrocket. At that point a true addict will do anything, steal anything, sell anyone out for a fix. Being able to throw a man into that kind of misery is real power. Being able to bring him back from it makes the power nearly absolute.

The door clicked open. We walked inside. Lucas shut the door and checked twice that it was closed securely.

The room was only about five by eight feet. A stainless steel sink and countertop, with a row of glass-front cabinets hanging above it, ran along one wall. The opposite wall was taken by a huge, double-doored stainless steel refrigerator. The cabinets were crammed with plastic and glass bottles, brightly packaged samples of Haldol, Mellaril and Xanax, boxes of surgical masks and latex gloves, and every variety of nursing aid— oxygen masks, hypodermic needles, nasogastric tubes, IV bags.

"We're in the ventricle of the heart," Lucas beamed. "The boiler room of the ship. Everything we need to beat Satan back is right here. I even found a little tool that should help with any messy blood vessels we encounter on our way through the cerebral cortex." He pointed at a transistor radio–sized plastic and chrome device in the center cabinet. It was an electric cautery used to singe small arteries and capillaries.

As I gazed up at the cabinet I realized we were truly alone. No one could reach us from the unit. And I knew that even in my weakened state I could overpower Lucas. I could kill him. I glanced at the corner of the steel counter. Then I looked at him and squinted as I pictured slamming his face into it, battering his eyes to mush, caving in his skull. The images were crystal clear to every one of my senses. I could feel his hair in my fist, his head bouncing back off the metal. I could hear the sounds of flesh and bone giving way. I could smell the last of his bodily fluids spilling out of his corpse. Everything I was experiencing was intensely pleasurable to me. I felt exhilarated. I leaned ever so slightly toward Lucas, as if drawn toward my own murderousness, into my own shadow.

He cocked his head as he looked back at me. "If you're thinking of doing me harm, keep in mind the men out there would tear you and the other hostages limb from limb without me."

I struggled to keep myself in check. I believed what Lucas had said was true, even if I didn't fully understand why. There were men much larger than he, after all, on the unit. They could try to torture him into telling them the combination to the medication room. They could steal doses of

methadone that he instructed them to hand out to
the other patients. They could try to escape. Was it
truly the mystique of the physician that gave
Lucas his authority? Did these extraordinarily
dangerous men, like men everywhere, fear auton-
omy and yearn to be led?

"Take me out of the equation, and they'll
explode," Lucas went on. "I'm the one who gave
them their freedom. I'm the one who diagnosed
their possession. I'm the only one who can win
their souls from Satan. I'm . . ."

Perhaps the biggest reason the patients followed him came to me as he ranted. Beyond doling out the drugs that quieted the turmoil in their
minds, that numbed their consciences, Lucas dispensed a kind of absolution. By asserting that
their common enemy was the devil, he allowed
them to believe they had no control over their
minds and behavior and, therefore, no responsibility for what they thought or what they did. They
had abandoned their free will to him and were free
not to look at themselves, not to feel their own
pain, not to think about how their lives had turned
to darkness. By conjuring the specter of Satan,
Lucas had created a collective delusion more powerful—and more liberating from reality—than any
individual's psychosis.

"Do you understand now the weight on my
shoulders?" Lucas demanded. "Do you see how

this war depends on me?" He reached out and pulled me flush to him. He was drenched with sweat. "Do you?"

"I understand."

He looked fiercely into my eyes.

I kept myself from pulling away. "I understand," I repeated quietly.

He seemed satisfied he had gotten through to me. He backed off, took a moment to compose himself, then reached into one of the cabinets. He took down an oversized brown glass prescription bottle. A white label identified the substance as methadone. He twisted off the cap, poured what looked like a five-milligram dose of the orange liquid into a paper cup and downed it. He winked at me. "I'll trust you not to report me to the Drug Enforcement Administration. I wouldn't want to lose my medical license." He poured another, bigger dose into the cup and handed it to me. *"Salud."*

I swallowed it in one gulp. "Where's the cocaine?" I asked.

"Not to worry." He reached into the cabinet again and picked up a much smaller clear glass vial with a rubber top—the way cocaine in solution is dispensed. The liquid is used to shrink badly inflamed nasal passages in case of sinusitis or to anesthetize wounds before minor surgical procedures. He held it out to me.

Even in my methadone-induced haze I could imagine the cocaine high. I hadn't touched the stuff for six months, but I had never stopped craving it.

"Go ahead," Lucas said.

I knew taking the vial from him could rocket me down the slippery slope of drug dependency. But the combination of seeing too much terror and swallowing too much methadone had left me in a state that was too dangerous to let alone—too dangerous for me and for everyone else on the unit. I had killed one man, there was no denying that. I could easily kill again. I took the vial from Lucas. I peeled off the rubber cap and poured a teaspoon or so onto my tongue. It went numb. My anxiety started melting away. I closed my eyes, took a deep breath.

"The wonders of chemistry," Lucas chuckled. "Look at you. You're becoming a new man before my eyes."

I forced myself to laugh with him, despite my thoughts. If I was becoming a new man, I wondered, what sort of man? I kept smiling even as I thought of what I had done to Bishop, what a large part of me wanted to do to Lucas. I poured another teaspoon of the cocaine between my lower lip and gums, then rubbed a bit into the laceration on my cheek. My jaw, mouth and throat slowly lost all sensation. My level of alertness began to rise.

Lucas took another swig of methadone directly from the bottle.

For the moment, Lucas was treating me like a drug buddy. I hoped he might give up some information about the takeover of the unit. "How can Kaminsky, Zweig and the rest of the patients out there be dependent on methadone already?" I asked. "How were they getting it before yesterday?"

An impish delight showed on his face. "I shouldn't say." He nibbled his lip and scratched the sutures in his stump, apparently deciding whether to let me in on the secret.

I waited.

"Nurse Vawn. Carla Vawn."

"Which nurse is that? What do you mean?"

"The poor thing at the nursing station. The one infested in the womb. I had her convinced I was detoxing off prescribed methadone, that I had been part of the Impaired Physician's Program on the outside—an addict in recovery. Just like you. My inspiration." He winked. "I made her see how I was being mistreated by the others on the staff. I told her I could sense she was brighter, kinder, more caring. Special. That's all she needed to hear. She's from a big family, lost in the crowd, as it were. Father and mother both bottom-dwelling drunks. She started dosing me up cautiously, just to take away the cramps I cried to her about, but she was good enough to smuggle more and more into my room. To calm my nerves. To make me stop shaking." He paused. "I distributed it to the others in need."

I had to speak through my revulsion at the reminder of Lucas' uncanny ability to charm, manipulate and ultimately help destroy fragile and sick women—including Kathy. To have fallen for a psychotic patient like Lucas, Vawn had to suffer severe psychological problems herself. "Why did she do as you asked?"

"The best reason of all. She's in love with me. On her night shifts, she gave me some of the best head of my life. She even smuggled the knives in here, helped me stash them under my bed. I believe she could see, at some level, that her coworkers weren't up to the challenge of engaging Satan in the final battle. It took a surgeon to show them the way." He took a deep breath. "I dare say I've fallen for her just as hard as she has for me. I'm a human being like anyone else, Frank. I haven't found many places to lay my head."

"Then why would you want to kill her?" An awful thought crossed my mind. "Is her child yours?"

"Kill her?" His face lost every hint of amiability. "Can't you see the truth? She's infested." He was nearly shouting. "I'm trying to cure her! I love her!" He screwed the cap back on the bottle of methadone and threw it into the cabinet, knocking over a half-dozen other bottles. He wheeled around and pulled open the doors of the refrigerator along the opposite wall. "Satan dwells in every one of these tissues."

I nearly stumbled back. Lucas' severed arm, the skin and muscles crudely dissected, lay on a stainless steel table. Above it, four shelves held an assortment of glass containers, some with specimens floating in murky fluid. I saw an ovary in a giant jar. The label on the jar read, *Elmonte, L, M.D.* I shuddered with the realization that Lucas had harvested the organ from her, that he wasn't beyond doing the same to Nurse Vawn. Next to it was a row of glass beakers filled with urine and blood. A rack of test tubes held what looked like samples of semen. I looked up a shelf, and my heart began racing faster. A wide-bottomed flask labeled *Winston, Ph.D.* held a tongue. I remembered Jack Rice leaning over Lawrence Winston outside the hospital. And I remembered his words: "His tongue's gone."

"Look at the black bile seeping out," Lucas said. "Lucifer's vital fluid." He pointed from specimen to specimen.

I didn't see anything but poorly preserved organs and bodily fluids.

He lifted his remaining hand chest level and stared at it. "The beast can hide anywhere." He turned his hand palm-up, then palm-down as he inspected it. He let it fall back to his side. "I need you to help me conquer him."

I knew Lucas' unconscious was projecting the demons that dwelled in his own tortured mind. And I knew the fact that he had kept me alive was evidence that part of him wanted to confront those demons. "To conquer Satan," I said, "you'll have to figure out how he sneaked into your soul. You'll have to figure out what happened to make you fertile ground for his evil."

"Psychobabble. No wonder your patient killed himself."

"You asked *me* to come onto the unit. A psychiatrist. You didn't ask for another surgeon."

"You're the one who took my life. You're the one who should help me win it back. It's only fair." He paused. "I'm giving you the chance to redeem yourself, Frank. That's more than you gave me." He closed the refrigerator doors, grabbed the electric cautery out of the cabinet and opened the door to the hallway. "We're wasting time. We have surgery to perform."

Eight

We walked to the last room on the right. Gabriel joined us at the bedside and stood with me, across from Lucas. The man earmarked for neurosurgery still lay face-down, in four-point restraints, the black *V* on his scalp outlining the planned incision. His whole body seemed to be trembling. "Is everything ready, Gabriel?" Lucas asked.

"Yes, doctor." He pulled a green paper drape off a bedside tray, revealing two scalpels, a set of retractors and a gray metal drill.

Lucas put the cautery down on the tray and picked up the drill. "Where did we come by this magnificent piece of machinery?"

"Maintenance. Second floor," Vernon answered.

"Excellent. As I remember, the amygdala lies fairly deep." Lucas pressed the trigger. The drill whirred, then screamed.

The patient cried out in terror.

I wasn't sure how to stop what was about to happen. Despite the fact that he had killed his eight-year-old son, I instinctively placed a hand on the man's arm to comfort him. He struggled to pull it away. I moved my hand to the mattress, realizing he couldn't consider my touch anything but threatening. I didn't even know his name. I read it off his hospital identification bracelet: Tisdale, Richard.

"This should get us where we need to go," Lucas shouted over the noise of the drill. He held the bit in front of his eyes and watched it spin for several seconds. When he let go of the trigger and tried to lay the drill back on the tray, his fingers stayed curled around the handle.

"Leave me alone," the man cried into the sheets.

"We'll leave you alone, sweet boy," Lucas answered him, still trying to let go of the drill. "We're going to chase Satan all the way back to hell."

Sweet boy. I remembered those words had been carved into Grace Cummings. I pictured her naked body sprawled on the concrete outside the hospital, the letters on her torso dripping blood. Given what I knew of Lucas' hatred for women, my gut told me the phrase belonged to his mother, the first woman in his life. I thought of the word Lucas had screamed before killing Lawrence Winston— *Harpy,* the mythological half-woman, half-beast. I had nothing to lose. The only way to reach him was to offer him the truth, which is always a reflection of God. I went out on a limb with my hunch. "Was she insane?" I asked.

Lucas was still occupied with the drill. He didn't respond.

"What did she do to you?"

He managed to release his fingers from the drill handle, but they were bent into a claw, as if crippled by arthritis. It wasn't clear he had heard my question. "You don't know what you're talking about," he said, without looking at me. He shook his hand to relax it.

"Was Satan in her, too?"

Lucas opened his mouth, but his words were obliterated by the PA system outside. "This is Lieutenant Patterson of the Massachusetts State Police," the speakers blared. "I am issuing a final warning. All hostages must be freed within ninety seconds."

The release of Lindsey Simons minus her tongue must have hardened, rather than appeased, Jack Rice. He had approved Patterson's plan.

Lucas turned and walked to the grated window at the head of the bed. "Dusk. How appropriate. The devil comes by night."

Kaminsky and Zweig walked into the room.

"Tell everyone to get down on the floor and stay down," I told Lucas.

Kaminsky's eyes flashed in my direction. Gabriel Vernon caught him by the neck and threw him back toward the door.

"Wait for the doctor's orders," Vernon said.

"And my orders are, assemble everyone in the Day Room," Lucas said. "This is the moment we have been waiting for. This is our Armageddon."

"You can't stop them," I protested. "They have too many men. They have guns."

He gazed at me as if lost in a dream. "We have the heavens. We have no need of the earth."

"Unlock the door," I argued. "Let the patients and staff go."

"We already have a place to go," Lucas said. "Satan won't find a single soul to steal when his army arrives." He walked out of the room.

Zweig began herding patients toward the Day Room. Vernon escorted me there. Some of the patients knelt and began chanting, others paced, still others milled aimlessly about. A few, including the former socialite Cecelia Gladstone, wept uncontrollably. Carla Vawn was still bound into her seat at the nursing station, breathing but seemingly unconscious.

Kaminsky marched three women and a man into the room. The four of them wore only hospital gowns. Their identification badges were clipped to the skin at their throats. I knew that one of the social workers taken hostage on the unit was a man. I assumed that was him. The women, I reasoned, were the dietitian and the two nurses who worked with Vawn.

Kaminsky directed everyone to form a single line facing the windows, stretching across the room. The last of a winter sunset cast its orange glow over them.

Lucas was nowhere to be found.

I heard the helicopter engine start. The blades began to whir. Patterson's voice blasted through the PA system again. "This is Lieutenant Patterson of the Massachusetts State Police. I am instructing everyone in the locked unit to lie on the floor, face down, hands crossed behind your backs."

The patients began chanting in unison. Zweig and Kaminsky joined the line.

I turned to Vernon. "We only have about thirty seconds. Everyone needs to get down on the floor. The police are going to fire through the windows at anyone left standing."

He squinted at me doubtfully. "Dr. Lucas gives the orders."

I grabbed each of his forearms. "You don't need orders from anyone to do the right thing. You know no one's going to be saved by getting cut up by Dr. Lucas or cut down by machine guns."

He didn't move.

I heard the chopper take off. I knew that SWAT teams were poised to invade the building just after the waves of bullets. I left Vernon where he stood and walked over to the row of patients and hostages. I tried desperately to pull them down, one by one, sometimes falling with them. None of them resisted me, but the patients stood back up as soon as I moved on to the next person. I could tell from the movements of their lips that they were still chanting despite the thunder of the assault helicopter rising toward us. Zweig was next in line. I tried to drag him down but he slashed my arms with his knife and threw me to the ground. I grabbed his pant leg and tripped him up. He fell to one knee, dropping the knife. Out of the corner of my eye I saw Gabriel Vernon had begun frantically sweeping people off their feet. He tackled half a dozen or more of them before the sun disappeared and the assault helicopter filled the wall of windows. I heard the first bullets crash through the panes of glass. If I had been thinking I would have stayed on the floor and buried my head in my hands, but I stopped thinking and started feeling the full horror of the state annihilating patients—even these patients. Every man is a story, and mine was about to be defined by a dizzying paroxysm of bloodletting I had helped set in motion. I had to defy it, even if that meant being consumed by it. I stood up and ran to the wall of windows, pressing myself against the glass, arms spread wide. The helicopter hovered directly in front of me. My ears ached from the roar of its engine, the beating of its blades against the sky. I could see the face of the pilot. And I could see Jack Rice seated next to him. Our eyes locked on one another's. I flashed back to his telling me that once I was inside the unit there was nothing he could do to help me. I closed my eyes and waited for the blaze of pain from a bullet, waited for the rest of my life to flash before me. It never did. The chopper hovered several seconds. I opened my eyes in time to see it swing right and left in the sky like a giant hornet before dropping out of view. The blades slowed, then stopped, the silence broken only by the continued chanting of the patients scattered around the room.

I spun around to gauge the toll of the assault. Most of the patients were standing or getting up, adding their voices to those still chanting. Others huddled in the corners of the room. The male social worker was on the ground, clutching a wound in his leg. There was glass everywhere. The plaster walls were marred by craters where bullets had landed. Kashoor, the huge man Lucas had kept from attacking me, was slumped against the wall nearest the door, shot in the head. I looked for Gabriel Vernon and spotted him face-down, spread-eagled in a pool of blood. I ran to him and used all my strength to turn him onto his back. His head flopped to one side. I saw that he had been struck twice in the chest. I called out for help. "C'mon, Gabriel," I muttered. "Don't die." I tilted his head back and listened for breathing. I ripped his shirt open and watched his chest for movement. There was nothing. I checked his pulse. His heart had stopped. I knelt by his side and tried to deliver CPR, but I heard the fractured pieces of his sternum crack against one another with each of my compressions. My breaths bubbled through the holes in his chest. I knotted his white orderly's top and jammed it into the wound, but air still escaped through the fabric. I yelled for help again. No one responded. Half a minute later he hadn't drawn a breath of his own, and I was gasping for air myself. I brushed my hand over his eyes to close his lids.

I looked up and saw Kaminsky and Zweig huddled together, whispering. They began reorganizing a row of patients across the center of the room, seemingly prepared to face a second assault. They separated the hostages into their own row, backs against the shattered windows, facing the others. I worried they might be planning to execute them. I struggled to my feet and ran into the hallway, looking for Lucas. I believed what he had told me. He was the keystone in the arch that kept the unit from collapsing into wholesale carnage. There were still lives to be saved—more than a dozen patients and six hostages.

I raced to check each room on the left and the right, revisiting the horror of Laura Elmonte's "surgery" and Richard Tisdale's planned neurosurgery. I fell back against Tisdale's doorjamb, exhausted. I was most of the way toward collapse. I gathered the last bit of my cocaine-fueled fortitude and headed back up the hall. I stopped at the medication room door, knocked, but got no response. I put my ear to the cold metal surface. Someone was moving around inside. "Trevor?" I yelled. "Are you in there?" I was answered by silence. I pounded on the door. "Trevor!"

"Get away," he snarled.

"Open the door."

He cried out in pain.

"Let me in!"

"I can't!" he screamed. His voice descended to despair. "My arm."

"What about your arm?"

There was silence again.

"What happened to your arm?"

"Lucifer has it." He let loose a deep groan. "His claws are ripping me apart."

I looked at the lock on the door. "Tell me the combination." I got no response. I was about to run back to the Day Room to try to get the sequence from one of the nurses when Lucas finally answered.

"3-1-1-5."

I punched in the digits, opened the door and stepped into the medication room, closing the door behind me. I turned and looked at Lucas. My heart nearly stopped. He was crouched in the far corner of the tiny room, one leg thrown over his forearm. His hand was contorted into a deformed fist with the fingers bent grotesquely over one another. His face was twisted with panic. Deep scratches ran from his right eye down the corner of his mouth. A bloody clump of his salt-and-pepper hair lay next to him, the wound on his scalp

still oozing. Brown shards of glass from a large
bottle covered the stainless steel countertop and
the floor. A half-filled 50-cc hypodermic syringe
was lying near his hand.

"Cut it off," Lucas said. "It attacked me."

I knew what he meant, but couldn't get my
mind to accept it. "Cut . . . what?"

"His hand." Lucas' arm strained to break free
from under his thigh. He pressed harder to keep it
from moving.

I picked up the largest piece of brown glass,
complete with most of the label from the bottle.
The bottle had held succinylcholine, a chemical
compound used to paralyze surgical patients who
are intubated and must not fight the rhythm of
their respirators. Without a machine to take over
breathing, anyone injected with the medication
would soon suffocate.

Lucas was watching me. "We can't leave any
souls for Satan," he said.

I saw that he had intended to orchestrate a mass
suicide. Maybe I had been wrong to think he
would help stop Kaminsky and Zweig. But I had
nowhere else to turn. I shook my head at that.

"Help me," Lucas said. He was breathing in
gusts.

The man I hated most in the world sat before
me, an eager victim if I cared to slice off his
remaining hand. Yet I felt no impulse to harm him.
Maybe that shouldn't have surprised me. Matt

Hollander had been right. Every murder, every evil, every act of terror and horror in our world is a projection of the perpetrator's self-hatred. Like a virus, that hatred seeks to infect anyone it can. But with Lucas' psyche visibly bent on his destruction, doing its own ugly work of vengeance, I was free to see him for who he was—a shattered man. Being locked up in prison had driven him over the edge, from sociopathy to psychosis. I had done that to him. And I had to help him find his way back.

"The devil you're fighting is some part of your *self* that you refuse to look at," I told him. "You can hack your whole body to pieces, cut up every staff member and patient on this godforsaken unit, and you still won't have found it."

"Then you find it!" he barked. He closed his eyes. "Why not, Frank? Maybe you'll find out something about yourself."

My heart leaped. Was Lucas really ready to let me try to heal him and to redeem myself? "I'm sorry I let you stay locked up." I waited.

"You lost something you loved. I took it. And that made you want to destroy me. We're even."

"No, we're not. Not until you let me help you." Because until that happens I can't love myself. "Tell me."

"I can't remember . . . anything. I don't know what opened the door to Satan."

I couldn't be sure whether Lucas was referring

to the recent or distant past. Did he not remember what had happened to him in prison or in his child-hood? "What's the first thing you do remember?"

He looked up at me like a terrified child. "Being alone."

I was taken aback by the starkness of the state-ment. "Alone," I repeated, hoping to sustain the momentum of his revelation without interfering with it, the way a parent will use the lightest touch to guide a boy almost able to ride a bike.

"I was on a plane. I was going to live with my father, may his soul rest in peace."

"Where were you headed?" I asked quietly.

His eyes never left mine. "We lived in Min-nesota."

"Where had you been staying before that?" I asked.

"Baltimore." He shook his head.

I wanted to ask about his mother again, but I suspected that might close Lucas down. And I might not get a second chance to reach him. Zweig and Kaminsky could strike out at any time. I crouched and leaned against the opposite wall, making sure to give Lucas as much space as possi-ble.

Lucas' jaws clenched and his breathing became erratic as his arm nearly wriggled free. He trapped it between his leg and the wall. Beads of sweat broke out on his forehead. "None of this matters. It's too late for me."

"Only if you decide it is."

He hung his head, staring at his hand.

I thought I was losing him. "Only if you give up."

He took a deep breath and swallowed hard, then looked back at me. "You ask for the courage of Job," he said with a strained smile. Several seconds passed. Pain took over his features again. "If you could figure out how the dark one chose me, how he got a foothold in my body . . . You could give me back my life. You could help rid this place of Satan."

We were closer to common ground. Lucas was still speaking the language of demonic possession and exorcism, but he was allowing that his life history might have ripened him for it. "I will," I said. I let the promise linger in the silence. "First we have to stop Kaminsky and Zweig," I went on. "They've lined up the hostages. I think they may kill them."

"It's not up to them to choose who shall live and who shall die. They don't know how to win this battle," he fumed. He tried to calm himself. "Take me to the Day Room. Take hold of my hand." He nodded at it. "Keep the beast from me."

I walked closer to him. I remembered the seemingly innocent invitation he had issued to Lawrence Winston. *Come talk with me.* A small part of me still wondered if Lucas was baiting me for the kill. The hypodermic syringe lay within his reach, half-filled with succinylcholine. But my gut told me Lucas' rage and hatred had indeed turned in on themselves, as rage and hatred always do, given time. Projection is only a temporary defense, a flame thrower atop a crumbling wall. Lucas was no different at that moment than Hitler in the bunker or Goering at Nuremberg. He called his self-loathing by the name Satan. Hitler and Goering called it the Jews. Serial killers see it in every one of their victims. John Wayne Gacey entombed thirty-three young boys in the crawl space under his home, but never succeeded in burying the tortured boy inside him.

I knelt down by Lucas and picked up the syringe. I laid it on the countertop. Then I slowly, firmly gripped his wrist. I helped him to his feet, careful to keep his hand safely down at his side.

"There's Xylocaine in the cabinet," he said. "Block the enervation to the arm."

As much as I believed that Lucas' renegade arm was fueled by his own psyche, not the devil, a nerve block with the local anesthetic Xylocaine seemed like a quick, albeit temporary fix; it would immobilize his arm a few hours at most. I held Lucas' wrist away from him as I reached into the cabinet. I used my free hand and my teeth to register 10 cc of Xylocaine in a syringe. I remembered from my surgical rotations in medical school and internship that the roots of the median, radial and ulnar nerves all course through the same region under the clavicle, just above the second rib. Pulling Lucas closer to me I buried the needle beside the collar of his scrub shirt, injecting the whole 10-cc dose.

He seemed immediately relieved. Within a minute his arm hung limply at his side. "Let's find Mr. Kaminsky and Mr. Zweig," he said.

We walked to the Day Room and quietly moved toward the rows of hostages and patients. Lucas' eyes scanned the room, pausing on Vernon and Kashoor's bodies. He used his foot to sweep away some of the shards of glass strewn over the floor, then looked up at the shattered windows. He turned and surveyed the bullet holes dotting the walls. He glanced at me in a way that seemed to put the whole scene into evidence as convicting Satan, then he continued on.

The four hostages were stripped and lined up opposite the patients. Their hands were bound in front of them with surgical tape. Cecelia Gladstone held a knife to the male social worker's throat as he struggled to stand on his wounded leg. Kaminsky and Zweig stood behind her, one to either side, their backs to the door, prodding her to kill him. They didn't notice Lucas and me until we were just three or four feet away.

"Whose orders are you following?" Lucas said softly.

Kaminsky and Zweig turned to face him. Gladstone dropped the knife. The row of patients slowly began their chant.

I have no life. I have no death.

Lucas cocked his head to one side as he studied Kaminsky and Zweig. "You know better than I do? You're ready to face Satan on your own?"

"No," Zweig answered immediately. He looked at me and bowed his head in a way that made me think he might have been moved at some level by my attempt to save him from being shot.

The row of patients broke into little groups as Lucas stepped within a foot of Kaminsky. He stared into his eyes, then leaned even closer. "Do I see the devil in your eyes?"

Kaminsky stood motionless a few seconds, then shook his head.

Never looking away from Kaminsky, Lucas ordered Zweig to prepare the patients and hostages to receive their medications. He waited until all of them had left the room, then continued talking to Kaminsky. "Are you becoming a servant of Satan?" His voice became louder with each word. "Have you lost your way?"

I saw that Lucas had many methods of maintaining his control of the unit. His underlying sociopathy made him expert at splitting off one potential adversary from another. Anyone he "demonized" risked being targeted by the rest of the group.

"Tell me what to do," Kaminsky answered.

Lucas nodded. "Get on your knees and pray. Pray for your soul."

Kaminsky kneeled before him.

"Our father who art in heaven," Lucas said.

"Our father who art in heaven," Kaminsky echoed.

As they prayed I walked to the wall of windows and looked down at the green. It was lighted like day, but the frenzied activity was gone, replaced with an eerie quiet. News crews had advanced to the perimeter road, a grove of white satellite poles growing out of their vans, their cameras pointed up at the fifth floor, bearing silent witness. The helicopter sat next to the State Police trailer. I knew that Patterson and Rice were inside planning their next move. I had to get to them. "It's time," I said, turning back to Lucas. "I have to leave to be of any use to you."

Lucas continued his repeat-after-me prayer a few more lines, then stopped. "Go help Mr. Zweig," he told Kaminsky. "Be thankful you still dwell in the house of the Lord."

Kaminsky stood up. "Will I be getting medication?"

"What you need will be provided," Lucas said. "Now go."

Kaminsky obeyed.

"Sheep," Lucas said, not unkindly. He walked to Gabriel Vernon's body. "And I am the shepherd. Leaving this good servant for Satan was my fault. I should have led him to a better place when I had the chance. I should have taken all of them."

I could tell Lucas was thinking of the succinylcholine. "Death isn't freedom," I said. "Suicide is no triumph. You have to battle darkness here on earth for the victory to mean anything." I paused. "Let me go. Let me find the door in your past that Satan walked through. Together we can force him out of your soul and out of this place."

Lucas looked around the room. "Why did they stop shooting? Why didn't Satan take them all?"

I hesitated, then told him the truth. "I stood in the window. They didn't want to kill me."

He nodded. "They think you're doing their work. Maybe you are." He squinted at me. "Why would you come back once you leave?"

I answered immediately. "Because I'm to blame for what's happened."

Several moments passed before Lucas answered. "We would have to keep this arm from doing evil," he said, considering. "There's one dose of Marcaine in the medication room. Salvage from the surgical suite downstairs. It's longer acting than Xylocaine, but it still won't last more than twenty-four hours. After that, there won't be anything left here for you to return to."

"Twenty-four hours isn't—"

"I won't wait to be torn apart by the beast. We'll take our leave of this earth at sundown tomorrow." He started out of the room, but stopped a few steps from the door. "You'll help us? Help me?" he asked quietly, without turning around.

I didn't know what I could learn of Lucas' past in twenty-four hours that could change the future. Jack Rice might not even give me the chance to try. "I'll do everything I can," I told him.

"Godspeed." He walked into the corridor.

Nine

It was after 7:00 P.M. when I walked off the unit alone. I heard the door lock behind me. The hallway was bathed in light from spotlights directed at the building's facade. My shadow loomed huge as I walked toward the elevator, then disappeared as I stepped inside. I took the elevator down five floors and walked the same corridor by which I had entered the building less than seven hours before.

I felt even more isolated leaving the place. I didn't feel anchored in hatred for Lucas nor allied with the police. As strange as it seemed to me, I now saw evil itself as my adversary—not the monster named Satan, but the potential for destruction in every one of us. I believed Lucas had indeed been captured by that seminal force early in life. Gabriel Vernon had been seduced by it some time before he dismembered his gay lover. Lieutenant Patterson had been moved by it when he contrived to assault the building without regard for human life. And the dark tide had nearly pulled me under on the locked unit. I had twenty-four hours to turn it back.

When I reached the lobby a spotlight shone directly on me. I tried to shield my eyes as I walked toward it, but I was blinded. The glass doors slid open, and gusts of winter air whipped through my clothes and hair. I took a few more steps and felt what seemed like a dozen hands grab me and force me forward at a run. As we moved out of the beam of light I caught glimpses of black SWAT uniforms around me. There were four officers, all with crew cuts like Patterson's. When my legs couldn't keep pace with theirs they grabbed my arms and carried me along, my toes scraping the hard earth.

About twenty yards from the hospital they let go of me. I stumbled, nearly fell, but managed to stay on my feet. They escorted me past the helicopter to the State Police trailer. The door was open. Jack Rice was standing just beyond the wooden steps, inside the door, looking down at me gravely. Without a word he walked to me and helped me inside. I was surprised and none too happy to see Calvin Sanger leaning against the far wall. He stared at me as I took a seat in front of Rice's desk.

"Whatever we say here is off the record," Rice said, walking to take his own seat.

"I thought I had an exclusive," Sanger said wryly.

"You do—to what's on the record. Otherwise

you've got a one-way ticket back to the mob of reporters standing out front in the cold. Understood?"

"Completely."

"What's he doing here?" I asked Rice.

"It was your friend Hancock's suggestion. We need somebody reliable to explain to the public why we're going to be carrying bodies out of the hospital."

I worried over how Sanger had burrowed his way to ground zero. What information had he swapped for a front-row seat? "Where is Hancock?" I asked.

"Working the copycat case," Sanger broke in.

I turned to look at him. He gave me a half-smile that unnerved me. I turned back to Rice.

He crossed his legs and sat Indian style in his desk chair. "That's a nasty cut there on your face, but you look OK otherwise." He squinted at my hands.

I glanced down at them. They were trembling, probably from a combination of exhaustion, cocaine and methadone. I tried to keep them still. "I'll be all right."

"How did you manage to get out?" he asked tightly.

"Lucas released me."

"As a reward for being a human shield?"

"I wouldn't rate a reward for that. Two patients

were killed before the shooting stopped. One of the hostages was wounded."

Rice said nothing, but his face lost some of its gaminess.

"I want to thank you for not—" I started.

"Don't," he frowned. "What I did up there was inexcusable. You got in the way of a strategic plan that could have ended this insanity once and for all. You made me put my men at risk for no gain. By every rule in the book I should have let the pilot fire away."

"Then why didn't you?"

"I don't know," he shot back. "I'm not proud of myself. And you shouldn't be either. You blocked an assault I told you was coming down if anyone on that unit got seriously injured. I'd say losing a tongue qualifies. Ms. Simons is over at Mass. General hoping some crackerjack surgeon can piece her back together." He paused. "How are the other hostages?"

If the injury to Simons had resulted in an assault on the building, I had to believe what had happened to Laura Elmonte would prompt another. "As well as can be expected," I said. "They're survivors."

Rice shook his head. "What exactly *were* you doing in that window, Frank?"

I took a few seconds to put my thoughts together. "We've still got almost twenty people up there at risk. Other than the hostages there isn't a single one of them who isn't very sick. Lucas has them convinced, to a man, that they're locked in a mortal battle with Satan, that Armageddon has arrived. They think he's the only one who can deliver them from evil."

Rice rolled his eyes.

"They're not refusing to surrender because they're outlaws. They're refusing because they're psychotic. They believe you're agents of the devil."

"Are we on the same team?" Rice asked. "Or did Lucas release you to negotiate on his behalf?"

"I don't want people to die who don't have to."

Rice leaned forward. "Nobody wants that. That's why we took our chance together, Frank. Now it's over. The only reason we're waiting to send the helicopter up again is to hear anything you might have to say that could help the SWAT teams when they move onto the fifth floor. That's the way you can help us save lives now."

"I might have another way."

"There's no room for discussion."

I went on anyhow. "Lucas has given me twenty-four hours to figure out what went wrong with him, what in his life history made him vulnerable to the force he calls Satan. He doesn't remember most of his childhood."

"Lucas doesn't have twenty-four hours to give," Rice said.

I forged ahead. "If I can find out the truth about what happened to him growing up in Baltimore and bring it to him . . ."

"What?" Rice asked. He looked betrayed, as if he had been supporting a lunatic.

"If I can bring him that truth then I might be able to move him toward dealing with his real trauma and away from the delusion that he's locked in a war with the devil. Then he might surrender. His Armageddon will turn into a personal reckoning with his own demons, not an overblown war for the soul of mankind." I paused. "I think unearthing his past is the reason he asked for me to begin with, whether he realizes it or not."

"Are you finished?" Rice asked.

"I'm asking for a day." I didn't share my worry that it would take extraordinary luck to unearth the key to Lucas' psychosis in that much time.

"You need rest," Rice said. "You've been through hell." He picked up the phone on his desk and dialed two digits.

"You told me you'd seen enough killing in Vietnam," I said.

"Lieutenant Patterson, please," Rice spoke into the receiver.

"The two patients who were shot to death were praying at the time."

Rice didn't respond.

"The pregnant woman is still up there," I said.

"Mike, it's Jack," Rice said. "I don't think we're

going to learn much more from Dr. Clevenger. So I'm going to—"

I stood up. "I'll give the whole story to the news. I'll tell them the patients are deep in prayer, that they're asking for one day before they surrender unconditionally. Five minutes after that helicopter takes off, you and the department will be a front-page story. Just like the ATF and Waco. When the bodies come out, the video will run on *Nightline* and *20/20*. And I'll be on the split screen saying it didn't have to happen."

Calvin Sanger got out of his seat and started pacing.

Rice glared at me.

"Ask Calvin," I said, nodding at him. "It's the story of a lifetime. Nobody cares what's happening on the ground. They care what's happening up there on the fifth floor. *USA Today*. A made-for-TV movie. The cover of *People*. No reporter from here to Seattle would turn it down."

"Jack?" Patterson's voice wafted from the receiver. "Jack? You there?"

"Give me a few minutes," Rice told him, still staring at me. He hung up the phone.

"Twenty-four hours. If I don't make it back here with the information I need, I'll make sure you have a room-by-room description of what I saw on the unit. And I'll stand up after the assault and say we did everything conceivable to save lives." Let me make this right, I begged silently.

Sanger walked across the room and out the door.

"Where the Christ is he going?" Rice said.

We heard shouting outside. Rice ran to the door and opened it.

Calvin Sanger was bounding across the green toward the hospital, stretching those marathon runner legs of his like a gazelle. Two officers were chasing him, but they had no hope of catching him. He opened up a ten-yard lead that quickly turned into fifteen.

I pushed past Rice. "Calvin!" I shouted at the top of my lungs. "Don't!" I noticed the bank of cameras across the way swing in my direction, then focus back on him.

He turned around for an instant, like a wide receiver catching a pass. Even from a distance I could see his eyes were wild with excitement. He was grinning. "Story of a lifetime!" he yelled back at me.

I wanted to say something to stop him, but I knew it was hopeless. He looked like a man possessed. Maybe evil really does beckon like a Siren. Maybe we were all—Winston, Sanger and I—paradoxically, mysteriously, irretrievably drawn to the dark force residing in Lucas. Maybe that explained why women so desperately wanted him inside them and why men like Vernon, Bishop, Kaminsky and Zweig followed him. Perhaps it even explained why surgical patients had once flocked to his practice to be cut up and sewn back together by him.

I thought again of Kathy's thirst to see Lucas once more, her certainty that he *needed* her. Was I losing myself in the same psychological undertow that had pulled her under? Had I been enticed into a competition for Trevor's soul?

Sanger sprinted to the sliding glass doors and, without any hesitation, walked into the hospital.

Rice was taking slow, deep breaths. His jaw was set. He looked up at me. "You're a very persuasive person. You just made that young man lay his life on the line for a story. I hope you can deliver the ending you think you can."

I drove away from Lynn State Hospital at 7:40 P.M., passing through a gauntlet of ambulances, police cruisers, fire trucks, TV vans and reporters that stretched a quarter mile. Teams from at least twenty television networks had staked out roadside camps complete with folding tables that held three-foot plastic drums of coffee and stacks of Dunkin' Donuts boxes. Again and again reporters advanced within inches of my door, targeting me with halogen beams and thrusting microphones against the windows. In the reflected light their mouths seemed disembodied as they screamed questions about what I had seen on the unit. Male reporters acting like traffic cops held up their hands demanding I stop my truck. A stunning young woman apparently anxious for a scoop smiled and flipped her long, black hair as I approached, then gave me the finger and shouted, "Die, asshole!" as I accelerated past her. When I stopped briefly at the same police roadblock I had passed through on my way to the hospital, a man and a woman in respectable clothes, holding microphones from New England Cable News and FOX, grabbed hold of my side mirrors, desperate to keep me from moving. Three officers had to pry them loose and pull them to the side of the road. I heard one of the officers scream, "You should be on that fucking psych unit!"

I focused ahead, trying to keep my hands steady on the wheel and my foot reliable on the brake and gas. Finally, the crowd thinned to curiosity seekers. They were gone in a few more blocks, and I was speeding down Jessup Road on a night that could have been any night but for the horror I knew had unfolded a mile behind me. For a moment I had the strange thought to declare the past day and night null and void by driving home to my loft in Chelsea as if nothing had happened, refusing to think of the locked unit, much less speak of it, hoping slowly to forget it. But I recognized that impulse more as a clue to Lucas' psyche than a road map for mine. It was a reminder that he had unconsciously attempted to relieve his unbearable psychic pain by burying it, a strategy always doomed because emotions mutate monstrously underground. As terrifying as the events on the unit—and in parts of the rest of my life—

had been, they were the most crucial memories connecting my thoughts and perceptions to the real world. Pain, not pleasure, grounds us. To disown one's traumas is to invite their distorted projections—imagined enemies, phantom visions, voices calling out from nowhere.

Twenty yards up the road, Emma Hancock's red Jeep Cherokee swerved from the oncoming lane and blocked mine. I jammed on my brakes and skidded to a stop.

Hancock got out and started toward my truck. She walked up to my window. I rolled it down. "Where is she?" she asked, expressionless.

"Who?"

"Kathy."

"Why would you bring up—"

Hancock reached into the truck and grabbed my shirt in her fists, pulling me toward her. Her arms were as powerful as any man's. "Don't make a mistake here, Frank. Obstruction of justice isn't a joke. You can go away a hell of a long time. State prison. And if you don't come clean right now, I'll make sure you do."

I had already accepted the risks of hiding Kathy. "I don't know," I said.

She pulled harder, nearly lifting me out of my seat. "Tell me."

I stayed silent.

Tears welled up in her eyes. She threw me back against the seat, then pulled me into the door. "My niece was killed, you son of a bitch." Her hands were shaking. "Tell me!"

My eyes filled up. Part of me, the part that had been conditioned to believe that vengeance can relieve a victim's pain, hungered to tell her where I had hidden Kathy. But the bigger part of me spoke. "I can't."

She was breathing like a bellows. She held me against the door a few seconds, then let go of me and took a step back. "I'll find her myself. Then I'll come looking for you."

"I'm sorry, Emma," was all I could think to say.

She shook her head. "No, you're not." She turned around and walked to her cruiser. She gunned the engine and shot past me, toward the hospital.

I put my foot to the gas and lurched into the night. Sweat soaked my neck and chest. I took lefts and rights I didn't need to in order to reassure myself I wasn't being followed, then snaked back toward the Lynnway so I could pick up 1A to Logan International Airport and my 9:05 P.M. flight to Baltimore. I couldn't know whether Calvin Sanger had dredged up information on Kathy's phony flight abroad or whether someone from Austin Grate Clinic had called in half a lead, maybe holding back on Kathy's exact whereabouts, trying to negotiate a reward. Matt Hollander had told me about one of the unit counselors meeting privately with Kathy from the very beginning of her stay. He might be the one. Or he might not.

With everything unraveling, my mind fastened on the slim chance I had to save the hostages. I figured Hancock would find out soon enough that Sanger had bolted for an even better story than she could offer him. That wrinkle gave me hope I still had my twenty-four hours.

I took a right onto the Lynnway. I saw the West Lynn Creamery building up ahead. Directly across from it, Webster Avenue led to the Y. I remembered the time I had spent there with Cynthia Baxter, a.k.a. Ginger, making love with her. I also remembered looking through her handbag and finding her driver's license from Maryland. My sense of isolation and my need to be comforted combined with my lifelong hesitancy to refuse the gift of coincidence. I have always felt the hand of a higher power in symmetries others might dismiss as chance. I took Webster Avenue and parked in front of the Y. I told myself that if Fate declared itself even more plainly and Cynthia were in her room, I would ask her to come to Baltimore with me.

Fate was bolder than I had imagined. I had just reached the front desk when the elevator doors opened and Cynthia stepped out with a distinguished-looking Hispanic man, fifty or fifty-five years old. I turned to her. She looked as if she were seeing a ghost. "Frank?" she said. "We just

saw you on TV." She was wearing tight jeans and
a black leather bomber jacket that looked a lot better on her than the soiled white wool coat she had
worn to my place. Her light brown hair hung in
shiny, damp curtains beside her chestnut eyes.
Compared to the worn, tortured women on the
unit, she looked brand-new.

The man smiled tightly at me. Other than a
wrinkled tab collar shirt, he was impeccably
dressed in a blue, double-breasted suit, Versace tie
and Gucci loafers. I figured he was probably an
attorney or a banker on his way home somewhere
tony like Boxford or Newburyport, twenty miles
north. Judging from the fear in his eyes I guessed
he had come to the Lynn Y, in the middle of a
crime-ridden wasteland, to be safe—safe from his
sexual appetite devouring the rest of his life. He
didn't want to meet me or anyone else. As irra-
tional as it sounds given Cynthia's profession, I
disliked him immediately for having had her.

"Hopefully none of the reporters followed me
here," I said, watching him.

The man grimaced and scanned the lobby.

"What happened to your face?" Cynthia asked.

I went to touch my wound, then realized my
hand was shaking badly and put it back at my side.
"A little run-in with a patient on the unit. It's not
important."

She nodded at my leg. "You lost a lot of blood."

I looked down and saw that my thigh was cov-

ered with dried blood—Craig Bishop's blood.
"Can I talk to you alone?" I asked. "Just for a
minute?"

She hesitated, then took a step away from the
man. "I won't need a ride, after all," she told him.
"Frank's an old friend. He can drive me."

He looked relieved. "Fair enough." He hurried
past me, headed for the door.

"What are you doing here?" Cynthia asked.

"My truck's outside. We can talk while we
drive."

We climbed into the Ram. I started the engine.
"I stopped on my way to Logan," I said immediately. "I'm flying to Baltimore to find out what I
can about Trevor Lucas. He was born there."

"Why does that matter?"

"I think what he's doing now is linked to something that happened there."

"Oh." She almost left it at that. "Why?"

"Because he can't remember *anything* that happened there."

She nodded, seeming to accept that theory. She
reached out and touched the blood on my thigh.
"Are you sure you're OK to go? You look really
rough."

I had the impulse to fall against her, to be held
like a child, then coaxed back into her room. But
that desire was just another escape fantasy that
would ultimately imprison me. I had to search for
the truth about Lucas. I had to try to help him. I

gripped the wheel with both hands. "Lucas forced me to take drugs on the unit," I said. I paused, admitting to myself that he hadn't forced me every time. "I took a lot of methadone and some pharmaceutical cocaine. I might come down hard, but I'll get through it."

"How long will you be gone?"

"Overnight. I have to be back this time tomorrow."

"Need a guide? I was born in Baltimore, too."

If I hadn't already put myself in the hands of Fate, I would have diagnosed Cynthia as self-destructive to do the same. Taking off for another state on the spur of the moment with a man she hardly knew was probably the kind of behavior that had landed her on the streets to begin with. But I was grateful for it at that moment. "I thought you were headed somewhere."

She reached into her handbag and took out her cellular phone. "One girl's as good as the next as far as this guy's concerned," she said. "I'll call the service and tell them I had to see my shrink."

We took the Lynnway past the Wonderland Dog Track in Revere, a pink neon temple to luck that was holding exactly $51,978.72 of my money in its coffers. For months I had kept the tally of my losses on a Post-it note in my wallet to remind me not to visit my friend Manny who worked the window there. At 8:30 we reached Bell Circle, the gateway to 1A, just five minutes from Logan.

Cynthia looked over at me. "When I used, I bought over on Shirley Avenue," she said. "If you need something to get yourself through tomorrow, we could swing by." She said it flatly, almost clinically, with none of the hungry, anxious drama of the drug seeker.

"What did you use?"

"Crack, mostly. It's been two hundred twenty-three days, but it's still one day at a time."

I wanted to say "no" to bolster Cynthia's sobriety and my own, but my muscles were cramping up and my stomach was starting to flutter like my hands. I could let my system fail in twenty-two hours, but not now. "Let's stop," I said.

Cynthia directed me through a maze of side streets to a parking spot in sight of a drab, off-white triple decker with an open front door. "It's more depressing than Lynn," I said.

"That's why the drugs have to be better."

We sat and watched three men and one woman come and go from the place within a few minutes. "I guess they're still in business," she said. "I'll be right out." She climbed down from the truck, jogged across the street and walked into the house.

As I waited two more people walked into the place. I started to worry when one left before Cynthia came out, but she was the next through the door. She jogged over to the truck, pulled herself inside and handed me five tiny Baggies. "Vun says to go easy. It's from Thailand. You shouldn't need much to keep your head above water."

I had never used heroin or any intravenous drug. "Am I supposed to inject this?"

"You could. But it's pure enough to snort."

"He didn't have any cocaine?"

"He has everything." She reached into her coat pocket and produced a small, triangular package fashioned from folded magazine paper.

I reached for it.

She held it away. "Do you swear not to touch any of this crap after tomorrow?"

"My word isn't what it used to be."

"It's good enough for me."

"My hooker, my healer," I winked. I meant no offense. "The Lord works in mysterious ways." I held my hand out.

She pulled the package farther away. "Is that a 'yes'? You'll get clean starting tomorrow?"

"I swear," I said—and meant it. "Do you swear not to touch it at all?"

"I do," she said.

I called Matt Hollander from a pay phone at the gate, just minutes before the 9:05 takeoff. It took the operator a while to find him. "I can't talk long," I said.

"Shoot."

"Emma Hancock knows about Kathy."

"Knows how much?" he asked.

"She seems to know what Kathy did, not where

she is. But Hancock's a pro. She'll work day and night to find out the rest. I've mentioned you and Austin Grate to her more than once over the years."

"I worried this might happen. I had to fire that counselor—Scott Trembley. He came in to talk with Kathy on a shift he wasn't even scheduled to work. He left me a message to call him. Maybe he's looking for a payoff."

"Or reward money. Whichever is richer."

"Or whichever comes first," he said. "I'm not above making an investment in my future. I'll call him back right now."

"I'm headed to Baltimore, Lucas' hometown," I said. "I've got to find out what happened to him growing up."

"He's letting you get that close?"

Hollander's choice of words made me think about the murderous jealousy my journey could provoke in Kathy. "Yes. He asked me to."

"Magnificent."

I took a deep breath. "Matt, there's no way Kathy can get out of there . . ."

"That may be the single thing you don't have to worry about," he said. "This place is a fortress."

"Right." I remembered the double iron door at the entrance to the unit, the half-inch plate glass windows, the furniture bolted to the floor. "The trip's about an hour long. My pager should still work in the air, but it'll definitely be working in Baltimore."

"I'll check in with any news."

The overhead speaker announced final boarding for US Air 515 to Baltimore.

"We better go," Cynthia said.

"Be careful, Matt," I said. "Hancock's grief over losing her niece is all rage now." I started to hang up.

"Frank," he shouted.

"Yup."

"Whatever happens, I'm proud of you," he said.

My lips pressed together. I swallowed hard. "Thanks."

Cynthia and I rushed onto the plane. We were two of about twenty passengers. We took seats just in back of a wing, several rows from anyone else. I felt less shaky, having inhaled a pinch of the heroin and a bit of the coke in the men's room prior to our departure. I had also washed the blood off my face and washed as much of Bishop's blood out of my pant leg as possible. I could feel the rest of the drugs where I'd stashed them under the arches of my feet.

We sat silently in the darkened cabin until after takeoff. I was glad Cynthia was beside me because I felt cut off from the rest of the world. Jetting away from Massachusetts, I worried whether Rice would stick to our deal—a deal I had blackmailed him into—and wait the full twenty-four hours before sending SWAT teams through the fifth-floor windows. And there was no way for me to be certain whether Calvin Sanger's presence on the ward would help stave off Lieutenant Patterson's assault plan or make Lucas more paranoid and move him toward a mass suicide.

"What do you think you'll find out about Trevor Lucas in Baltimore?" Cynthia asked.

I checked my watch. We had been flying ten minutes. "I'm not sure I'll find out anything. I'm looking for an explanation why Lucas' psyche fractured in prison while he waited for his trial to start. I'm looking for the first cracks in the foundation of his mind, the roots of his religious delusions. I need to know the reason he crumbled into psychosis."

"Does there have to be a reason? Can't you just be born with bad nerves?"

"No." My quick answer surprised me. In discussions with other psychiatrists, I would equivocate, allowing it was conceivable that some people come into the world with weak nervous systems prone to collapse under routine pressures. But Cynthia, unadorned as she was, called forth my naked belief. In my heart I had no doubt that trauma is always to blame when a man loses his mind. "The nervous system is no different than shocks on a car," I said. "It wears out when you hit too many bumps in the road. Some people may be built like Ferraris, born with fragile suspensions, but treated with care they wouldn't fail."

"I've hit a few too many potholes myself," Cynthia grinned. "How do you get your shocks replaced?" She suddenly looked tired to me. She let her head fall onto my shoulder.

"I think psychotherapy is the best way," I said. "A priest would tell you that prayer can work." I felt her breath against my neck. "Love can probably do it, too." I closed my eyes. "They're probably all the same thing."

Cynthia gently kissed my ear. The warmth of her lips, then her tongue was enough to make my emotions overflow, the way a tight abscess will burst at a surgeon's first touch. Tears ran down my face. She brushed her hand over my cheeks and jaw, wiping the wetness away, then buried her fingers in my hair and brought my mouth to hers. I relaxed as she pressed herself inside me. I wanted to be filled up by something other than fear and hatred and violence. I ached to feel human again. I inhaled as deeply as I could of the subtle perfume at her neck as she ran her hand between my legs, then unbuttoned and unzipped my jeans. Making sure no flight attendant or passenger was nearby, she freed me and made me hard with her wet palm. My breathing quickened with the motion of her hand. The delicious need for release built in my groin. Before I came she bent over my lap and took me inside her mouth, each caress of her tongue reminding me I could

still feel, each stroke of her lips promising I
could pour myself into her, that I was neither poisoned nor poison myself, that God had not for-
saken me.

Ten

The plane touched down at the BaltimoreWashington International Airport at 10:20 P.M. We took a taxi down Route 295 to the city. I had the driver drop us at the Stouffer, a well-appointed hotel close to City Hall, equidistant from the trendy Inner Harbor shopping complex and Baltimore's red light zone, and not far from the Johns Hopkins Hospital. I had stayed there nearly two decades before when I'd interviewed for a psychiatry residency at Hopkins. Wherever my search for Lucas' roots led, I wanted a safe base at the center of things.

"What now? How do we start?" Cynthia asked after we stepped into our room.

I walked to the windows. New buildings stretched as far as I could see, testimony to Baltimore's newfound vitality. For a moment I felt defeated, as if it was folly to think I could find one boy's story alive in a city that had died and been reborn itself. But I reminded myself that Lucas' childhood pain had had enough staying power to reach through the years and capture him—and me.

I was no more lost in Baltimore than I had been sitting with the buried traumas of men and women Lucas' age and older who I had treated in my psychotherapy office. After listening to a pat life story, I had to summon the will to ask my first penetrating question, to begin our work in earnest by putting the patient's mind on notice that I knew the truth was still encoded deep in some web of neurons and that I meant to have it. Sometimes the question had to be shocking—an assault at the door of denial. My own therapist, Dr. James, had used the verbal equivalent of a battering ram after listening to me jabber about an on-again, off-again romance for the first half of our initial session together: *How can you expect to be properly loved, Frank, when you hate yourself?* "We start with the first question," I told Cynthia. "Then we ask another and another and another." I walked to the desk, opened the top drawer and pulled out a phone book. I flipped to the letter *L.* There were dozens of Lucases listed. "How do you feel about playing census taker?" I asked.

"At least it's an original fantasy. I'll try anything once."

I smiled. "I want you to reach as many Lucas families as possible. Ask whoever answers whether Trevor Lucas is one of their relatives. Say you have him listed on the census at that address."

"Won't they be a little shocked to hear from a census worker at midnight?"

"We don't have the luxury of timing. And catching people half asleep may not be a bad thing; somebody might actually talk to you."

"What are you going to do?"

"I'm going to the police station to find out whether the name Lucas rings a bell with anyone. I'll swing back here before I head anywhere else."

I walked down Lombard to Gay Street then over to East Fayette, passing the ten or eleven bars and couple of X-rated video arcades that made up the Baltimore "zone." A few vagrants clutching bottles in brown paper bags and a group of teenagers dressed in black sweats eyed me, but inspired no fear. The area was lighted like a carnival, and Baltimore Police Headquarters was a block and a half away.

Headquarters itself was darker. Citizens I would not want to meet on the streets were milling about, presumably waiting for news of loved ones in the lockup. A man seated on a bench just inside the door was bleeding through a gauze patch taped to his eye. Another, wearing a leather vest emblazoned with the words *Live Free and Die*, had coils of barbed wire tattooed up every finger, both hands and both forearms.

The counter that stretched across the main room was manned by three cops presumably collecting bad news and doling out half-answers, like tellers in a foundering bank of humanity. I approached the one in the middle because he was the oldest, and his lined face and white hair suggested kindness. He was still filling out a form sparked by the last story he'd heard. "How can I help you?" he asked, without looking up.

"I'm Dr. Frank Clevenger," I started.

He glanced at me. His brow wrinkled as he tried to square the "Dr." with the gash in my face, my ponytail and my black Harley jacket. "What kind of doctor would you be?" He went back to filling out his form.

Right about then I was thinking I *would* be a dermatologist if I had followed my head, rather than my heart, in medical school. My roommates and I used to joke that a single rule governed the whole specialty: If it's wet, put something dry on it; if it's dry, put something wet on it. But I had been bored on the surface of things. "I'm a psychiatrist," I said.

"We could use one around here." He looked up again, then back down. "You don't look like any shrink I've ever seen."

I'd heard that line more times than I could remember. I didn't look like any shrink I'd ever seen, either. "I'm here from Boston," I said, knowing that really didn't explain the incongruity. "I work with the police in Lynn, Massachusetts."

"Clevenger?" a black officer to our left said, looking over at me. He held up a hand to stop the wiry man in front of him from speaking. "Give me a minute."

"All I'm saying," the man persisted, "is that Harry's got sugar." He shrugged inside his faded Orioles baseball jacket and pulled nervously at his graying, scraggly beard. "You put a Breathalyzer in front of him when he's real bad off, it lights up. I seen it happen once before. Don't matter that my brother . . ." His own alcohol breath wafted my way.

"Shhhh," the officer demanded. He looked barely thirty, with pale blue eyes, a goatee and a shaved head. He looked over at me again. "We got a call about you from the State Police up there."

I wasn't sure whether the call had been to help me or hurt me. I stepped closer to him. "And . . ."

"We got nothing on any Lucas. At least nothing in our computer."

"How long do your records go back?"

The thin man began rocking against the countertop. "My brother Harry been around. He knowed—" he said.

"On the computer, ten years," the officer interrupted.

"What I'm looking for would have happened much longer ago."

"Fuckin' Ronnie Lucas," the man blurted out.

I turned to him.

The officer had tuned him out. "You could check police archives in the morning, but that's in City Hall. You'll need to go through proper channels over there. You may need a court order."

"You know somebody named Lucas?" I asked the man.

"Piece of shit broke Harry's jaw."

"Ronnie Lucas?" I asked. *"L-u-c-a-s?"*

"Ronnie Lucas," the older officer echoed.

"You know him?" I asked.

"Small-time bookmaker, loan shark. Hung around Fells Point. Drove a lemon yellow Pontiac LeMans convertible. White seats. Real low profile."

The black officer chuckled. "You never forget a goddamn thing."

"They didn't have computers when I was on the street."

"Have you heard of a Trevor Lucas?" I asked him.

"Nope."

I turned back to the thin man.

He shook his head. "I only knowed Ronnie owing to I chased him away from my garage with a tire iron when I caught him laying for Harry, maybe five years ago. This is after he already busted my brother's jaw. OK? Then he comes back with two other guys lookin' to mess *me* up. So I paid him." He looked at the young officer and shrugged. "What the fuck was I gonna do?"

"Call the police?" he suggested.

The man rolled his eyes.

"Where's Ronnie now?" I asked.

"I ain't seen him."

"He's got to be seventy, if he's still around," the older cop said.

I didn't want to waste time on Ronnie Lucas if Trevor was no relation. "Would your brother know more about Lucas than you?"

"Probably so. He was into Ronnie a long time. Bad with the ponies and the dogs, you know?"

"Yes, I do."

"But he don't drink."

I looked at the young black officer. "Can I talk to Harry?"

"He's drunk."

"*I* drink," the man interrupted, shaking his head. "Like I told ya, Ronnie's got sugar."

"Can I give it a shot?" I asked again.

"You can try. I doubt you'll get anything from him until he dries out." He anticipated an argument from the thin man. "Quiet. I'm not going to tell you again."

I figured it must have been Jack Rice who had called from Massachusetts. If Lieutenant Patterson had phoned I wouldn't have any chance of visiting a subject in custody.

The officer directed me to a door at the end of the counter. He let me in. "Anderson," he said, extending his hand.

I took it. "Frank Clevenger." His handshake was one of the most powerful I had ever felt.

We began walking down the flight of stairs leading to the holding cells. I was behind Anderson and noticed that he limped badly, favoring his right leg. His weakness surprised me, making me more conscious that the rest of him—a barrel chest, thick neck and rippling forearms—was built as if to withstand assault.

"I have a titanium knee and pins in my tibia," he said, reading my mind the way people with physical defects sometimes can. He answered my next question, too. "Attempted robbery of a U.S. Trust branch on Orleans Street. I got hit twice. The bottom of my femur shattered."

I wanted to reassure him I didn't see him as handicapped. "Looks like you've got most of your strength back."

Anderson stopped on the stairs and looked up at me. "My leg is coming back," he said. "That's not my problem." He paused, pointed at his shaved head. "I have things wrong nobody but me can see. Nightmares. Flashbacks. I might be at the counter out front and, all of a sudden, no warning at all, start bawling like a baby."

My skin turned to gooseflesh. I was standing in a stairwell in the middle of the night, hundreds of miles from home, while a man I had known just minutes revealed himself. If exposed ten thousand times I do not believe I will ever become immune to the raw, awful beauty of the human psyche in distress. Dermatology would have been a desert for me; I have a vampire's thirst for the suffering of others. My other addictions pale in comparison.

"Crying over a bullet ripping into you isn't anything like being a baby," I said softly.

He pursed his lips, nodded.

"Have you seen anyone about the memories?"

"They want me to. They might make me."

"Why would you need to be forced?"

He shrugged. "I don't know." Just as suddenly as he had turned toward me, he turned away and continued down the stairs.

I caught up to him and walked with him. I tried to summon the panic of being struck by a bullet—the shock, the pain, the helplessness of the inevitable collapse, of life and death spinning like a roulette wheel. I had to concentrate in order to avoid imitating his gait, a knee-jerk and futile way of trying to edge into his experience. How many of us have not closed our eyes and attempted to navigate a room to appreciate the lot of the blind man? And how petty is that effort knowing we can open our eyes the next moment and see?

One or two of the prisoners in lockup seemed truly dangerous, but the rest looked like hapless thugs and drunks who might have been nabbed for disturbing the peace, simple B & Es or, like Harry, driving under the influence. We stopped at a two-man cell. "Harry's the big one," Anderson said.

Harry was snoring loudly, lying on his side on the lower bunk. He was wearing a long brown leather coat, but I could tell it covered at least two hundred fifty pounds. He had grown his crown of hair shoulder-length on one side to comb over his bald spot, and the tress hung limply down his face. He looked like a bizarre cross between a skid row bum, a rock drummer and the Buddha. A black man about twenty was perched on the edge of the bunk above him, watching Anderson and me.

"What's the other guy in here for?" I asked.

"Possession of cocaine. Intent to distribute."

"How much?"

"Half a gram."

"Oh." I had more than that in my boot, not to mention the heroin.

"It doesn't sound like anything," he went on, unlocking the door as he spoke, "but he was near a school. He could go away five years. Maybe more. And it's federal time."

"That should cure him." I worried I might have shaken our alliance, but Anderson surprised me again.

"The 'War on Drugs' is a joke," he said. "This guy needs a halfway house, not the big house." He leaned closer and dropped his voice. "Half the cops in this building smoke dope or do a line of tootie now and then. One thing I can't stomach is holier than thou, Scarlet Letter bullshit."

"You're a hundred percent right, and you'll never make chief," I said.

"I'm barely makin' it as an Indian." He pulled open the door to the cell. "Like I told you, good luck getting anything out of Harry. I couldn't make head nor tails of what he was saying."

I walked in. Anderson waited at the door. I nodded at the black man in a way that asked for reassurance he wouldn't jump me. I was entering his space, even if it was borrowed from the penal system. He nodded back. I knelt by the side of Harry's bunk. "Harry?" Nothing. Louder, "Harry." I grabbed his shoulders and shook him. "Harry!"

He opened his eyes, then shut them again.

I shook him harder. "Your brother sent me to see you."

"I got nothin' to say, Charlotte Anne," he said, his eyes still closed, his words slurred. "Your mother's a good woman. Heart of gold." He shook his head. "Mary?" His eyes scanned back and forth under his lids, then opened wide and met mine. He reached out and took my hand in his. His skin was clammy. "Mary, turn off the sprinklers. I'm getting soaked here."

"Told you," Anderson said from the door.

I concentrated on Harry's odor. He didn't smell of booze. His breath, even his clothes, carried the chemical-sweet smell of ketones, produced by the liver when diabetics go without insulin too long, and blood sugar skyrockets. I moved my fingers to his wrist. His pulse was erratic. I turned to Anderson. "He's got bigger problems than being drunk—if he is drunk. I think his brother was on the money; his diabetes is completely out of control. He needs to get to a hospital right away."

"Is he gonna die?" the black man asked.

"I don't know," I said, glancing up at him. He was leaning over me, gripping his mattress to keep from falling.

"He sounded drunk just now," Anderson said.

I looked back at him. "I know, but that's probably because he's delirious. His blood chemistry is so far off that his brain can't function. His heart isn't beating real well, either."

"You know for sure he isn't just smashed?"

"No. I can't be absolutely sure. But if I end up being right, he could end up being dead."

"Shit," the black man said. "I knowed it, too."

"Let's go. We'll get him over to Hopkins," Anderson said.

I rushed back upstairs with Anderson, whose bum leg didn't keep him from outpacing me. I sat in front of his desk as he called to arrange for an ambulance. "The paramedics won't transport a patient alone," he said, hanging up. "I have to ride over with them. You want to go, question him once he's making sense?"

It was 1:20 A.M. I wondered whether I should head back to the Stouffer and make half the calls to Lucas families from the lobby while Cynthia used the phone in our room. I couldn't afford to waste time. I'd already been away from Lynn State six hours. But I reminded myself to listen to the city the way I would listen to a patient. I had asked a question by visiting police headquarters. I couldn't know whether the answer was about to unfold. "Let's go," I said.

I rode the ten or so blocks to Hopkins in the back of the ambulance with Anderson, Harry and Jim Maloney, one of the two paramedics who'd arrived at the police station. Harry's wrists were shackled to the gurney. I gave Jim my tentative diagnosis—diabetic ketoacidosis—which he scoffed at until he threaded a catheter into Harry's bladder, yielding a few milliliters of urine that turned the chemical dipstick bright pink from glucose. When he saw that color, he radioed the Hopkins ER for orders. A doctor with a Texas accent told him to start an IV of lactated Ringer's wide open for rapid hydration and to inject Harry with 30 units of regular insulin. I watched the cardiac monitor. Harry's heart was barely clinging to its rhythm, occasionally sputtering like an engine burning gas tinged with maple syrup.

As we turned on to Broadway, the dome of the hospital's original building rose like a beacon amidst Baltimore's poorest streets. My skin turned to gooseflesh as I pictured the ten-and-a-half-foot white marble Jesus standing inside it, robes flowing, palms outstretched. Lights are mounted to shine on His face. His bare feet border a plaque carved into the base that reads, *COME unto ME*

*all ye that are weary and heavy laden and I will
give you REST.* Though I had already sworn off
organized religion by the time I interviewed at
Hopkins, I was overwhelmed (in truth, nearly
brought to my knees) when I saw that statue. I
imagined how patients confronting cancer and
stroke and schizophrenia might find hope, might
even begin their cures, standing in its presence. I
thought of the Hebrews fleeing Egypt, some of
them swallowed into the earth for worshiping
graven images en route to the promised land.
Why, I wondered, would the God of Abraham
destroy any of his chosen people in a turf battle
against an idol they had fashioned from gold? And
once God had killed to defeat the idol, how could
anyone believe it consisted of nothing but metal? I
sat down on one of the armchairs facing the Lord,
doubting the miracle of His conception, yet revel-
ing in the humble majesty of men carving ten and
a half feet of stone into an object of devotion and
siting it so magnificently in a place of healing.
And I saw clearly for the first time that it doesn't
matter what you worship, as long as it helps you
focus your love for others and for yourself. A willing and great man will do. So will a golden calf.
Or a piece of rock. Or the kind of psychiatry I had
once been privileged to practice myself.

The ER staff was waiting for us. Two nurses
and a young, female physician I assumed was a
medical resident whisked Harry into one of the

curtained cubicles. Above the cloth I saw them hanging more bags of IV fluid. The cardiac monitor came to life with a green fluorescent tracing that continued to threaten death.

A tall, slim man with perfectly parted jet black hair approached Anderson and me. He wore a starched white lab coat that hung to his knees, a light blue shirt and a blue-black tie embroidered with silver Texas longhorns. He reached for Anderson's hand and shook it vigorously. "You guys better get an in-house doc down there in lockup, or I'm gonna have to put bars on my ER," he drawled.

"You can bunk with us anytime," Anderson said. "How's the knee?"

"I'll make it." He nodded at me. "Dr. Blaisdell, this is Dr. Frank Clevenger from Boston. He's a criminal psychiatrist."

"Good," he smiled. "I'm tired of the law-abiding kind." He bowed slightly in my direction. "Welcome. If I get a break in the action, I'll give you the two-penny tour."

Blaisdell went to work on Harry, Anderson left to grab coffee and I went to find a pay phone to call Cynthia.

As soon as I walked into the hospital's main corridor I saw that Hopkins had grown at least as much as the city had. A labyrinth of old and new buildings had been connected to create a gleaming mall. Stainless steel ceilings topped corridors

thirty feet across. Lighted etched glass signs
affixed to the walls marked the way to medical
meccas like the Wilmer Eye Institute, the Halsted
Surgical Department and the Oski Pediatric Center.

I used a stall in a men's room to snort half a bag
of heroin, then wandered a bit before I found a
bank of phones outside a coffee shop called the
Corridor Cafe. Our hotel room's extension was
busy the first few times I tried it, so I used my calling card to dial the Lynn Police Station for an
update. Before I could decide whether I wanted to
be, I had been patched through to the State Police
trailer on the grounds of Lynn State Hospital.

"Captain Rice," Jack Rice answered.

"It's Frank," I said, unsure whether he would
even stay on the line.

"Oh." A pause. Then, coldly: "What do you
need to know?"

"I'm just checking in. Everything holding
together?"

"From what we can see down here, which isn't
much." A slightly longer pause. "That it?"

"What about Calvin? Any word?" I pictured
Calvin Sanger turning around as he raced toward
the hospital, yelling the words I had hooked him
on. *Story of a lifetime!*

"No. No word. We done?"

I tried to offset his tone by imbuing mine with
amiability. "Listen, Jack—"

"No. You listen. You got what you wanted. Provided nothing changes, we won't take the unit for another sixteen and three-quarters hours. In exchange, you won't be burying me or my department in the press—ever. That's the deal. Don't ask me to hold your hand after you push me into a corner and threaten to fuck me."

I nodded to myself. He was right. But I couldn't resist reaching for his hand again. "I think I'm making a little progress down—"

"Anything we can use here, now?"

"Well, no. Not yet."

"Then I'll see you when you get back." He hung up.

"OK," I said to no one. "See you then." I slammed the receiver into its cradle. Two nurses passing by turned to look at me, but looked quickly away and kept walking. Between my jacket, my hair and the wound on my face, I probably seemed like a bigger problem than they cared to handle on a coffee break. I stood facing the booth several seconds, then picked up the receiver and dialed the hotel, hungry for a bit of good news about Cynthia's search.

She picked up. "Where are you?" she asked.

"Hopkins Hospital."

"I thought you were stopping back here."

"I stumbled on someone at the police station who knows a man named Ronnie Lucas. The trouble is, I couldn't get anything more from him. His diabetes had gone out of control, and he was nearly unconscious. He's being treated in the emergency room right now." I took a deep breath, thinking how tenuous a lead I had followed. "Have you found out anything?"

"I might have. You tell me."

"Shoot."

"I've called twenty-three Lucas families so far."

"OK."

"Nobody answered on nine of the calls. On twelve others, someone at each address talked to me just long enough to say they had no idea who Trevor Lucas was. One other woman said she knew him well, that he played tight end for the Ravens and that she was carrying his twins."

"We can probably refer her to Montel. That's twenty-two calls. How about the twenty-third?"

"Michael Lucas on Jasper Street. The guy hung up the second I mentioned Trevor. So I called back. He put me on the spot before I could get a word out: Who was I? Why was I bothering him? I gave him the party line—I was a census taker—but he just hung up on me again. When I called a third time he let the phone ring." She paused. "You think he's more than some random paranoid person?"

"You talked to him. What do you think?"

"I'm not sure."

"Then I think we should find out."

Eleven

Cynthia had suggested she save us time by visiting Michael Lucas herself, but I told her to keep making calls from the hotel room until I got back. When you enter someone's life story on the wrong page, the plot can turn viciously on you. I had learned that the hardest way of all—losing Rachel in the final chapter of Kathy's violence.

The instant I crossed back into the emergency room I heard the sounds of impending doom. Staccato electric tones filled the air. A gurney squeaked in the unmistakable cadence of CPR. Dr. Blaisdell was yelling orders for epinephrine, lidocaine and bretylium—medications I knew were parts of the treatment for severe cardiac arrhythmias. What had to be six sets of feet danced nervously under the curtain pulled around Harry's cubicle. I looked up and saw the green line on the cardiac monitor bending into the frantic, sawtooth rhythm of ventricular tachycardia. Harry's heart was squeezing down on itself again and again and again, never pausing to fill with blood, pumping air.

His brother suddenly appeared at my side. "What the hell is going on?" he asked.

"They're having trouble," I said, turning toward him. His lined, unshaven face suddenly looked very old to me. "Harry's heart isn't beating the right way."

"Ain't beating right?" He squinted at the cardiac monitor. "He'll make it, won't he? I mean, he ain't gonna . . ."

"Four hundred joules," Blaisdell ordered from behind the curtain. "All clear!"

Beneath the curtain, I saw feet step back. Harry's brother started moving forward. I caught him by the arm. "There's nothing you can do. Let them work." He stopped and stared blankly at the curtain. I knew he couldn't see through it the way I could. I could see Blaisdell with the defibrillator paddles in his hands, could picture Harry's chest heave off the mattress as the metal disks touched down. I could see eight blank faces, frozen, waiting, as if *they* had been shocked.

The gurney clattered under the weight of Harry's torso slamming back onto it.

"What was that?" his brother asked. Before I could answer, he crouched down against the wall next to us, holding his head in his hands.

I glanced up at the monitor and saw what he must have seen. The green line had gone flat. The electric tones in the air had become a constant hum.

"Four hundred," Blaisdell said calmly. "Stay back."

Silence descended as Blaisdell fired more current through Harry. The gurney clattered again. The green line traced a mountain range of sawtooth beats that lifted Harry's brother halfway to his feet, then dropped him right back down as it fell flat again and restarted its funereal hum.

"Four hundred," Blaisdell said.

The gurney clattered, but the line didn't budge.

"Four hundred."

Clatter. Nothing.

Harry's brother's face had gone white.

"Intracardiac epinephrine, please," Blaisdell said.

I pictured him registering the "epi" in a syringe and shooting the first bit into the air. I saw him bury the needle just below the sternum, then push down and away, angling directly into the ventricle of the heart.

I waited. The monitor's hum was unrelenting.

A female voice: "Call it?"

Blaisdell's voice stayed dead even. "Go to five hundred joules."

Harry's brother, grease-stained proprietor of a Baltimore garage, proud owner of an oversized Orioles' jacket with cracked orange and black vinyl appliqués, man worn thin by life, supplicant to the Hopkins shrine, stared at me with a profound prayer in his eyes.

I crouched next to him because I felt out of place on my feet. I wished I knew his name. The monitor hummed for what felt like many seconds, but what was probably only a few. Then, like a bird back from winter, it started to chirp. I looked up. The green line traced a few hesitant, deformed beats, then broke into a normal rhythm of blips across the screen. Harry gazed up at it as if he were looking at his first sunrise. His face flushed. I watched him, wondering whether a man can die and be reborn with his brother.

The curtain swayed with the frenzy of activity behind it. Feet changed places. Hands wearing the trappings of life—wedding bands, red and pink nail polish, watches, chains of gold—reached up to swap bags and bottles. Voices spoke in tongues—ccs, IVs, sub q, SMAC 12, CBC, CPK, EKG, ABG, ICU, CICU. Then, all of a sudden, I heard deep groans, followed by the first word of a newborn twohundred-fifty-pound man: "Louie?" He coughed. "Louie!"

"I'm here," Louie said, his voice breaking. "I'm here, Harry."

Blaisdell stepped from behind the curtain and pulled off his surgical gloves. His white lab coat was gone. His sleeves were rolled up. His necktie was tucked away between two buttons of his shirt. He saw Harry's brother standing next to me and walked over. "Dr. Blaisdell," he said, extending his hand. "You're a member of the family?"

"I'm the brother. I'm Louie," he nodded. "Louie Stokes." He took Blaisdell's hand and shook it, but wouldn't—or couldn't—let go.

Blaisdell didn't try to pull his hand away. "Your brother's heart took a rest. That's what all the commotion was about. It's running like clockwork now. Hopefully, it'll keep running that way."

"What happens next?"

"We'll get him up to CICU—cardiac intensive care—and make sure his sugar is under control. The first twenty-four hours are the most important."

"When can I see him?"

"He's right over there," Blaisdell said, nodding behind him. He winked.

Louie released his grip on Blaisdell and walked around the cubicle until he found an opening in the curtain. He disappeared inside.

"Strong work," I said.

"Well, you know, it's cookbook medicine," Blaisdell said. "You could write out the whole shooting match on a flow chart."

"Except deciding to go the extra mile. There's no recipe for that. Plenty of people would have called the code at four hundred joules. Plenty more would have called it after the intracardiac 'epi' didn't work."

Blaisdell literally blushed. "Plenty wouldn't." Great doctors are usually embarrassed by their gifts, precisely because they can't be diagrammed on any chart, can't really be explained at all. He looked down at his shiny black wingtip shoes, then back at me. "You were the one who picked up the ketoacidosis. That's way beyond the call for a psychiatrist."

"Blind luck. I listened in lecture that day."

We stood in an uncomfortable silence for a bit, as if suddenly remembering we didn't know one another, at least not in the traditional sense. At some more basic level, of course, we did. "I do have one question for Harry. Is he stable enough to answer it?"

He seemed to hesitate, but then shrugged. "Go ahead. You're not gonna throw him into another arrest with a question."

I walked to the cubicle and stepped through the break in the curtain.

Harry's clothes had been cut off. He lay naked on them, his midsection barely covered by a paper chuck. Louie was at the head of the bed, smoothing his brother's tress of hair back over his bald spot. The nurses and medical resident were finishing up their work.

"Dr. Blaisdell told me I'd be able to speak with Mr. Stokes," I said to no one in particular. I walked to the side of the gurney.

"Who's this, Louie?" Harry said. He coughed, then grimaced in pain. "My chest feels like somebody took a sledgehammer to it."

"That's from the CPR," I said. "They pretty much do take a sledgehammer to it."

"He's OK," Louie said. "He's a shrink from Beantown. Works with the cops up there. All he's lookin' for is he wants to know if we know any guy named Lucas. I told him Ronnie, but that ain't the one he means. So I thought maybe you'd know if Ronnie had brothers or this or that."

"Ronnie? Ronnie's name ain't Lucas," Harry said. He closed his eyes, exhausted.

My heart sank.

Louie squinted at him. "What do you mean? *Ronnie Lucas.*"

"Loomis. Ronnie *Loomis.*"

Louie nibbled his lower lip. "I'm talking about the bookie."

My pager went off. It was Matt Hollander's private number at Austin Grate.

"Yeah, Ronnie Fucking Loomis," Harry said. He opened his eyes and stared up at his brother. "What's wrong with you, Louie? You don't remember a guy's name comes looking to bash in your head over my stupid shit? You gotta lay off the booze. You can't remember nothing."

I felt dazed. Following the fictional Ronnie Lucas had given me hope that I might be closing in on Lucas' history. Now, past 2:00 A.M., I had hit a dead end. I didn't know where I was in relation to my goal anymore. How could I have thought that I would stumble so quickly onto the correct path? I summoned enough false cheer to wish Harry and Louie well and walked out through the curtain.

A nurse let me use one of the ER phones to dial Hollander.

"Frank?" he answered.

"Everything all right?"

"Only if you consider a cop car at your gates all right. Commissioner Hancock is out front waving a warrant for the arrest of one Kathy Singleton."

"How did she find—"

"Hard to say. I never did reach my renegade counselor."

"She's alone?"

"As far as I can see. Maybe she has something in mind other than bringing her niece's killer to the station. Maybe a pit stop in the woods. A little workout with the baton. Maybe they never get to the station."

"Kathy's a serial killer. Hancock shouldn't try to transport her without backup."

"I'm sure she considers this a personal matter."

I checked to be certain no one was in earshot. "Listen, Matt. Hancock won't be able to prove you hid Kathy. She could have used a pseudonym when she was admitted."

"You trained under me. Anyone would assume I'd been properly introduced."

"That doesn't mean Hancock can prove it."

A few seconds passed. "She won't have to prove anything."

"What do you mean?"

"I'm not going to deny what I did."

"Huh?"

"I admitted Kathy Singleton because she was ill. I knew she was a murderer. I also knew she needed help. Those are the facts. I'm not budging from them."

"Hancock will arrest you."

"She has to make it over my threshold first. And that gate out front is hundred-year-old, three-inch wrought iron. Twelve feet high. She'll need a locksmith. By the time she gets one, I'll be deep into my second brandy."

"You have to let her in. She's got a warrant. It's a court order."

"I have my own marching orders. This is my hospital. A place of healing. The police have no business here."

"Matt . . ."

"Listen to me. We started down the road to this moment the night you brought Kathy to Austin Grate. I agreed to keep her here. In case you were wondering, friendship had nothing to do with it. Zero. I did it because it was the right thing to do. Natural law. So don't worry about me. Every reporter dreams about being thrown in the slammer for not revealing a source, for sticking to his professional ethics. I'm doing the same. I'm not turning over any patient to the penal system. Let them punish me. It'll be an honor to do every last minute of my time."

I closed my eyes. "Well, I'm not going to let you do it alone."

"You better fucking believe I'm doing it alone. My patient. My hospital. My moment." He paused. "I can't stomach the system, Frank. That's why I'm behind these gates to begin with. You're more suited to it. Mr. Inside-Outside. You can get things done. You could actually teach the bastards to think. Maybe even to feel."

"I think you should let Hancock in. It's over."

"Thanks for the consult. Here's mine: What you're doing down there is God's work, pure and simple. You're trying to bring someone his truth. You're showing concern for a man who showed no concern for others. Or himself. That's glorious. Keep listening with the third ear. It'll never fail you." He hung up.

My mind was a fog. I walked out to the ER lobby.

Anderson was waiting for me. "Find out anything?"

I had to remind myself what he could be talking about. "Apparently Louie has a problem with his recall," I said listlessly. I shook my head. "Ronnie *Loomis* is the bookie Harry owed money to."

"Oh, shit."

"That cop you were working the desk with

backed up everything Louie said. He remembered Ronnie *Lucas*, too. He said he even remembered his car: 'A lemon yellow Pontiac LeMans convertible.' "

"He sure did. But his memory's shot. That's why they took him off the streets in the first place."

My neck felt stiff. My hands were trembling again. The heroin was wearing off. "You complimented him on his memory. You told him he never forgot a thing."

"What was I gonna tell him? That he's over the hill? That I check every report he fills out before it gets officially filed? That we all joke his next transfer's gonna be to the Guilford Assisted Living Center?" He folded his giant arms. "I figured since he and Louie agreed on the name, it had to be true."

I was starting to sweat. "Whatever."

"Hey. I screwed up. I'm sorry."

"I didn't mean to blame you."

"Blame me all you want, it won't change anything. What's next on your agenda?"

I didn't feel like telling him I had no agenda. "A friend of mine from Mass. has been over at the Stouffer making calls to all the Lucases listed in the phone book. One of the people she reached—Michael Lucas—got defensive when she brought up Trevor." I let out a long breath. "I guess I'll go by his place."

He nodded. "You're luffing."

"Bluffing? Bluffing about what?"

"No. *Lu*ffing."

"What's that?"

"You feel OK? You look like you're going to faint."

"I'll be fine. What's luffing?"

"You don't sail. I thought being from Boston . . ."

I wanted to get back to the hotel. "No. I don't. Listen . . ."

"I started last year. It really does clear my mind. So I bought a little wigeon. 'North's Star,' out of Baltimore harbor. That's my first name."

"North?"

He nodded. "But that's got nothing to do with the point I'm trying to make."

He obviously wanted to tell me something, and I did owe him for letting me tag along to Hopkins, even though it turned out I had no good reason to be there. "OK," I said, "what about me 'luffing'?"

"It's when your sail is angled wrong, and the canvas starts flapping. It happens when the wind shifts suddenly, or when you stray out of it, usually because you're not sure where you want to head."

"North, I don't know where the wind is, period. I'm just trying to keep my boat afloat. If you want to help me out, give me a ride to the hotel."

"You don't want to look for Michael before we leave?"

"He was home less than an hour ago. I don't think he's an inpatient."

"Not today. But maybe he was."

I started listening harder.

"Maybe he was even born here," Anderson went on. "Maybe the whole family's been in and out of this place."

I silently chastised myself for losing faith in the power of the third ear. It had carried me to the police station, to Anderson, to Harry and to Hopkins. I'd given up on it because of what I had just heard about Ronnie Loomis. But the third ear can work in mysterious ways. What if I was standing in the building with Anderson for another reason? "Can you get me into medical records?" I asked him.

"Nope." He winked. "But I'd be willing to ask Dr. Blaisdell."

"We're at Hopkins," I said. "That's like asking to look at a safe deposit box at the Chase Manhattan Bank."

"I wouldn't be shy about asking that either, if I really needed to see what was inside."

The walls of Blaisdell's office were covered with gold-framed degrees and certificates of membership in medical associations. I had planned to get mine prettied up, but had never gotten around to it. I guess the parchments never meant that much to me. Blaisdell was at his desk, entering a final note in Harry's chart. He waved us in and listened to Anderson's request as he finished writing. "Patients have rights, North," he said, swiveling to face us. He nodded at me. "Dr. Clevenger knows that. I can't show you a record without a release of information."

I let Anderson do the talking. I was still waiting for relief from the heroin I'd inhaled in the men's room a minute before. And I was ambivalent about pushing another doctor to violate his professional ethics.

"We don't even know whether there is a record," Anderson said. He took a seat on a small couch along one wall. I sat next to him. "If there is, all Dr. Clevenger wants to check is whether Michael Lucas has a brother named Trevor. He's not interested in whether he has syphilis or was a crack baby."

Blaisdell was unmoved.

"It's important to the case he's working on. There are hostages," Anderson said.

Blaisdell looked at me. "I wish I could help you. I really do. But there's a protocol to follow here. If the police need a chart, they go to court to get it."

"Unfortunately, there isn't time for that," I said.

"Ask for an emergency hearing. I've seen records released in thirty minutes."

"There's not a clear enough link," Anderson admitted. "We wouldn't get the court to act."

Blaisdell held up his hand. "Then you shouldn't get the chart."

I focused on the sense of connectedness with Blaisdell I had felt after Harry's resuscitation—a connection I continued to feel. I knew the emotion was rooted all the way back in my medical school years. Once doctors have dissected a human body, watched people die young and seen miraculous cures, we develop an "us-versus-the-world" mentality, not unlike Marines—or cops. It is an insular, seemingly unavoidable and potentially very destructive mind-set. Telling Blaisdell that almost twenty people, including three nurses, a dietitian, a social worker, a reporter and more than a dozen psychiatric patients, were at risk in Lynn wouldn't tap into that fraternity. Telling him that one of the nurses was pregnant wouldn't either. "There's a surgeon's life at stake," was what I told him. "If I don't get the information I'm looking for, he's going to be killed."

The resolve in Blaisdell's face began to fade. "One of the hostages is a doctor?"

I didn't answer the question directly. "He won't last until tomorrow morning," I said.

Anderson offered Blaisdell a way out of the stand he had taken. "If you were to order a patient record delivered to the emergency room, that's not like giving anyone permission to look at it. It would sit with the rest of the charts in that wire bin on the counter out front."

Blaisdell glanced at me, then stared at Anderson. "What you do is your business," he said. "Don't get me caught up in it." He swiveled back around to face his desk and picked up the phone.

"Fair enough." Anderson stood up and walked out.

I followed him to the lobby, suddenly half-filled with people who looked as desperate as the ones I had seen at the police station. A few, too drunk or high to sit up, had draped themselves over several chairs. A little boy and girl with soiled faces, neither of them older than six, chased one another while a woman who might have been their mother or older sister held her swollen jaw and cried. The doors opened, and an elderly man stepped through, half his face red and droopy from what looked like a fresh stroke or a fresh beating.

"This place never stops," Anderson said.

"Neither does yours."

"That's because they're both emergency rooms. I'm no different than that woman over there." He nodded at the nurse interviewing the old man who had walked in. "The people on our turf are just sick in another way. For some reason I didn't get that when I was working the streets."

"Too busy?" I said.

"Maybe. Maybe too angry. I grew up on the streets myself." He stepped over to the Coke machine a few feet away. "Want anything?"

I wanted to be in two places at once—Hopkins

and Austin Grate. "Diet, thanks," I said. "You think Blaisdell will get the chart for us?"

"We'll have to wait and find out. But you did a nice job in there. I'd be surprised if he didn't come through," he said. He fed quarters into the machine, handed me my drink. I opened it and drank until my throat couldn't take the burning anymore. He grabbed a can of Mountain Dew. "We should get you to come in as a consultant on some of our interrogations at the station," he said. "I could talk to the captain. I've seen him bring in forensic experts plenty of times. They fly you here, put you up—the whole nine yards."

"Thanks, but you might be a little late. I think I should be out of this racket."

"Why?"

I didn't have the time or the desire to spill my guts about Trevor and Kathy and Rachel. And I wasn't about to tell him I might be headed to jail when I landed back in Boston. "Too much stress dealing with cops," I said.

He laughed. "What would you do instead?"

"I don't know." Then, out of the blue: "Get back into private practice?"

"You miss it?"

"I guess I do."

"I don't miss the streets. I'll tell you that. And I don't think I ever will, certainly not while my head keeps replaying horror films."

I wanted to help him talk about what had happened. It didn't seem like the ideal time or place, but he had chosen it. "What exactly do you see?"

"The whole scene. I go over it and over it."

"But is it that you see yourself being hit? Or falling to the ground? Do you focus on yourself bleeding?"

He looked away, toward the sliding glass doors that opened on to the street. "No."

I waited.

He glanced at me, then stared down at the floor between us. "I see them falling."

"Them?"

"The two guys who held up the place. I hit one in the neck after I took the first bullet to my knee. I got the other one between his shoulder blades after I was already on the floor." He squinted and shook his head. "One was seventeen. The other one was nineteen. Tyrone Billings and Jerry Corkum. Neither of them made it."

Sometimes people replay traumas to find out how they could have managed to change the ending. "They were both armed?"

"Semiautomatic pistols. Just like mine." He glanced down at the gun on his belt.

"They fired on you first."

Anderson seemed to understand I was digging for the part of his trauma that troubled him most. He let out a long breath. "I got hit before I got off a round." He paused. "But I think the second one, Jerry, was ready to pack it in before I shot him. I think he was going to drop his weapon. His buddy was already down. He had his arm at sort of a forty-five-degree angle to his body. I didn't focus to see if his hand was letting go."

"Could you have? From the ground? Wounded?"

"I didn't even try."

"He had a gun. What if he had . . ."

His face tightened with what looked like a combination of rage and grief. "I wanted to kill him. Understand? I *wanted* him dead."

So there it was. The center of the storm. North Anderson had seen the darkest part of himself, and his mind's eye was stuck there, like a projector chewing on the same two inches of film. Now the storm was sucking at me. I couldn't resist it. "Yes, I think I do understand," I told him. I remembered the fury that had possessed me as I faced Mr. Kashoor on the locked unit, just after cutting Craig Bishop. "You figure you're a murderer at heart."

His eyes filled up. He cleared his throat and scanned the lobby to make sure no one was looking at him.

"I'm going to tell you something, North, because I know it as a fact and because we don't have the luxury of sitting around for twenty or thirty sessions so you can slowly come upon it yourself. Men who enjoy killing don't replay the scene over and over again unless they want to, for a good laugh or to impress a buddy or to get themselves hard so they can fuck something that isn't dead. I've never been shot, so I don't know what would go on in my mind looking at the guy who had done it to me, especially if he still had a gun in his hand. But my guess is I'd want to shoot the bastard where he stood. You can go around thinking you're a murderer, tearing yourself apart because you're not a saint, or you can start admitting you're a human being and let it go at that."

He swallowed hard, nodded once. "I never thought of it the way you're saying—that I wouldn't have flashbacks if I wasn't basically OK. Like, I wouldn't be screwed up if I wasn't normal. Or something like that."

"That's about right." I felt as if I had said too much, not because North didn't need to hear it, but because it had poured out of me, which always left me feeling exposed and depleted, at least for a while. And I didn't have energy to spare. I started to walk away, but turned back. I wasn't quite done bleeding my truth and still wasn't in control of how it flowed. "I can't say if you belong on the streets now, North, but you must have been a great gift to them back then." I smiled. "Take that to the bank with you next time your mind wanders there."

Fifteen minutes later a clerk from medical records emerged from the lobby elevator and wheeled a shopping cart full of charts past Anderson and me.

We watched her continue to the front counter and check a list on the clipboard she was carrying. She took a few minutes to select four charts from the stack in the cart and dropped them into the wire basket.

"Either it's one of those, or we struck out," Anderson said. "Wait here. If the nurses see the two of us fishing around they might get their backs up. At least I'm in uniform."

"I'll be over there." I nodded at a couple of seats tucked into a corner, away from the rest of the waiting area.

Anderson walked to the wire bin on the counter and quickly rifled through the four charts. The medical resident glanced at him as she hurried between cubicles, but didn't try to stop him. He grabbed one folder and brought it back with him. "Michael Lucas," he said, handing it to me. "Nice to know that when you get a feeling, it sometimes turns out to be on the money. Makes a believer out of you." He sat down.

"Unless you're at the track, then it makes a degenerate out of you." I held the thick chart a few seconds, not wanting to open it and find myself at another dead end. "He must have been here quite a bit. This thing's heavy." I slowly turned back the cover.

The demographics sheet indicated Michael Lucas was forty-three years old during his most recent Hopkins admission, from January 12, 1997 to January 16, 1997. He lived where Cynthia had reached him—at 2304 Jasper Street. His religion was Protestant, his insurance coverage "self-pay"—hospital lingo for the uninsured. Other dividers in the chart were for stays of about the same length during 1995, 1992, 1987 and 1983. A sticker on the inside back cover indicated more records were stored on microfiche.

"Tell me about Jasper Street," I asked Anderson.

"The old Baltimore. Row houses in disrepair. High crime. Low rent," he said. "It's like walking into the past."

That comment sent shivers down my neck. I flipped back to the first admission. My pulse quickened as I read from the "Initial History and Physical":

January 12, 1997
Chief Complaint: "I'm just here to finish the work on my lips."

History of Present Illness: Mr. Michael Lucas is a 43-year-old white male with prominent facial deformities. He is admitted to the plastic surgery service for revision of grossly disfiguring scars to his upper and lower lips. The patient has undergone 18 previous procedures to address injuries to the head and neck caused by severe chemical burns sustained as a 5-year-old.

"What does it say?" Anderson asked.

"He was admitted for plastic surgery. His face is badly scarred from chemical burns." I shook my head, stunned at the link between Michael Lucas' medical needs and Trevor Lucas' medical specialty. I fanned through the chart, my eyes locking on line drawings of the procedures Lucas had undergone. "It looks like all of his admissions were for different facial surgeries."

"Didn't you say Trevor Lucas is a plastic surgeon?" Anderson asked.

I nodded, still fanning pages. I stopped on two side-view photos of Lucas labeled "Before" and "After." In the top photo his ear looked like an irregular triangle with folded corners, and his nose was skeleton slim, as if most of the flesh had melted, leaving skin and bone. The bottom photo showed marked improvements in shape, coming closer, but not very close, to what nature had intended. In both photos, the visible part of Lucas' scalp was a patchwork of shiny scars and fine clumps of hair. I couldn't tell from either shot whether Michael Lucas resembled Trevor.

I turned to the "Personal, Social and Family History" portion of the first admission. Typical for a surgical write-up, the biography consisted of a few sentences:

This unmarried, unemployed male with no children has never worked, describes himself

*as a "hermit." Denies alcohol and illicit
drugs. Lives alone. No hobbies. Extended free
care since 1969 due to grave medical need.*

On the next page I found a genogram charting
three generations. A box with an arrow pointing at
it signified the patient. Slash marks through the
box and circle one level above him indicated his
parents were deceased. According to the diagram,
he had no siblings. "Damn," I muttered.

"What?" Anderson said.

"It says he has no brothers or sisters." I quickly
found the family histories from the other admissions. Each listed the patient the same way.
"Every one of these write-ups lists him as an only
child." I looked at him.

"Well, I certainly wouldn't take that to the
bank," he grinned.

Twelve

Anderson pulled to the curb in front of the Stouffer around 3:15 A.M. "If you want a ride to Jasper Street, I could manage to get out of the rest of the shift. It's over at seven, anyhow."

"A police escort might spook him," I said. I held out my hand. "I'll call if my own luck runs out."

"Fair enough." He shook my hand. "Thanks."

"Same here." People who have shared the truth are like atoms that share electrons. You feel the force of the bond most powerfully as you take leave of it. I got out of the cruiser, but poked my head back inside. "Be careful, will you?"

"Nobody's attacked a police station yet." He winked.

I watched him pull away, then headed into the hotel. I figured I would hook up with Cynthia and taxi over to Jasper Street. If Michael Lucas' plastic surgeries turned out to be coincidence, and he turned out to be irrelevant, we could make it to City Hall by the time it opened at 9:00 A.M. Anderson had promised to help us with access to the police archives there.

I knocked at the door to our room, but there was

no answer. I knocked again. Nothing. I assumed
Cynthia had fallen asleep or headed downstairs for
food or coffee. I had one of the card keys for the
room with me. I slipped it into the high-tech lock,
pulled open the door and stepped inside. The room
was empty. The phone book was open on the desk.
A paper airplane was wedged, nose down, in the
binding. I walked over, picked it up and read the
note Cynthia had left me: "You're late. Flew to
check out Michael L. Back ASAP."

I dropped the note and raced for the elevator. I
pored through all the horrors imaginable—Cynthia being abducted, raped, murdered. I knew my
mind was in overdrive partly because Rachel had
been killed in the crossfire of my life, but recog-
nizing that afforded me no comfort. Personal histories tend to repeat themselves, like the histories
of nations, until the lessons they would teach are
fully learned. Paranoia gripped me. I started to
fear that Trevor had again maneuvered me into
sacrificing the woman I needed in my life.

I ran to the semicircle in front of the hotel and
climbed into the first taxi in a line of four or five.
"Jasper Street," I said.

The driver, a gaunt, half-shaven man in his
fifties, turned around. "Know how to get there?"

"No."

"Me neither. Maybe you should ask that guy."
He pointed at the cab behind us.

Cab drivers sometimes feign ignorance to avoid a short run and wait to score a fare to the airport. I had a feeling this was one of those drivers and one of those times. I reached into my pocket and pulled out two twenty-dollar bills. I tossed them over the front seat. "Get me there."

Within ten minutes, without a single wrong turn, the taxi came to a stop across from 2304 Jasper Street, a brick row house indistinguishable from dozens of others lined up on either side of it. Metal signs that read NO TRESPASSING and PRIVATE were wired to the chain-link fence surrounding an overgrown, postage-stamp front yard. I jumped out and walked up the stairs to the door. I gently tried the handle. Locked. I leaned over the railing, trying to see inside the first-floor window, but a paper shade stained yellow and brown, crumbling in places, blocked most of my view. The glimpses I did get were of books—hundreds of them, some stacked neatly against the walls, some thrown into a three-foot pile beside a sooty white marble fireplace.

I thought I heard voices. Or had I? I listened harder. The sounds seemed to be coming from the back of the house.

I hopped the fence and plowed through waist-high grass and weeds to reach the backyard. I stumbled over something that turned out to be a rusted tricycle old enough to be in an antique shop.

A child's two-wheel bike of the same vintage lay
next to it, a decomposing mud-brown baseball
glove still tied to its seat. I heard crying. I picked
up my pace, but when I made it to the backyard
the only sounds were the creaking of branches
and the fluttering of an American flag hanging
from the fire escape. I looked up and saw that all
the shades in the back windows were drawn. Then
I heard a man's voice. I couldn't make out his
words, but they were drifting from the basement.
My eyes scanned the foundation and locked on a
half-window that had been painted black, but was
cracked like a spider web. There was a jagged
two-inch hole in one corner.

I crouched next to the window and peered
through it. I saw Cynthia, her face wet and flushed
from crying, her eyes filled with terror. She was
standing on a dirt floor beside what looked like an
animal cage, older and more substantial than the
wire ones sold today, large enough to house a
Great Dane. I could just see the tip of a man's bare
shoulder, closer to me, off to the right. The man
was talking, but I still couldn't hear what he was
saying. My racing thoughts filled in the blanks. I
pictured him holding a gun or a knife, demanding
Cynthia climb into the cage. I imagined him con-
cocting lurid plans. I scrambled to my feet and
scoured the back of the house for a weapon. The
only thing I could lay my hands on was an old

baseball bat. I ran to a set of wooden doors built into the ground—the opening, I guessed, onto stairs to the basement. A padlock held them closed, but it seemed to be rusted through, like everything else around the place. I didn't hesitate. I smashed the lock with the bat. It broke apart with the first blow. I reached down and flung one door aside, then bolted down a set of concrete steps and kicked in the flimsy door at the bottom of them. I rushed past Cynthia just as Michael Lucas, perfectly muscled and naked to the waist, his face even more grotesque in life than in his photos, rushed at me. Cynthia's screams filled the musty air. Lucas planted his knee in my abdomen. I doubled over. His fist landed above my eye. I felt my skin rip. His hands closed around my neck. I summoned every ounce of strength I could and drove my shoulder up into his chest, knocking him off me. I gripped each end of the bat and used it as a plow to drive him against the cement wall of the foundation. I pressed the wood hard across his neck. Now he was the one who looked terrified. Now he could think about losing his life, instead of me losing someone I loved. I watched his smooth, shiny, melted skin turn pinker for want of oxygen. I stared into his eyes—Trevor's black eyes—and pushed harder with the bat. And only then did I realize that Cynthia was screaming more, not less, than before, that her fists were rain-ing down on my shoulders. I was so deafened by my fury that I had to force myself to listen to her actual words.

"Frank! Stop it!" she pleaded. "Leave him alone!"

It took me a few seconds to trust what I was hearing over what I felt. I moved the bat an inch off Lucas' neck. He coughed and gasped for air.

"He wasn't hurting me," Cynthia cried. She yanked at my jacket. "Let him go!"

I backed up a few steps and let the bat fall to my side. Lucas dropped to his knees and watched me as he caught his breath. Half his face bore a strong resemblance to Trevor's, but the other half was reconstructed into something that looked like a high school art student's C+ rendering from clay. The flesh looked layered on in places, the contours of jaw and cheekbone irregular. His upper lip pulled noticeably to the damaged side. One eyelid drooped, the fleshy pocket cradling a tiny pool of clear fluid—an eternal tear. His hair was the patchwork I had seen in the medical record.

I let Cynthia drag me another couple of feet from him. I was trembling. "I thought he was trying to put you in there," I said, glancing at the cage.

"He wasn't," she said. "He was showing me where his mother kept Trevor."

"Kept . . ."

"As a penance. He had to pray morning and night . . . for his salvation." She took a moment to catch her breath. "Trevor was eight. Michael was five. They were chasing each other through the kitchen, past the stove. Trevor reached up and knocked a big pan of cooking oil off its burner. Michael was right behind him."

I thought of the ritualistic prayer Lucas was demanding of patients and hostages on the locked unit. "How long did she keep him in there?"

"Almost a year."

I stood there, thinking about the nightmare it must have been for Trevor Lucas to be kept behind bars awaiting trial for murder. It had to bring all the fear and guilt and hatred of his tortured childhood crashing back. I remembered visiting him at the Lynn jail shortly after he had surrendered. He had been seated Indian style on the floor, chanting, a pose I saw as an overblown display of false self-possession. But perhaps it was not arrogance, but desperation I had witnessed, an attempt to mentally escape the confines of that cell—of the cage—to keep the past from overtaking him. After he was transferred to the state prison, as the days and weeks and months dragged on, it was easy to understand how meditation would fail to keep the past at bay, and his mind would stumble upon the ultimate way out, liberating itself wholly from reality. Psychosis is the supreme vanishing act.

Michael Lucas struggled to his feet. He cleared his throat and massaged his neck. "Dr. Clevenger, I presume." His voice was cultured, almost melodic, not unlike Trevor's. A hint of a smile played across his mismatched lips. "Cynthia mentioned you might stop by. You could have knocked. It worked for her."

"I didn't understand what was going on. I'm sorry."

"Not that I dare counsel a psychiatrist to *think*, but had you, I would be saved a bruised windpipe, and you, that ugly cut."

I touched my brow and felt the warm, wet opening in my skin. "Forgive me."

"Not my place, I'm afraid."

"Has Cynthia told you why we're here?"

"She told me what my brother has done."

"I'm trying to help him. I need to know more about him."

"I have neither seen nor heard from Trevor since he left home." He paused. "Of course I'm not shocked he would wreak havoc in the world. He did in mine."

"If I can't convince him to surrender, he'll be killed."

Several seconds passed in silence. "At least he was free for a time. I've been imprisoned my whole life. This house. This face." He turned and took a few steps toward the staircase to the first floor. "I'll trust you to let yourselves out," he said, without looking back at us.

I stood there with Cynthia as Lucas walked

slowly up the stairs. A door opened, then closed. "Did he tell you anything else?" I asked her.

"I wasn't here long enough. It took him a while to admit he knew Trevor at all. When I told him about the locked unit, he brought me to see the cage."

I needed every page of Trevor's life history I could get. "I'm going upstairs."

"He came to the front door with a shotgun when I rang the bell."

"He could have turned you away with a simple lie when you called him at midnight. He could have not answered the front door at all when you rang the bell. And he certainly didn't have to bring you down here." I shook my head. "He's not going to shoot me. He's got his own questions about Trevor's life—maybe about his own." I thought back to Harry yelling out for Louie in the Hopkins emergency room. "They're brothers, no matter what happened." I started up the stairs, then realized that Cynthia was right behind me. I turned around.

She heard my objection without my speaking it. "I didn't come this far to hide in the basement," she said. "If it's safe enough for you to go up there after you attacked him, it's got to be safe enough for me."

I realized I wasn't sure what would happen

when I confronted Lucas again. I was still wary of replaying Rachel's demise. "I'm going alone."

She shook her head. "It's too late for that."

I tried staring her down, but lost. I started to tell her I loved her, partly because I felt that way, partly because I hadn't gotten to tell Rachel. "In case you don't know . . . ," I said.

"I do," she said. "Save it, though. Tell me when I can show you."

We found Lucas seated on a threadbare couch in the living room, surrounded by his haphazard library, staring into the fireplace. A dozen or more crucifixes adorned the walls, along with dime-store framed passages from the Bible. Charred books and a few half-burned split logs lay cold on the andirons. His shotgun was on the cushion next to him. I kept a respectable distance, just inside the room, with Cynthia behind me, off to my right. I moved slowly to the nearest stack of books and picked up a copy of Plutarch's *Lives*, revealing Saint Thomas Aquinas' *Summa Theologica* beneath it. A tattered copy of the Pentateuch, the five books of Moses, was at the top of the next stack. *The Hunchback of Notre Dame, Invisible Man* and *The Complete Works of William Shakespeare* lay askew atop the third. I was in the company of a learned man. "An impressive collection," I said, keeping my voice soft and even. "Which ones get burned?"

He didn't respond.

I noticed a copy of J. D. Salinger's *Franny and Zooey* near my feet. I slowly crouched and picked it up. "A kindred spirit?" I asked, holding up the book.

He looked at me, but said nothing.

"I wonder what Salinger would say about me standing here. You think he'd dismiss it as coincidence?"

"Certainly not."

"Then there must be a reason to talk more."

He moved his hand to the butt of the shotgun. "Not necessarily. Perhaps you're here to end your life," he said. He tilted his head up and to the right, the same mannerism that accompanied his brother's grandiose ruminations. "The sign out front says NO TRESPASSING. You broke into my home. Cynthia told you, no doubt, about this gun. And here you are standing in close range."

The comment reminded me of others made by Emma Hancock and Matt Hollander and Trevor Lucas himself, all of them wondering whether I was unconsciously orchestrating an elaborate suicide. I thought of the Harpy surrounding me on the grounds outside the hospital, of the assault helicopter hovering in front of me after strafing the locked unit. Was I asking to be killed? Was some fatal mixture of grief and guilt driving me to my own demise? Or is the search for a broken man's soul always a journey toward destruction? "I'm here for the truth," I said. "If you shoot me, I'll have part of it—that what went on in this house so utterly crushed two little boys that, hundreds of miles apart, they both became killers." I shrugged. "Maybe that's what really brings me into 'close range.' Maybe I'm *your* destiny—to find out you're no different than your brother."

Lucas' jaws worked against one another. His eyes stayed locked on mine. I worried I had pushed him too far. But then, all of a sudden, he moved his hand away from the gun. His gaze lost its menacing quality. "Well put," he said. He seemed lost in thought for a time. When he finally spoke, his voice had a hint of warmth in it. "The books that get burned are the ones full of lies. I've warmed my feet beside everything from *Mein Kampf* to *Das Kapital* to *Listening to Prozac*. If it gets any colder outside, I've got a nice supply of Jerry Falwell and Pat Robertson."

I smiled. Cynthia took the few steps to stand at my side. "I'm looking for the biography of Trevor and Michael Lucas," I said.

"I've told you what I know. My brother made me a freak. Our mother apparently turned him into a monster." He stared into the fireplace. "Or maybe he was already a monster."

There it was, I thought to myself—the real question that Michael Lucas needed to answer. "You think he might have meant to hurt you, that he did it on purpose."

"I don't care anymore." A twitch in his lip said otherwise. "It doesn't matter."

"He was eight," Cynthia said.

"I was five," Lucas shot back. "My mother's favorite. Her 'sweet boy,' she called me. That was my crime. He hated me for that."

My skin turned to gooseflesh. Those were the words we had found carved into Grace Cummings after she leapt from the fifth floor of Lynn State Hospital. Were they the words that an eight-year-old Trevor Lucas, shivering in his cage, wire and dirt underfoot, had heard his mother call lovingly to little Michael?

"How can you know he hated you?" Cynthia asked.

"Has he truly repented? Has he knocked once at my door since he left this house? No. Not him. Not my father. Not even after Mother died."

"How did he end up living with your father in the first place?" she asked. "Why did she let him go?"

"She didn't, as I recall. Keep in mind, I was a child. But I believe she fell ill at work. Her appendix, or some such thing. My aunt came by and found Trevor locked up in the basement. I remember her making frantic arrangements."

"Did you miss him?" Cynthia asked.

Lucas seemed taken aback by the suggestion. "No one ever spoke of him again," he said, neatly avoiding her question. "It was as if he never

existed—except for one rather stark reminder."
He reached up and ran the tip of his index finger
down the disfigured half of his face.

"What sort of work did your mother do?" I
asked.

"She was a nurse," Lucas smiled. "A saint."

I thought of the pregnant nurse, Nurse Vawn,
bound into her seat at the nurses' station on the
locked unit.

Lucas looked into the dormant fireplace again.
"What has my brother done with his life?" he
asked. "What did the monster do before losing his
mind entirely? Pave roads? Write ad copy? Rob
banks? What?"

I glanced at Cynthia, realizing she hadn't told
him his brother's profession. All of a sudden, the
room and everyone in it seemed absolutely still
and bursting with energy at the same time, as if
longing for the revelation. "Trevor went to medical school," I said. I closed my eyes briefly, feeling the presence of a higher power. "He trained as
a plastic surgeon."

Lucas squinted at me. "A . . ." He swallowed
hard. "A plastic surgeon." I could see him struggling to remain untouched. Within half a minute,
the divine symmetry overwhelmed his resistance.
A tear slid down his cheek.

I let several moments pass. "It sounds to me like
your brother's been trying to come home for a
long time. In a way, maybe he finally has."

Lucas didn't respond.

I realized what I really wanted from him. "Would you come back to Massachusetts with us? Will you help us talk Trevor into surrendering?"

"Not a chance."

"They'll kill him," Cynthia said.

Lucas smiled indulgently at her. "My brother died thirty-five years ago. And I have no desire to raise him from the dead."

I thought of Louie and Harry again. "You might end up reborn yourself."

"Not in this body, thank you."

I noticed a copy of Shakespeare's *King Lear* on the mantel. I nodded at it. " 'Pray you now, forget and forgive,' " I quoted. "It's one of my favorite lines from *Lear*."

His eyes locked on mine. " 'The wheel is come full circle,' " he quoted back. "That's my favorite." He stood up. "It really is time for you to leave."

I pressed harder. "I think it's time you left— time you left your childhood and this . . . mausoleum."

He picked up the shotgun but didn't raise the barrel. "I want you to go away now."

"Michael . . . ," Cynthia started.

I held up a hand. From the cold resolve in Lucas' eyes, his past history of trauma and his choice of words, I worried pressing any further really could cost us our lives. Maybe the foundation of his psyche was no more stable than Trevor's. "I understand," I said. "We appreciate you letting us in at all." I took Cynthia by the elbow. "We need to go," I told her.

We walked to the front door. I gently guided her ahead of me, onto the landing outside. "Just out of curiosity," I said, turning back toward Lucas, "which side of the kitchen was the stove on? Would Trevor have reached up to the pan of oil with his right hand or his left hand?"

"Why?" he asked.

"I'm just trying to imagine the whole thing. That's all."

He shrugged. "It would have been on the right. He used his right hand."

"That's the way I pictured it," I said. I paused. "That's the arm he cut off after he took over the locked unit. He cut off his right arm." I didn't wait for a reaction. I started down the steps with Cynthia, hoping Lucas might call out to me, that he might reach out for his brother.

The door slammed shut behind us.

Cynthia and I started walking south on Jasper Street, looking for a pay phone to call a cab.

"The police found the real killer," I said.

"They . . . Where?"

"A unit for violent patients at Austin Grate Clinic. My friend runs it."

She looked down. "What happens now?"

"I can't say. For all I know, they'll be waiting for me with cuffs at the airport in Boston."

"They wouldn't *arrest* you."

I smiled at Cynthia's naïveté. "The power of the state is an awesome thing. Stand in the way, you'll generally be crushed beyond recognition."

She glanced at me with a kind of desperation in her eyes, as if she was searching for words to put me at ease but had none.

I took her arm and pulled her closer. We kept walking until I spotted a pay phone inside the Balmer Cafe, a greasy spoon that was already bustling with a blue-collar trade. Construction workers in overalls and padded canvas jackets packed the counter, steeling themselves with fried eggs and pancakes against another icy day. A wiry man at the grill yelled out orders as he filled them and comments on the Baltimore Ravens football team as he thought of them. Cynthia ordered breakfast for us while I made the call. Before I headed back to our booth I stopped in the men's room to get at the stash of heroin in my boot to keep withdrawal at bay.

"The taxi will be here in about twenty minutes," I said, taking my seat by the front window. My coffee was waiting for me. I sipped it. It was just hot enough and just sweet enough and served in one of those well-worn, heavy white ceramic mugs with no glaze left at the lip. I wrapped my fingers around it. The window was fogged at the edges, cold and a little wet to the touch. There was magic in the place, and it relaxed me enough to think about what would happen next. "It's time to fly home. I have as much information as I'm going to get. The question is whether I get the chance to use it to coax Trevor back toward reality."

"They could have stormed the unit already," Cynthia said.

"I called the State Police from Hopkins. Things were holding together."

"Maybe you should call again."

I looked at the clock on the wall. 8:55 A.M. Six hours had gone by. I thought of checking in with Rice, but decided against it. I didn't want to tell him by phone what I had learned about Michael Lucas. If he didn't think it was enough to change anything, he might be tempted to move the assault up. Of course if Emma Hancock had gotten to him, nothing I could offer would be enough. "I don't want to answer any questions while I'm here and they're there," I said. "If Captain Rice is still willing to give me my shot, he may not understand how I can use what you and I found out to end the siege."

Cynthia nodded tentatively. A few seconds passed. "Why *do* you think telling Trevor about Michael would make him less crazy?" she asked.

"I'm not sure it would. But the truth can extinguish even the most bizarre psychic dramas."

"You think the truth is that powerful?"

"The mind is lazy by nature. It uses the least possible psychic energy to keep itself chugging along, to keep us eating, sleeping, working. Its first choice is always to see things for what they are, to stick with the facts as life unfolds. Because reality is free for the taking."

"Which is why an hour with me runs two hundred dollars," she said. She looked embarrassed.

"It always costs something to create a fantasy. Only when reality seems unbearable does the mind spend the creative energy to make up a cover story—like painting a pretty scene over an ugly crack in a wall. If you're a beaten, abandoned kid who can't stand to think of it, your mind might create an inflated ego that keeps you from feeling worthless. When the pain is much more extreme, your mind could try to bury it once and for all by making you believe that you're royalty or that you're Superman."

"And Trevor?"

"Trevor's truth is that he destroyed his brother. His unconscious mind has been working overtime to keep him from feeling overwhelming guilt— that's the crack in the wall of his psyche. He was only eight when Michael was scalded. I doubt he even remembers the accident—presuming it was an accident. He may not even remember Michael. But somewhere deep inside, he knows what he did, and he knows that his mother, who was supposed to love him, started torturing him and ultimately abandoned him because of it."

Our breakfasts arrived. Fried eggs, crispy hash browns and toast brushed with butter. I thought of my breakfast with Matt Hollander before I entered the locked unit. I was worried for him and I missed him. I had the feeling he would have been able to get further with Michael Lucas than I had. "Good thing I'm not on a diet," I joked. I swallowed a forkful of hash browns.

"You need the calories," Cynthia said. "There's no nutritional value in anything you can snort." She ate a bit of her food, then paused. "So why didn't Trevor go crazy before this?"

"Because he was able to stay one step ahead of the truth. His mind was essentially running like a Ponzi scheme, trying to cover up reality wherever it started to show. I would guess being shipped out of state allowed him some distance from his guilt for a while. Maybe his father assured him the whole thing was a nightmare, that it had never happened. His developing narcissism helped him to not look back. He probably used sex as an anesthetic, losing himself in passion. Becoming a plastic surgeon, basking in the public eye, bought him more time. But when he was kept in prison, stripped of his professional identity and his women and his possessions, none of it was enough to carry him through. The bars of the cage were

right in front of him. Every hour. Every day. For
months. Unbearable memories about what he had
done to Michael—and what his mother had done
to *him*—surged toward the surface. The crack
started to widen. Eventually the whole wall felt as
if it might fall, unleashing a tidal wave of guilt,
despair and shame. So his mind came up with a
last-ditch fiction to prop it up. It disowned the
very arm he had used to knock that boiling oil off
the burner. That arm wasn't part of his 'self' any
longer. It was part of Satan, captured territory in a
sham war between good and evil. That made it
easy to cut it off, to bury it—and the truth—under
the rubble of Armageddon."

"But cutting it off didn't stop him. It didn't end
anything."

"No. Because the whole puffed-up drama was
nothing more than another mural on a crumbling
wall. A bigger lie. The truth keeps pressing to be
known. It slowly eats at anything in its way. It will
not be held back forever. Trevor Lucas could chop
himself to pieces without getting rid of the guilt he
has locked up inside."

"And if you tell him the truth, that could stop
him?"

"Possibly. It could short-circuit his pathologic
defense mechanisms, dissolving his delusions. I
told you the mind is lazy. With the past uncovered
and all the facts on the table, it becomes much
harder for a man's mind to resist reality."

"What if he'd rather die than accept it? What if it's too overwhelming?"

That cut to the heart of the matter. I took a deep breath, let it out. "That's the danger." I thought of Trevor's plan for mass suicide. "Trevor's already talked about killing himself and everyone else on the unit." I shook my head. "But I have to believe I would never have met Michael Lucas if Trevor was dead set against learning the truth himself. I don't think he would have given me enough information to start looking for it."

"Still . . ."

"It's a risk. Anything can happen. That's the main reason I wanted Michael to come back with us. If Trevor saw that his brother had begun to forgive him, he'd be more likely to begin forgiving himself."

Cynthia turned and looked out the window.

"What are you thinking about?" I asked her.

She shrugged. "Nothing."

"C'mon."

She turned back to me. "If he goes through with it—kills himself, I mean, or kills every one of the patients and hostages—will you be able to live with it? Will *you* be able to forgive yourself?"

Hearing Cynthia lay out the possibility of failure so starkly made me focus on it, instead of rushing to think of ways to prevent it. I thought of Nurse Vawn, of her unborn baby. "I don't know," I said. I pictured the locked unit absolutely still, bodies scattered everywhere. And the terrible thought came to me that I would be left with the precise feelings Trevor must have experienced after burning his brother. Guilt. Despair. Shame. What if I was on a collision course with Lucas' psyche, one step away from becoming a mirror of the emotions he had buried at age eight? What if he was giving them to me like a virus? The ultimate projection. I ran my hands down my face. "I don't know if I could forgive myself. I hope I never have to find out."

Thirteen

North Anderson had left his home phone for me on our voice mail at the Stouffer. I called him from the room after I had booked the next USAir flight to Boston at 1:30 P.M.

"Hit pay dirt?" Anderson asked.

"Pretty much," I said, pacing back and forth in front of the windows overlooking the city. The winter sun was cooling itself over the harbor, turning the water a brilliant green-blue. The wind raised emerald swells with snow-white caps. A new day graced a new city. I glanced at Cynthia, curled up like a cat, asleep on the room's brown velvet chaise. She hadn't lasted two minutes once we were inside the door. "They're brothers," I told North. "Michael's injuries were caused by Trevor when the two of them were kids. It sounds like it was an accident. Trevor knocked a pan of cooking oil off the stove. They haven't seen each other since."

"Lord. Talk about guilt."

I knew North was no stranger to that emotion. I certainly wasn't. I had been taking it to bed with me and waking up with it ever since I had let

Trevor Lucas stand trial for murder in Kathy's place. "It's an ugly adversary," I said. "Grief is a pushover by comparison."

"I hear that." He paused. "So what's next?"

"I'll try to use what I know to get Trevor to surrender. I wanted to use Michael himself, have him make a plea to his brother in person at Lynn State, but he wouldn't go for it. He escorted us to the door with a shotgun."

"He what?"

"We overstayed our welcome. I pushed him a little further toward the truth than he was ready to go."

"Well, you've got bargaining power there, if you want to use it. Pointing that shotgun at you was assault with a deadly weapon. That carries a ten-year sentence in this state. Swear out a complaint, and I can have a couple of the guys pick Lucas up, maybe make a deal for his cooperation. Who knows if he's even got a license for that thing."

I thought about that, but not for long. "What I need Michael to do would have to come from his heart. He'd have to make the choice to help, for the right reasons. The last thing I need is him blowing up at Trevor and blowing our chances of getting people off the unit alive."

"Can you perform this next act with a bullhorn? Do you have to do it face-to-face?"

"Lucas sees everyone outside the hospital as the

enemy—the forces of Satan," I said. "I've got to go back inside. That is, as long as I'm still invited." I still didn't see any reason to tell him about Hancock and Kathy. "The last time I called to check whether things had blown up was when you and I were at Hopkins."

Cynthia stirred, opened her eyes and watched me on the phone.

"Nobody blinked," North said. "I called Captain Rice on-site before I left the station at seven. They're expecting you."

"Good." Some of the worry I was feeling dissolved, replaced immediately by rising anxiety about confronting Trevor again. The distance between Baltimore and Boston collapsed. I pictured Lindsey Simon's mutilated mouth, Craig Bishop's open neck stretched over my knee, Gabriel Vernon dead on the floor at my feet. I swallowed hard and focused on Cynthia, like a visual antidote. Her beauty cleared my mind of terror. "Did Rice tell you anything else?"

"Not a thing. He's a man of few words." He paused. "You almost get the feeling he doesn't much care whether you come back or not."

"My flying to Baltimore wasn't his idea," I said. "I forced him into it."

"I never trusted the state guys myself. You better watch your back. If they've got it in for you, you never know. Anything can happen. Friendly fire kills just as quick."

It sounded to me like Anderson's post-traumatic stress had left him paranoid. "I'll be careful," I said. "And if you talk to Rice again, tell him I'll be there."

"No problem." He didn't sound ready to hang up. "Hey, listen. I just wanted to square one thing."

"What's that?"

"You probably don't remember, but when we were talking at the hospital, I said I didn't miss the streets."

"I remember."

"Well, that was a lie. I do miss 'em. I miss standing up to crime . . . or evil, or . . ."

"I think of it all as illness—an epidemic."

"It sure feels that way. And I still want to help fight it." A couple of seconds passed. "I don't know why I needed to tell you all this."

"You wanted to square things. You want me to know where you stand."

"You can go nuts if you don't tell somebody what's really going on in your head." He paused. "I'm thinking I should take the department up on their offer. Get myself a shrink. Then, maybe, I'll get back to work—real work."

"Seems like the right move."

"You stand tall up there in Lynn," he said.

"Thanks. I'll see you again." I hung up.

Cynthia sat up. "That was the cop you met?" she asked.

"Right. North Anderson."

"What did he have to say?"

"He talked to Captain Rice. Things are status quo at the hospital. They haven't stormed the unit."

She seemed relieved, but then her expression changed to a mixture of sadness and worry. "Frank, when this is over, I . . ."

I figured she was nervous we'd be over. "You want to fly somewhere far away together? A long weekend in Paris, maybe. A week in Monaco?"

She let out a long breath.

"C'mon, pick."

"Disney World."

"I'm serious."

"So am I."

"I offer you Paris, you take Orlando?"

She feigned irritation. "It's my fantasy, all right? I thought I got to pick."

"You do. Disney World, here we come. But at least tell me why I'll be shaking hands with Pluto instead of spinning a roulette wheel with Sly Stallone."

"I used to watch all the commercials for it when I was a kid. My house was about three miles from Jasper Street—a row house like Michael Lucas', just like all the others. I used to dream about running away to that castle they show at the beginning of all the Disney movies. The one the fairy flies in front of."

"Nobody would take you?"

"Take me to Disney World? My parents were too drunk to take themselves to bed half of the time." She shook her head, remembering something. "You know what a 'fly-up' is?"

"Are we talking baseball here?"

"No," she laughed.

"Then, no. I don't." I sat down in the desk chair. "What's a fly-up?"

"It's a ceremony." Her voice was flavored with the slightly embarrassed, tentative tone of a child speaking of something close to her heart. "It's when a girl who's in the Bluebirds becomes a Campfire Girl."

"So Bluebirds are like Cub Scouts?"

"Only better."

"OK. So a fly-up is like a graduation, or getting a merit badge."

"You got it. Anyhow, the day I was supposed to fly up neither of my parents could take me to the ceremony."

"Because . . ."

"Because neither one of them could stand up." She squinted at the ceiling. "I was already in my uniform, set to go. Blue cotton dress. Blue cap. Badges. I remember each of them trying to get up. I mean, they really did try. Twice. Dad, maybe even three times. But they kept falling back into their seats at the kitchen table."

My eyes had filled up. "I'm sorry," I said, my

voice as solemn as if I were praying. The ability
of one human being to feel the pain of another is
the best evidence I have found for the existence of
the soul.

She winked. "You had nothing to do with it."
She looked away, then back at me. "I make it
sound terrible. It's just the way it was."

"Well, it shouldn't have been. You deserved
better."

"My parents didn't have it any better themselves when they were kids."

The words, *"That's no excuse,"* were on my
lips, but I did not speak them, because I knew
they were untrue. If you've never had the chance
to be whole, it's tough to give someone else that
chance. My scalp tingled as I thought of the creed
that had kept Rachel from being consumed by bitterness over her childhood injuries. *There's no
original evil left in the world. Everyone's just
recycling pain.* "Where are they now?" I asked.

"My parents? Here." She nodded at the phone
book, still open on the desk. "At least they're still
listed."

"Did you call them?"

"It's not time. I have to have my feet planted a
lot better. A different profession. A real place to
live. A life."

"You still want to make them proud."

She shrugged. "They never got to see me fly up.
You know?"

"I do." It is a terrible and exquisitely human irony that children inadequately nurtured almost never give up on the breast. The thirst for love from a mother or father who cannot provide it is seemingly unquenchable. I have treated sixty- and seventy-year-old business executives, politicians and physicians still desperate for approval from shriveled, emotionally barren men and women in their eighties and nineties. "Maybe them not seeing you fly up is the reason you like that Disney fairy so much."

"Maybe," she smiled.

"When did you leave Baltimore?"

"When I was sixteen. I ran away." She paused. "I'm not telling you anything else until after this is all over."

"Fair enough." I meant it, but my words sounded sharp.

She must have felt as if she needed to explain. Her eyes locked on mine. "I'm not the person you seem to think I am, Frank. I don't have any reason to be proud of *myself*. And I don't have a handle on how to do the right thing yet. I keep screwing up."

"You're not alone. I know something about how that feels." I looked at Cynthia lying on the chaise. The terror I faced back in Lynn made me want her more, not less. "Come over here," I said.

She got slowly to her feet. Without another word she unbuttoned her jeans and stepped out of them, leaving her in a black spandex bodysuit.

The light from the window shone on her light brown hair and the taut curves of her hip and leg.

It is testimony to the incalculable designs of Nature that men and women will find each other even at the edge of an abyss. There are lovers to rival Romeo and Juliet in every violent, run-down housing project in America. There are lovers carrying on amidst hopelessness and chaos in Bosnia. There were lovers in the death camps of Nazi Germany.

Cynthia walked to where I sat in the desk chair. I reached for her hips—for control—but she stepped away. "Don't," she whispered. I let my hands fall back to my sides. She came close again, reached down and pulled my black turtleneck out of my jeans. "Arms up." I lifted my arms, and she pulled my shirt over my head and tossed it on the bed. She knelt down and pulled off my boots and socks. She unbuckled my belt and unbuttoned my jeans. "Now lift up," she said, almost sternly. I did. She pulled my pants off, then my boxer shorts. I was naked, and she was not, which was a first for me. With my excitement showing I felt vulnerable and in loving hands, a blissful combination. She stood up in front of me. I reached for her again, but she shook her head. She felt between her legs and unsnapped the strap of cloth covering her. "Keep your hands by your sides," she whispered. She stepped flush to my knees, then straddled me, bringing us slowly together. Her softness and scent brought me closer to the memory of Rachel rather than further away. And as she rose and fell in the rhythm of our passion, I gave myself to her again and again.

We had the time to shower, holding each other under the spray, using the tiny bar of translucent hotel soap to clean one another's backs and legs. Cynthia combed my hair and tied it in a ponytail using a gold elastic band from her handbag. I called the front desk for a razor and shaved for the first time in three days. I poured alcohol over the gash in my cheek and felt it burn in the raw, red-pink places where the scab had fallen away.

Neither of us said much in the cab to the airport or for half the flight to Boston. Cynthia broke the silence. "If things don't go well," she said, "should I do anything? I mean, is there anything you'd want me to do?"

I thought about that. "I don't have a lot to settle. I've traveled pretty light lately." Then I thought about it a little more. "There is one thing. My mother lives at Heritage Park on the Lynnway. We don't have much to do with one other. Partly, my trouble with drugs. Partly, a lot of other garbage. If I don't make it, let her know that . . . with all of it, I . . . Just tell her 'goodbye' for me."

"I'll tell her both things."

"Thanks." I lifted the middle arm between our seats, and Cynthia moved close. Then, like a hiccup from my unconscious: "I wish I had a brother." ·

She sat back a bit. "What?"

"Nothing. I don't know where that came from."

"You wish you had a brother?"

I held up my hands. "It's foolishness. Forget it."

"No." She looked annoyed. "Why would you have wanted a brother?"

"I think my life might have been different. That's all."

"That's a lot. Different in what way?"

I shook my head, thinking back to Louie and Harry in the Hopkins ER. "I think I might have been able to deal better with some of the crap that came my way as a kid if I'd had a partner from the beginning. Maybe everything wouldn't have hit me as hard. When you're an only child, you're destined to be alone, in a certain sense, your whole life."

"I know what you mean. I'm an only child."

"But of course," I said.

She laid her head on my shoulder.

I closed my eyes. There was nothing I could do in the air to change what was awaiting me on the ground in Boston. I let myself doze off.

The chirping of my beeper woke me. I looked at my watch. 2:20 P.M. Cynthia was still asleep by my side. I pressed the button to light the beeper's numeric display and saw Matt Hollander's direct number at Austin Grate. I grabbed the airphone, slid my VISA through the slot on the receiver, dialed and waited.

"Frank," he answered.

"Yeah. I'm on a flight back. What's up?"

"I've heard from Kathy." His voice sounded unsteady.

I figured Hollander must be taking Kathy's arrest pretty hard. I was glad he hadn't confessed everything and been hauled off to jail himself. "I'm surprised Hancock allowed her a phone call," I said.

"She's making as many calls as she wants. She's free."

The blood left my head. "What?"

"She got away from Hancock."

"Got away? How?"

"I don't know when, where or how. But I have to admit, as terrible as it is to say it, I'm almost enjoying the irony."

"Enjoying? Matt, she's a killer. There's no telling . . ."

"That's not our fault. You need to remember that. We had her locked down tight. Then the law decided to intervene, presumably in the name of public safety. It seems to have gone rather badly."

"What did Kathy say?"

"She said she just wanted me to know she'd do the right thing. Whatever that means. I tried to coax her back here, but it was no use." He paused. "It's bound to be a bad scene down at the police

station. You may be in store for an unpleasant
welcoming party. If Hancock's there, tell her I
said, 'Great work, Ms. Commissioner.' "

I hung up. The fact that Hollander was gloating
over Kathy's escape made me sick to my stomach.
Then fear began mingling with my feelings of
horror and disgust. My exploration of Trevor's
past, the intimacy I had achieved with his life
story, could make me the next magnet for Kathy's
jealous rage.

Cynthia stirred. "Are we almost home?" she
said sleepily.

"Almost," I said. For better or worse.

The jet touched down at Logan. In the chaos of
people grabbing their bags to deplane, I grabbed a
package of heroin from my boot and used a few
pinches to steady myself for the next couple of
hours.

There were no cops waiting to arrest me at the
gate. I took Cynthia's arm and nervously scanned
the crowd for Kathy. We walked as quickly as we
could to the parking garage.

I worried about a roadblock at the airport exit,
but it was smooth sailing right onto Route 1A
North. I coursed out of Revere and into Lynn. I
was beginning to believe I'd make it all the way to
Lynn State Hospital when a siren began blaring in
back of my truck.

I checked my rearview mirror and saw Sam

Keane's well-weathered face. He was a distinguished street cop at the tail end of his career. We'd worked a few cases together. He'd always done right by me. At least I could thank Hancock for sending a friend to bring me in. "Looks like this is as far as it goes," I said to Cynthia.

"I'm sorry," she said. She started to cry.

I summoned enough false cheer to wink. "You had nothing to do with it." I pulled into the breakdown lane, got out and walked toward my fate.

Keane leaned against the front grill of his cruiser and crossed his wasting, but still-muscled arms over one another. As I got closer I saw that his eyes were bloodshot. His expression was somber. I stopped three feet from him. "Glad I was the one to find you, Frank," he said. A hint of Irish brogue had survived fifty years in Lynn.

"What's up?"

"Who you traveling with?" he asked, nodding at my truck.

I followed his line of vision and saw that Cynthia was watching us through the rear window. "Her name's Cynthia."

"Very pretty girl. You always have a pretty girl." His facial expression grew even more bleak. He ran a hand through his silver hair and stared out over the expanse of marsh on the opposite side of the road. "I don't know how to deliver news like this," he said. He shook his head. "I guess there's no sense beating around the bush." His hand fell to his waist, his fingers resting where a set of cuffs dangled from his belt.

"You know me, Sam. I like mine straight up. Just tell me."

He pursed his lips, nodded to himself and faced me. "Commissioner Hancock is dead."

I staggered back a foot. My skin went cold.

"She was found lying next to her Jeep two and a half hours ago, out back of the old Rowley Box Factory, up 95 North. She'd been shot once in the head."

"God, no."

"There was another body found nearby, a couple yards into the woods, with a wallet full of ID. A twenty-nine-year-old white male named Scott Trembley, from Newburyport. He was shot twice in the back. A gun registered to him was at his feet."

It took me a few seconds to remember that Trembley was the counselor at Austin Grate who Matt Hollander had let go. He must have somehow followed Hancock's car and tried to free Kathy. That bit of gallantry had cost him his life. I pictured him running into the woods after Kathy had murdered Emma. Obviously he hadn't run fast enough.

"There's something more," Keane said.

I stood there.

"It's bad."

"Tell me."

"Your initials were at the scene . . . painted . . . smeared onto the windshield." He paused. "The killer used Emma's blood."

I bent over and held my stomach and chest to keep from vomiting.

Keane grabbed me and held me up. He waited until I seemed steady on my feet. "Somebody obviously wanted to send the department—and you—a message. But we don't know anything else yet. Not a blessed thing. We don't even know where Emma first ran into trouble. No one had spoken with her all morning." He paused. "If we're dealing with this copycat psycho, he's changed his weapon of choice."

I was breathing too fast and knew it but couldn't stop. Everything looked wavy. "What now?" I said.

"We've got all available men working it. You're welcome aboard anytime. But I know the state guys are waiting on you up at the hospital."

In the past Kathy had only targeted lovers of Trevor and mine. Now her violence had exploded outside that circle, like a cancer metastasizing to other tissues. Who else, I wondered, would die at her hand? Keane didn't know me well enough to know I had lived with Kathy. "Look for a Kathy Singleton," I said.

"Huh?"

"Kathy Singleton. Blonde hair. Green eyes. Slim build. Five feet six. Thirty-two years old.

She used to work at Atlantic Hospital. She's an obstetrician."

"That's where Dr. Lucas worked. You think the copycat is a doc, too? Was this a lead you and Hancock were checking out?"

"Yeah. Hancock and I."

"We'll get right on it. You'll be OK alone?"

I nodded.

He reached out and squeezed my arm once. "I know you and Emma were close." He turned and walked away. He climbed into the cruiser and sped off.

I walked back to my truck, numb. I got in and stared through the windshield at nothing. The image of my own initials, written in blood, made me rub the heels of my hands into my eyes.

Cynthia was still in tears. "I wanted to tell you," she said. "I tried to tell you."

My thoughts were too jumbled to generate any words.

"Calvin said I could be charged as an accessory to the crime. I didn't understand why you'd done what you did. I was scared."

I turned and squinted at her. An unfocused, unwieldy anger began to take hold of me. "What are you talking about?"

"I didn't want to take his money. He threatened me. He said I could go to jail."

Cynthia obviously thought Sam Keane had just tipped me off to the fact that I'd been sold out.

"You told Calvin Sanger about Lucas not being guilty, about me hiding the killer?"

"I told him she was somewhere she could get help."

My fists clenched. "How much did he pay you?"

"I'm screwed up," she wept. "I don't know why I do the things I do."

"How much?" I yelled. "How much did he pay you?"

"Two hundred dollars."

"Two hundred . . ." I let my head fall onto my knuckles. Why hadn't I seen this coming? Was I so desperate to have Rachel back that I had tried to reinvent her in Cynthia? Had I used her like a drug, to numb my grief? Or was my problem the old one, the one that had led me to live with Kathy in the first place, the false safety I felt in the arms of a stranger?

Now I knew how Hancock had arrived at Hollander's gates. Once she learned that Kathy was *somewhere she could get help* she was most of the way toward finding her. Matt Hollander owned two of the seven freestanding psychiatric hospitals within ninety miles of Lynn.

I remembered Jack Rice telling me that he'd given Calvin Sanger an exclusive to the inner workings of the operation at Lynn State Hospital. I figured Hancock had made that happen as payment for Sanger sharing what he had learned about Kathy.

I started the truck and pulled on to the road, keeping my eyes straight ahead so that Cynthia wouldn't even enter my peripheral vision. There was a subway station less than a quarter mile down the road. I stopped in front of it. The blue line ran within a few blocks of the Y.

"I love you," Cynthia said.

My eyes stayed focused on the road. "Get out."

She sat there. "I didn't mean to ruin everything."

I didn't respond.

She climbed out and raced toward the platform.

I turned and watched her disappear into the crowd waiting for the train. A surprising and unwelcome heavy-heartedness invaded my anguish and rage. "Forget her," I said aloud. "Do what you came to do." I stepped on the gas.

As I drove I was besieged by flashbacks: Trevor brandishing his bloodied stump, showing off the organs he had harvested, ranting about Nurse Vawn being infested by Satan. Then my initials painted in Hancock's blood appeared again across the windshield. I jerked the wheel and lurched into the opposing lane of traffic, nearly hitting a pickup that swerved to avoid me. I barely wrestled control of the truck. I pulled over.

Emma Hancock was dead. Kathy was free. And it was my fault. My hands shook uncontrollably. Sweat soaked my clothes. Twisting aches spread up my lower back and around the curves of my rib cage. I couldn't separate which symptoms were

from grief and panic and which from heroin withdrawal. I managed to fish one of the tiny plastic
bags out of my pocket, snorted a pinch, then
another. That shifted me down a few gears. The
trembling stopped. My muscles slowly relaxed. I
gave the wave of calm a minute to loosen the
knots tied around my spine, then accelerated back
on to the road.

I staved off thoughts of what it had already cost
to hide Kathy on Matt Hollander's Secure Care
Unit and concentrated on what had to be done. If I
could save the hostages, save Nurse Vawn and her
baby, maybe I could live with myself.

I took the final turn onto Jessup Road. The
gauntlet of reporters began a full mile from the
Lynn State Hospital grounds, but the monotony of
twenty hours with no increase in the body count
had left them listless, like anemic vampires. Some
huddled in little groups, hugging themselves and
shifting foot to foot to stay warm. Others milled
about the litter-strewn canteen areas, the ground
now inches deep in coffee cups, paper plates and
donut boxes. I thought I saw Geraldo Rivera pacing back and forth across one of them, kicking up
garbage with each step.

I made it about half a mile before a man outside
a tent emblazoned with a bright red painted
MSNBC logo screamed, "That's Clevenger!" and
ran after my truck as if I were escaping with his
wallet. In a way, I suppose I was. Sometime dur-

ing the '90s journalists stopped being truth seekers and started being prospectors, trolling for anything titillating they could peddle to viewers. You
can net yourself decades in prison for selling people drugs or selling them sex, but you can fashion
a magnificent career hawking a coward's vicarious
high.

I kept my speed around 15 mph as a thicket of
microphones formed around me. So many cameras flashed against the car that its silver paint
seemed to glow. I knew some of the men and
women staring through my windows would beat
me into an interview if they could get away with
it. At this time and in this place I wasn't a person.
I was a thing, a commodity, an animated character
walking the earth.

Three or four cameramen trying to shoot tape
while running backward in front of me lost their
balance and tumbled to the ground at the side of
the road. One vanished under my front end. I
jammed on my brakes. The mob crushed in, a
dozen or more reporters climbing onto my hood
and into the back of the truck. Lenses and microphones targeted me from every conceivable direction.

I heard my back window crack. A wall of hands
pushed on my door. The truck started to rock. I
have no doubt I would have been overturned,
ripped from my shell like a soft crab and
devoured, had a State Police helicopter not

descended within twenty yards of the street, its blades whipping the air into a freezing windstorm, driving my would-be interviewers off the road in search of cover.

Two cruisers sped down the road toward me. One turned around in front of my truck to lead, the other passed me on the shoulder of the road and circled back, taking up the rear. They escorted me to the State Police trailer. Even more military equipment was scattered around the hospital grounds. Three sand-colored Desert Storm–style Hummer pickups with what looked like Gatling guns mounted on the cargo beds were parked in the semicircle out front. In the far corner of the green sat an M-1 army tank.

I looked over at the shattered windows and bulletriddled facade of the hospital. SWAT teams crouched at the corners of the roof.

A state trooper I hadn't met before escorted me into the trailer. Jack Rice sat solemnly behind his desk. Lieutenant Patterson leaned against the opposite wall. Rice motioned for me to take a seat.

I glanced at Patterson, then turned my back to him and took one of the two chairs in front of the desk.

"The Lynn Police Department told me they would notify you about Commissioner Hancock as soon as you got back," Rice said.

I couldn't be absolutely certain Hancock hadn't told him about Kathy. "They notified me."

"You and I both know this never should have happened," he deadpanned. His eyes were filled with anger.

I wasn't sure where he was headed. I didn't respond.

"A solo practitioner of forensics and a local police department just don't have the horses to handle something as complex as that copycat investigation. It should have been turned over to the state a long time ago." He shook his head. "Don't start blaming yourself."

So Hancock hadn't told him. I nodded, even though I knew I *was* to blame. I let several moments pass. "Thanks for the help out there with the press," I said tentatively. "How did you know I was in trouble?"

Rice pointed over my shoulder. I turned and saw that a television monitor had been mounted to the far wall. The volume was off. On-screen, a reporter was apparently giving his play-by-play at the edge of the hospital grounds. The CNN LIVE insignia glowed red at the bottom right-hand corner of the picture. As I watched, the words SKY EYE flashed in the upper right-hand corner, and the video cut to an aerial replay of my truck being mobbed. I tried to cover up the churning in my gut with a one-liner. "Thank God for cable," I said.

"Absolutely. You're a star," Patterson said. He walked past me and perched himself on the corner of Rice's desk. His upper lip quivered, and the muscles in his jaw tensed. "If you can milk it long enough, maybe you can walk off the unit alone, the only one left standing. Then you can have every camera focused on you."

Rice seemed uncomfortable with Patterson's remarks, as if he wasn't ready to stand completely with him, completely against me, but he said nothing in my defense. "Did you find out anything in Baltimore?" he asked, finally.

"Enough to make it worth going down there."

"What does that mean?" Rice said. "What did you find out?"

"I found Trevor's brother, Michael."

Patterson shrugged off the news.

Rice leaned slightly forward. A cautious interest showed in his face.

"I think I understand why Trevor believes he's fighting a war against Satan," I said. "I think I know what made him snap."

"Are you going to let the rest of us in on it?" Rice asked.

"When Trevor and Michael were children they were playing a game of chase in the house. Trevor ran by the stove, reached up and knocked a pan of boiling oil off a burner. It nearly melted half of Michael's face. He's been badly disfigured ever since."

"So what?" Patterson scoffed.

I kept my eyes on Rice. "That tragedy is the root of Trevor's delusion about being taken over by

Satan; he's never wanted to believe he was the one who maimed his brother. I think he's suppressed the whole thing—utterly buried it in the furthest reaches of his mind."

"Then how does he think Michael ended up looking the way he does?" Rice asked.

"Trevor left the state and lived with his father after the accident. He hasn't seen Michael since. I doubt he remembers he has a brother at all. But the burns on Michael's face are the unconscious reason Trevor became a plastic surgeon. And they're the reason he disowned and then amputated his own right arm—the same arm that knocked that boiling oil off the stove. He's projecting his destructiveness and self-hatred onto an outside force—Satan."

Patterson shook his head. "You're saying this psycho burning his brother explains everything that's gone on here."

"There's more. Trevor's mother kept him in a cage after the accident." I looked down, picturing the heavy wire mesh, the dirt floor. "In the basement. It's the kind of thing you'd keep a rabid Rottweiler in."

"A cage?" Rice asked, squinting at me. "For how long?"

"Months. She made him pray day and night for his salvation."

"Lord God," Rice said.

"How is this supposed to explain Lucas murdering two people?" Patterson said. "Or did you forget that's why he was locked up in the first place?"

"I'm not sure how this figures into his prior charges," I said. "But I think being locked up awaiting trial brought Lucas much too close to the horror of scalding his brother and being tortured by his mother. He felt himself being dragged back to that boiling oil, to that cage in the basement. A terrified, fractured child. His mind fled, all the way into psychosis."

Patterson chuckled. "What crap."

Rice let out a long breath. "Let's say your psychological theory about Lucas is true," he said skeptically. "That doesn't mean he's going to accept it and surrender."

"No, it doesn't," I admitted. "But I think it's our best shot."

"Our best shot is with a fucking thirty-eight," Patterson exploded. He turned to Rice. "I can't believe you'd even consider letting this whack job deliver psychotherapy to a goddamn killer."

"I wouldn't call Lucas the picture of mental health, would you?" I said.

"I'd call him a piece of human garbage," Patterson sputtered. "And you're not much better. If it weren't for you and the bullshit you've been spreading around here, Lucas would be in the morgue right now, and the hostages would be home—including Calvin Sanger and that lady doctor. Singleman, Single . . . whatever."

Chills blanketed me. I stared at Rice. "You let someone else onto the unit?"

"Katherine Singleton," he said. "She's an obstetrician. Apparently, she used to work with Lucas. She read about the pregnant woman in the *Item* and got word to us that she'd be willing to go up and help. She's been there over an hour."

The room swayed. "Why would you agree to that?"

"Every media outlet from here to L.A. has been focused on that baby," Rice said. "Saving the child equals victory here, at least as far as the public is concerned."

Kathy's pathologic jealousy had led her to kill Lucas' lovers before. If she intuited that Nurse Vawn had slept with him, that she was carrying his child . . . I thought of telling Rice about Kathy's history of violence, but I knew that would end all negotiation and trigger an assault on the building. And I knew Trevor was prepared to sacrifice everyone. "You shouldn't have let her go up there," was all I said.

"Don't worry," Patterson said gamely. "I doubt you'll have to share the limelight. Ten-to-one she's already dead. We keep feeding this maniac victims."

Maybe it was my own guilt that left me without control, that ignited all my pent-up rage at my father, at my mother, at every neighborhood bully I had bloodied myself standing up to, at life's bogus balance sheet of what is due each of us and what each of us must pay. Maybe I'd used up every ounce of my self-control on Michael Lucas. Or Cynthia. Or maybe I'd sucked up a little too much cocaine, or not enough heroin. Whatever the reason, I looked down at the floor, summoned a mental picture of where I stood in the room and where Patterson sat, and rushed him.

He was no pushover. Before I reached him he was up on his feet, fists cocked martial arts style at his sides. He landed a jackhammer right to my shoulder, but I managed to use the force of the blow to transfer all my weight onto my right leg. I channeled every ounce of strength I could summon into a karate kick that found the sweet spot of his abdomen. He doubled over. I grabbed him by the belt and rammed him headfirst into the wall of the trailer. He went down on both knees. I yanked his head back and would have slammed it against the wall even harder had Patterson not reached behind him and wrapped one of his arms around both my legs, pushing off the wall at the same time and dropping me onto my back. In an instant he was straddling my chest, his torso twisted like a discus thrower, his huge fist held aloft.

"Don't do it!" Rice yelled. He leapt up.

Patterson was powerful enough to kill me with a single blow, certainly with two or three. His whole arm—*his right arm*—shook as he wrestled with the killer inside him, with the potential vio-

lence he had transmuted into a job hunting crimi-
nals. At a level deeper than my fear, seeing that
primal struggle satisfied me and actually made me
smile, because I knew in my marrow that Patterson was in touch with Trevor Lucas' soul, even if
he could not see it and would never admit it. And
that perfect psychological symmetry is the voice
of my God. At that moment I knew he was still
with me. I closed my eyes. The distinctive, metal-
on-metal sound of a barrel being pulled back registered in my head.

"Get off," Rice said.

I opened my eyes and saw that Rice had drawn
his Glock semiautomatic. The nose of the barrel
was pressed against Patterson's right shoulder.

"Three, two . . ." he counted.

Patterson sprang to his feet. He stood over me,
looking down with disgust as my chest heaved to
get air to my lungs. "I'll do everything I can to get
you off the unit alive," he said. "Then you're
mine." He marched out of the trailer.

I turned onto my side, crowing my neck and
arching my back to get more air, faster.

Rice stood watching me a few moments. "You
shouldn't start things you can't finish," he said. He
knelt beside me, then helped me to my seat. It
took nearly a minute before my breathing slowed
toward normal. Another half-minute passed before
my vocal cords started working again. "I need to
go back in there," I said.

He glanced out the trailer window at the hospital. It was growing dark outside, and a row of lights had begun burning across the fifth floor. "I told Dr. Singleton exactly what I'll tell you," he said. "I won't hesitate to use lethal force if Lucas harms anyone else. PR problem, or not."

I nodded.

"And if it comes to that, and you play human shield again, you won't be left standing."

"How long do I have in there?" I asked.

"Until midnight." The animosity in his voice was mostly gone.

"Guaranteed?"

"It is on my end. I can't speak for Lucas."

Fourteen

I took my first steps toward the hospital as the sun closed its eyes at 6:20 P.M. The light from the street lamps lining the parking lot, along with an array of halogen beams emanating from the army of reporters massed at the perimeter road, threw my shadow thirty yards across the green. Patterson had deployed dozens of state troopers who knelt behind concrete barriers to either side of the hospital entrance, along the roof of the building and around the helicopter, tank and Hummers. When I was halfway from the trailer to the sliding glass doors of the hospital I glanced up at the fifth floor and saw several figures that seemed to be watching me from behind the shattered windows.

I was frightened to my core, but I kept moving, on a collision course with Kathy Singleton and Trevor Lucas, who I now recognized as blood relations of the crippled parts of myself. I had lived with Kathy, a tortured child who grew into a serial killer, probably because she unconsciously reminded me of the attempted murder of my soul by my father. And I had treated Lucas savagely, letting him stay imprisoned for murders he did not commit, probably because I had yet to overcome my rage at having been a kind of prisoner in my own childhood home.

Human beings sick with violence look like monsters only when we refuse to acknowledge our own terror and hatred and fury. Then it becomes easy to disown them, even to execute them, with the same sense of certainty and relief Lucas must have felt severing his own arm, believing it to be that of Satan. We fail to see, as he did, that the cutting off leaves us less than we were, not more. For our souls to be truly saved, we have to do what we can to save theirs.

For the first time since I had closed my psychotherapy practice I felt confident I was working as a healer. I knew that fact was no insurance against any misery that might await me, but I also knew that pain and adversity are signposts on the road to every cure. Pilgrims make a drama of this fact when they travel miles on bent knee to pray at holy shrines. A fire walker understands that crossing the red-hot coals before him—not leaping over them or darting around them—is the only route to a higher spiritual plane. And surgeons show similar faith whenever they cut the body in order to restore it. Whatever separated Lucas, Kathy and me, I felt I could count on at least that much common ground.

I crossed the metal threshold into the lobby and stopped, checking for the Harpy. The fact that

Lucas had invoked the memory of that mythological creature, half-bird and half-woman, bent on eating its young, made perfect sense to me now: His mother had psychologically devoured him, almost certainly beginning her feast long before locking him away in the basement. A woman capable of caging her young son is capable of many things.

Several seconds passed with only the random complaints of an old building breaking the silence. I started down the corridor. The sounds of my heels against the floor echoed off the cinder block walls. Within seven or eight yards the light drifting from the crowd of reporters and from the street lamps around the green petered out completely, leaving me in darkness. I stepped closer to the wall and ran a finger along a line of grout to keep myself steady as I walked toward the elevator.

I turned a corner, and saw three sets of UP and DOWN buttons glowing in the distance. I let myself wonder fully what had happened on the locked unit since I had flown to Baltimore. The injection I had given Lucas should have kept his remaining arm paralyzed, but it could have worn off, leaving Lucas—and everyone else on the fifth floor—at the mercy of the ferocious affliction he called Satan. Calvin Sanger might be on his way to a Pulitzer Prize written from the belly of the beast, or the beast might have destroyed him. The hostages left on the unit, including Nurse Vawn, could be alive or they could be dead.

I stepped within reach of the buttons. I took a deep breath. Standing there alone, I knew I might be living the last pages of my life story. But even if that were the case, I still had the chance—more, the responsibility—to shape my ending. I forced myself to trade all the images of carnage and defeat racing through my mind for the image of the fire walker, who I pictured, strangely (or perhaps not strangely at all), as a lanky young Abraham Lincoln in a sober gray suit, pants rolled up past his shins. He wore no beard, but the jutting jaw and forehead were as unmistakable as the deeply set Atlantic blue eyes. I smiled in spite of my fear, swallowed hard and pressed the UP button.

The elevator doors opened with a blast of white fluorescent light that made me shield my face. I took the few steps to the center of the car and watched the numbers climb on the stainless steel panel in front of me. Before my vision had fully adjusted to the brightness, the doors slid open again, and I walked back into the dark, headed toward the locked unit.

Peter Zweig, the nineteen-year-old who had made an offering of his victims' remains at a church, moved his head to each side of the glass square in the steel door as I approached, apparently checking that I was alone. When I reached the door, he turned and yelled something I couldn't make out. Fifteen or twenty seconds later I saw Lucas emerge from the room at the end of the hallway—the room he called the *quiet room*.

Zweig pressed his face against the glass. The supply of methadone on the unit obviously hadn't run dry; his pupils were pinpoints. They flicked left and right a few times as he searched the space around me. Then he pulled the door open just enough to grab my arm and drag me inside. The door slammed shut behind me. Dead bolts slid home.

I hardly noticed Zweig running his hands over my arms and legs, stomach, chest and back, checking for weapons. My attention was focused on Trevor Lucas as he walked the last twenty feet toward me. His left arm wasn't moving, which gave me hope that the injection had held, but then I noticed what looked like fresh blood splattered over his hospital scrubs. My heart sank. A warm, sick feeling spread from my gut to my head and made me lean against the wall next to the door-jamb.

Zweig grabbed me and slammed me back against the door.

"Off," Lucas barked.

Zweig let go, but stayed flush to me. His rancid breath made me turn my head.

"Join the others," Lucas said. "Now."

Zweig finally stepped away. I watched him

walk into the Day Room and take his place in a double row of patients and hostages who knelt facing the windows, their heads tucked to their knees. They were chanting what Lucas had called the Samurai warrior's prayer.

I have no life. I have no death.

I saw Calvin Sanger was among them. Kathy was not. I glanced at the nurses' station. Carla Vawn, the pregnant nurse who had been bound into her seat, was gone.

"You came back," Lucas said.

I turned to him. His face glistened with sweat. His pupils were pinpoints, just like Zweig's. "I promised I would." I squinted at the ruby splotches running down his surgical top. "Where's Kathy?" I asked.

"Working in service to the Lord." He caught his lower lip between his teeth and chewed on it. "We're losing ground. Satan has the upper hand."

The *upper hand.* I pictured Lucas as a child, reaching up with his hand and knocking the pot of boiling oil off the stove, scalding Michael. "I want to help you take control again."

He shook his head. "You should leave. You'll become infested." He paused. "You'll become what I am."

My throat tightened. There are few moments that testify more eloquently to the endurance of the human spirit than when the afflicted worries for the healer. When I was a medical student, a patient of mine named Max Sands, wasting away from lung cancer, gagging on a ventilator tube stuck down his raw throat, had scrawled out a note at 3 A.M. saying I looked tired and ought to get a little rest. I have not forgotten and will not forget that man. And it matters not whether the suffering is with cancer or leprosy or murderousness. It matters not whether the vector spreading disease is a bacterium, a virus or the psychological dynamic called projection. When one man's body or mind is under siege, the magnificence of his soul will occasionally make itself plain to another. Sometimes the gift is received, sometimes refused. Witness Karla Faye Tucker.

Trevor Lucas, maimed, gripped by psychosis, had touched me. His humanity still whispered from behind the mask of lunacy. "I'm not leaving until this is over," I said.

Several seconds passed. "It won't be long," he said. "We're nearly ready to place ourselves in the hands of God." His gaze drifted to the wall just behind me and to my left, and something between worry and confusion showed on his face. Then he focused on me, again, staring vacantly into my eyes.

I glanced over my shoulder at the cinder blocks in his line of vision, but noticed nothing unusual. I wondered if he was hallucinating. "I did what you asked," I said, hoping to anchor him in the moment. "I went to Baltimore."

He shook his head. "That doesn't matter anymore. It's too late."

I could sense Lucas' unconscious girding against the knowledge I had brought back with me. I put as much confidence into my tone and bearing as I could. "I found out how Satan entered you," I said.

"How he entered is irrelevant. The cancer has spread."

"We can still cure it."

"That's why you're a psychiatrist, and I'm a surgeon." He tried to smile, but his upper lip trembled wildly and made him look even more grotesque. "I know when a case is inoperable. You'll hold a hand until it's gone ice cold." He turned around and started down the corridor, his arm hanging limply at his side.

Hold a hand. Maybe I was making more of the words than they deserved, but it seemed to me that the walls of denial Lucas had built to contain the past were already leaking bits of his truth. I took a breath. "I'm not the one who's in denial," I called out. "You are."

He stopped abruptly and stood with his back to me for several seconds before turning slowly around. His jaws worked against each other. One eye twitched spastically.

I worried I might have pushed him too far. But

I could not back away. Nor could I stand still. I was already walking the hot coals. "I met Michael," I said.

He squinted at me. "You saw Michael? You saw him, as you see me now?"

My skin turned to gooseflesh. "I did."

He took a few steps toward me. His eyes were wild with excitement. "Did he say he would take us under his wing? Did he say he would guide us, as he did the Jews?"

It took me a moment to understand. In the Old Testament, Michael is the guardian angel who shepherds Moses and his followers across the desert. I remembered having thought of the Hebrews' flight from Egypt while admiring the statue of Jesus in the Johns Hopkins Hospital lobby. The parallel felt like more than coincidence; I took it as a sign I was on the right path.

"Did he say he would help us?" Lucas pressed.

I needed to keep tiptoeing the line between delusion and reality, coaxing Lucas toward the truth. "Michael said he's been with you right along," I said. "He told me you've been wandering too many years." I made sure to look him squarely in the eyes. "He told me the reason you left home."

Lucas' features softened from manic excitement toward sadness for an instant, and I thought I might have reached him, but then his gaze drifted back to the cinder blocks over my shoulder. He kept looking at them as he spoke. I wondered whether his mind was conjuring demonic voices or visions as a last-ditch effort to keep away his real demons—the memories of what he had done to Michael and what his mother had done to him. "My life before this day is irrelevant," he said, finally. "All that matters is that my flock reach the promised land." He turned and started down the corridor, again, walking faster this time.

I knew I had to follow him, but I hesitated. I dreaded the horrors that lay to either side of the hallway and I could not be certain whether Kathy, fresh from another kill, lurked four, ten or twenty feet away.

Lucas stopped in front of Laura Elmonte's room. He looked back at me.

I caught up to him at her door. The buzz of the fluorescent fixtures overhead suddenly filled my ears. The sick, warm feeling started rising in me again.

Elmonte was still naked in four-point restraints, her torso bisected by the prickly line of sutures Lucas had placed from her neck to her groin. Her breathing was shallow and erratic. A new IV catheter had been inserted into the base of her neck, at what looked like the location of the jugular vein, just above the collarbone. Plastic tubing carried her deep blue blood to a urine collection bag strapped to the foot of the bed. The bag could easily hold three units and was nearly full.

"Black bile," Lucas said. "It just keeps coming." He glanced up at the corner of her room. "It's starting to seep through the walls."

That vision must have been what distracted Lucas at the door to the unit. I chose my words carefully. "Maybe it's better," I said, "to let Satan show . . . his whole hand." I paused. "Maybe it's better to let the bile through."

"Insanity," he crackled. "We would all drown."

"No, you wouldn't. You've escaped catastrophe before. Michael told me. You can do it again."

Lucas didn't respond. He stood silently, watching Elmonte. Then he looked back up at the corner of her room. "We're running out of time."

"Tapping the jugular is no cakewalk," I said, hoping to help him focus. "How did you get the catheter into her without the use of your arm?"

"I have no arm," he said, without emotion. "Satan took my arms."

"How, then?"

"Calvin."

"He's a reporter," I said, as much to myself as to Lucas.

"He came here for glory. He ended up a soldier for the Lord," Lucas said. "The young man turns out to be a Harvard Medical School dropout. Failed biochemistry during the first semester, as if that matters. Harvard cocksuckers. He's a surgeon if I've ever seen one. He has the gift." He closed his eyes. "What thou need shall be provided." He took a deep breath, then looked straight at me. "Now that Kathy has arrived, the last of our work can proceed." He turned abruptly and continued down the hall.

I stayed right with him. We walked past the medication room where he had stored his harvest of body parts. We stopped again two doors down, outside his "O.R." Fresh blood covered the floor between the older, congealed mounds of ruby-black jelly.

He saw me looking at the puddles. "I'm afraid Mr. Kaminsky became infested, like the others. Like me. We had to remove the spleen. Calvin and I." His expression reminded me of the one doctors reserve for relatives of terminal patients. "I don't know that he'll pull through," he said.

"Have there been other surgeries since I left?"

"Of course. Would you expect us to sit, locked up like animals, waiting to be consumed?" He seemed to expect an answer.

I said nothing. But the reference took me right back to the basement of Lucas' childhood home on Jasper Street. Back to the cage. To the Harpy.

"I have one more procedure to complete before we escape this hell," Lucas went on. "I want to salvage every soul we can. If you really mean to stay with us to the end, I'll rely on you to help." He headed down the hall.

I thought of Richard Tisdale, the man who had killed his son. But Tisdale's room, the next to the last on the right, was empty, save for his blood-soaked gurney. Partially dried blood was splattered over the far wall. The floor was covered with it—a field of red dots, shoe prints, streaks from a mop. My eyes drifted to the spot where the streaks converged. A pile of bone fragments, hair and what looked like gray-white pieces of rubber sat just beyond the gurney, near the far wall. I knew that gray-white tissue was brain, but couldn't quite admit it to myself.

Lucas was standing at the door to the quiet room. "I know you felt for him," he said, looking back at me. "I did, too. Trust that we tried everything to save him. Heroic measures were taken."

"What measures were those?" I asked weakly.

"You understand we're working in something less than an army field hospital here. No X-rays, no CAT scans, no MRI, no halo devices, no needle biopsies. Even so, with Calvin's help I reached the necrotic tissue. The amygdala. We managed to excise a good deal of it. I'd venture a pathologist would have told us we had nearly clean margins." He pressed his lips together. "I can't state the exact cause of death. I know he was still alive when we closed."

My forehead pounded. I couldn't begin to fathom the suffering Tisdale must have endured before succumbing. Violent thoughts raced through my mind—thoughts I had had before. Maybe the thing to do was to take Lucas out while

I had the chance. Maybe I was colluding with Satan by letting Lucas live and breathe. The surgeon's strategy, not the psychiatrist's, might indeed be the humane one. Cut the cancer out. Limit its spread. Would it not have been moral to murder Charles Manson or Andrew Black or Jim Jones before they murdered? Can anyone prove that so doing would infect us with their evil? Can anyone prove the teachings of Gandhi, or Saint Thomas Aquinas, or of Christ? No. No such data exists. Yet with everything that had happened on the locked unit, with everything I had seen of the world and its darkness, with pieces of a man's skull and brain as evidence of Lucas' pathology, my heart still protested the kill. And I had learned through many and painful lessons to let my heart's voice be data enough for me.

I knew one thing beyond a shadow of a doubt: Violence is illness. As a physician—as a human being—I had the right neither to ignore it nor to mirror it. I had to treat it. A line from Dante's *Inferno* came to me.

> *Here must all distrust be left behind; all*
> *cowardice must be ended.*

"You can see what we face," Lucas said. "You can see why we need your help." He turned his head and nodded over his right shoulder. "There's still a chance to save this one."

I took a few deep breaths and joined him at the door to the quiet room. My heart fell.

Kathy, wearing scrubs, stood over Nurse Vawn, who lay naked on a gurney, her wrists and ankles buckled into leather restraints. Her belly was swollen with what was almost certainly Lucas' child. A scalpel and an assortment of makeshift metal instruments—the ten-inch shank of a screwdriver, a crescent wrench, half a barber's scissors—lay on a tray at the bedside, along with packages of blue nylon sutures.

Vawn was struggling to free herself. "Please." She began crying, repeating, "Let me go. Let me go."

Lucas walked in ahead of me, chewing his lower lip. "Just as soon as you're well," he said.

As I entered Kathy turned. Volcanic anger flashed across her face, stopping me cold.

Lucas walked to the side of the gurney opposite Kathy. "We were just getting started."

"With what?" I managed.

"Dilation and curettage," he answered. "She's begun to bleed again. D and C is the treatment of choice."

I tore my gaze away from Kathy's piercing eyes. "She's pregnant. The child needs help."

"She's infested!" Lucas sputtered. "Satan may be curled inside her womb, sucking his hoof, but nothing human slumbers there." He paused, his jaws working against one another. "Kill it first, then remove it," he instructed Kathy.

Vawn screamed.

Kathy picked up the screwdriver. "You bitch," she rasped, resting the gray metal shank against Vawn's inner thigh, but looking at me. "This is all your doing. You tried to split us up." Her voice was murderous. "Did you really think you'd get Trevor all to yourself?"

Nurse Vawn had become the rope in a psychosexual tug of war. And I had the sense that if I didn't let go, the rope would snap. "No. I should never have come between you. It wasn't for me to lock either one of you up."

"Too late. You should never have come back here. What Trevor needs he can get from me."

Kathy loved Lucas, twisted as the affection might be. And Vawn's baby was part of him, derived from his flesh, his soul. That fact might be the only one to stop Kathy from killing the child. But it might instead pour fuel on her primitive jealousy. I swallowed hard. "The child is Trevor's," I said.

"Liar!" he roared.

Pain filled Kathy's eyes. She pressed so hard on the metal shank that it punctured Vawn's thigh.

"No!" Vawn shrieked, jerking frantically. "Please."

Kathy moved closer to the head of the gurney.

She grabbed a handful of Vawn's hair. "Is the baby his?" she asked.

Vawn's eyes filled up. Tears ran down her cheeks.

Kathy placed the tip of the screwdriver at Vawn's throat. "Answer."

"Yes," Vawn choked.

Kathy stared at her several seconds, then walked back to stand over her abdomen. She looked at Trevor.

"I love you," Trevor said. "Stand up for the Lord."

Kathy put the screwdriver down on the bedside tray and picked up a scalpel.

"The child isn't Satan's." I began to weep, too. I turned to Lucas. "You were eight years old when you knocked that boiling oil off the stove. With your right hand."

Lucas' face convulsed in pain, as if I were screaming in his ear. The look in his eyes had changed from rage to panic.

I grabbed him. "You didn't do it on purpose. Do you understand?"

He stared at me for several seconds, then closed his eyes. His jaws ground against one another.

"You didn't deserve to be locked up in a cage."

Without warning, Lucas used his whole body to drive me against the wall. His face was just inches from mine. His eyes were wild.

I forced myself not to turn away. "No child is evil," I said.

A new sound filled the room. Lucas wheeled around to face the gurney. Then the sound came again. And this time I recognized an infant's cry.

Kathy held a baby boy in her arms. The scalpel, its blade bloodied, sat on the bedside tray.

Nurse Vawn lay unconscious.

"That is no human thing," Lucas said shakily. "Please, Katherine. Kill it."

Kathy looked at Lucas with a mixture of sympathy and longing. "He's your son," she said softly. "He's part of us. So is she." She held the boy gently to Vawn's breast.

All of a sudden, the unit was flooded with light from outside the building. It poured through every window.

My stomach convulsed. Rice had lied to me. The attack was under way, hours before my midnight deadline. North Anderson had been right; I'd been set up for the kill. I shook Lucas. "If you die here you'll never know the truth about your life," I said.

Lucas looked up at the corners of the room, then past me, into the hallway. "The devil comes for his little prince," he said, with no emotion. "Judgment Day."

I had nothing left. I stepped back against the doorjamb. "They're going to fire through the win-

dows. Just like they did last time. Save the lives
you can. Tell everyone to lie on the floor. Tell
them to get down and stay there."

Lucas didn't respond. He walked slowly out of
the room. As he did, Jack Rice's voice blared
through the bullhorn. "Trevor Lucas, this is Captain Rice. Come to a window. No one will harm
you."

Lucas stood still, staring toward the green.

Rice was making it easy for Lucas. He could
take a bullet and go out believing himself a martyr
in a holy war. "You have my word," Rice went on.
"As God is my witness. No one will fire a shot."

Lucas cocked his head to the left. He glanced
back at me. Then he walked toward the Day Room.

I started toward the baby and Nurse Vawn, then
realized they were indeed safe, not in spite of
Kathy's illness, but because of it. Her pathology
had embraced them. I turned and ran down the
hallway.

Fifteen

I made it to the door of the Day Room just in time to see Lucas walk through the rows of kneeling patients and hostages to the wall of windows. The ceaseless chanting, together with the lights flooding the building, could only fuel his delusion that he was about to shepherd his flock to the afterlife. He looked over the green, though I doubted he could make out anything in the glare.

"Your brother Michael is here to speak with you," Rice bellowed.

My heart began to race. Breathing became an act of will. Like most witnesses to a miracle, I told myself it couldn't be, even as the possibility filled me with hope and wonder. I moved past the patients and hostages to a window several feet from Lucas. I had to shield my eyes.

"Trevor, this is Michael," Lucas' brother began. Despite the PA system, his voice sounded tentative, almost shy. "I came from home to see you."

Lucas opened his eyes wider, staring directly into the blaze of light. He began to take deep breaths, arching his back to fill his lungs.

"I want you to come out of the building," Michael went on.

Lucas moved forward until he was nearly flush with the sheets of broken glass. He raised himself onto his toes.

I couldn't tell whether he was struggling to get a glimpse of Michael or getting up the nerve to jump. And I couldn't know whether his mind had begun to accept his brother as a human being or was still caught in webs of denial about a biblical guardian angel by the same name. I was afraid to say anything that might push him over the edge. I took a cautious step toward him and held out my hand.

Lucas stood motionless several seconds before turning around to face the patients and hostages. They fell silent. He glanced at me and smiled, but it was the vacant smile of an automaton. "Be at peace," he told the group. "The time has come for us to take our leave."

The patients stood up. They pulled the hostages to their feet. Zweig and the other two men took their places among them.

"Please come talk to me," Michael pleaded.

"Satan shall not inherit the earth," Lucas went on. "The Lord is God."

"The Lord is God," the patients echoed.

Lucas' voice built to a shout. "He maketh me to lie down in green pastures. He restoreth my soul.

Yea, though I walk through the valley of the shadow of death . . ."

Michael's voice over the PA system was still louder: "We've both been hurt enough. Please."

Rage surged in me. I made no attempt to contain it. I was out of time and out of strategy. "You'll go straight to hell!" I shouted.

Lucas jerked his head in my direction. His face was pure fury, but he looked at me askance, hardly making eye contact at all.

That subtle surrender of will was enough to make me roll the dice again. I stepped closer to him. "This is the moment you've been ranting about—the final battle for your soul. If you don't face up to your pain, if you project it onto your brother, then you're Satan's through and through. Michael will have to pay for your evil in this life. And if there's any justice, you'll pay for it in the next. Like every coward and fraud."

Lucas ducked for cover in the Bible. "Was Jesus a coward because he carried his own cross?" he said, his voice wafting high and low, as if he were reciting poetry. "Would you pillory him as you do me? Let he who is without sin among us cast the first—"

I stayed on the attack. "You're no Christ," I seethed. "You won't even face your own sins, let alone die for anyone else's. You want your brother to absorb your guilt while he watches you fall five stories. It wasn't enough you threw boiling oil on him and turned him into a freak."

"Stop!" Lucas screamed.

Zweig and two other patients stepped out of line and started toward me. I reached back and broke a shard of glass off the shattered pane behind me, holding it like a dagger at my side. I felt the edges cut into my palm. I transferred it to my other hand. It sliced me again. My fists grew warm and wet.

Zweig stopped coming forward and started to pace right and left, like a hungry lion stalking its prey. He drew a knife. The two other men stayed just behind him.

"Haven't you tortured Michael enough?" I peppered Lucas. "You never even went back to see if he was alive or dead in that godforsaken row house on Jasper Street. You hated him because he was your mother's 'sweet boy.' " I watched Zweig while I gave the words a few moments to sink in, then increased the pressure another notch. "You remember. 'Sweet boy.' She used to call out to him while you were locked in that cage in the basement. Cooped up like a dog."

"I don't . . ." Lucas started.

"You left him behind for her to feast on."

Zweig stopped pacing and stared at Lucas.

"I don't remember that," Lucas said softly.

I glanced back at him and lost my breath. Tears were streaming down his cheeks, turning the blood-red splotches on his scrub top pink in places. He looked baffled by his own grief.

The patients and hostages stood motionless, watching him.

He closed his eyes and shook his head, then squinted at the floor. The tears didn't stop. "I remember that cage." He finally raised his eyes to mine. "You say my brother is here to see me?"

I still couldn't be certain that Lucas was using the word *brother* in the biological, rather than spiritual, sense. But I wasn't certain it mattered. "Michael. He never forgot you. He came here from Baltimore." I felt as if I could push further. I pointed to the hostages. "These people have families, too."

Lucas' gaze traveled over the rows of patients and hostages.

"Shepherd them home," I said.

He turned to the wall of windows again.

I knew in my heart that Lucas was making his decision between life and death, between facing reality and literally flying in its face. Strange as it seemed to me, I knew I would forgive him if the rest of the truth was too much, if he couldn't bear to look upon Michael's face. Because the mind buries some traumas so deeply that the excavation is more torture than a person can stand. "You didn't mean to hurt him," I said, in case it was the last thing he heard. "It was an accident."

Several seconds passed. "Mr. Zweig," Lucas

said, without turning around. "Give Dr. Clevenger
your key." He waited another moment. "Bring me
to him, Frank," he said. "Bring me to this man you
call my brother."

Lucas released the four hostages who were well
enough to walk, along with Calvin Sanger. He left
Laura Elmonte where she lay. Despite my
protests, he insisted Kathy and his child remain in
the quiet room with Nurse Vawn. Then he had me
medicate the patients and lock them in their
rooms.

No one fought us, not even Zweig. No one
asked a question. Maybe dose after dose of
methadone had left them listless. Maybe the fever
pitch of violence on the unit had sated them.
Maybe neither. Lucas had an irresistible force of
his own. He had converted a ward of hopeless
cases into soldiers in a great war against the devil.
Caught in the drama of Lucas' psychosis they
were liberated from their own tortured minds,
allowed for a brief time to joust their demons, like
Don Quixote tall in the saddle, tilting at wind-
mills. To keep the wind through their hair a
moment longer, to keep denying that the monsters
were inside them, not in front of them, I believe
they would have played out any final scene for
Lucas—suicide, murder or surrender.

At 8:24 P.M. Lucas and I stood together, just

inside the sliding glass doors of the hospital. The green was lighted like a football stadium. In the glow, Lucas looked cadaverous. The yellowing stump of his right arm hung like a dead weight at his side. His lip twitched feverishly while he took in the scene—the M-1 tank, dozens of police cruisers, the Hummers outfitted with Gatling guns, Jersey barriers shielding at least fifty officers shouldering high-powered rifles, legions of reporters choking the perimeter road. The blades of the assault helicopter turned slowly, at the ready.

"Look at Satan's army," Lucas said. He shook his head. "So hungry to destroy us. They won't let us get five feet from the door."

Us. If I had any doubt how deep into Lucas' world I had traveled, that word erased it. I knew his dire prediction might be right, had known it ever since North Anderson warned me about friendly fire. With most of the hostages freed, Patterson and Rice were already heroes. They didn't need to take Lucas into custody or get me out of the hospital alive. Whether I took a bullet on the locked unit or on the green, I could be written off as a casualty of an assault on the building. I wouldn't rate two sound bites on New England Cable News. "Going back inside wouldn't stop them," I said. "Our only chance is to keep moving toward the truth, toward Michael."

Lucas looked down at his left arm.

I saw that his hand had begun to tremble. My stomach fell. The Marcaine was wearing off.

He looked out the doors again. "Michael," he whispered, not so much to me as to himself. He started forward.

I caught up with him. The doors slid open. A gush of icy air swept over us. We walked out into the light. The police aimed their rifles. Sharpshooters atop the State Police trailer knelt down. My eyes closed for an instant, but I forced them open and concentrated on keeping my legs moving—one foot, then the other, forward toward the past.

I noticed Lieutenant Patterson standing beside one of the Hummers. He had a clear shot at me if he wanted to take one.

When we had walked about ten yards, Michael, dressed in a brown barn jacket and jeans, emerged from the trailer and started toward us. Jack Rice appeared in the doorway. Then he stepped aside, and North Anderson joined him on the landing.

Shivers fanned over my back and up my neck. Anderson, himself an injured man, had brought Michael from Baltimore to Lynn. He had been the one to convince Michael to rise above his suffering, to try to heal his brother.

Lucas walked faster. I glanced at his hand, clenched into a fist.

Thirty seconds later Michael and Trevor Lucas stood in the center of the green, not five feet apart, staring at one another. Michael's layered flesh and patchwork hair still shocked me. I watched his eyes fall to Trevor's severed arm. Neither man spoke a word. I took a few steps back, to give them space to fuse the past with the present.

Trevor's arm rose slowly, fell, then rose again. His fist unfurled. His open hand trembled midair. Tears streamed down his cheek. He reached toward Michael's face.

Michael leaned back slightly so that Trevor's fingers just brushed his ragged skin. No one other than a burn victim really knows the horrors of melted flesh, but perhaps a plastic surgeon, perhaps a brother, can begin to understand.

"I'm sorry," Trevor said. "Please forgive . . ."

My eyes filled up. When a man finally embraces his pain he ennobles all of us.

Michael's deformed lip quivered. "I've tried," he said, his voice breaking. "I want you to know that."

Trevor hung his head.

The rest happened so quickly that my mind replays it in slow motion, going over it and over it and over it, sometimes in my sleep.

Michael reached behind his back. When his hand reappeared, it held a .44 Magnum. He aimed and fired.

The bullet blew off the right side of Trevor's face and the back of his skull. Blood sprayed over me. I fell to my knees next to him.

"Drop it," Patterson shouted.

Michael stood still, but held on to the gun. Another shot rang out. He crumbled to the frozen ground, a gaping hole through the base of his neck.

I looked up and saw a wisp of smoke drift from the muzzle of Patterson's rifle, still perched on his shoulder. He tilted his head away from the telescopic sight, smiled at me, then tilted his head back in line with it. I froze. He fired again. The bullet ripped into Michael's back. Patterson lowered the rifle. He raised his hand in the air and dropped it, signaling the other troopers to advance.

Hell broke loose. The Hummers scrambled over the green and perimeter road. The helicopter's blades whipped up to speed. The tank rolled forward, its gun craning skyward. What seemed like hundreds of figures in black stormed the building, some dropping from ropes on the roof, crashing through what was left of the windows.

Jack Rice and I stood together near the sliding glass doors of the hospital, waiting for the remaining hostages to be taken to safety. He'd gotten word on his walkie-talkie that the patients were found locked in their rooms. None of them had been harmed.

"You're a huge hero in this thing," Rice said. "You'll be flooded with cases. All over the country."

"I don't want another case," I said. "I'm through."

He looked at me with concern. "You say that now, but you'll be back. The phone will ring, and you'll answer. That's just the way it is."

I stayed silent.

Laura Elmonte, her chest still rising and falling almost imperceptibly, was wheeled out on a stretcher into a waiting ambulance. Nurse Vawn was next. Then I saw four troopers escorting Kathy down the corridor toward the lobby, Vawn's baby in her arms.

Rice had allowed a dozen television and newspaper photographers to record the moment. Their lenses spun in unison to focus on the scene. I knew all the horror of the last seventy-two hours would be distilled down to a few images. The obstetrician and the baby was sure to be one of them, partly because it spoke of life springing amidst death, partly because it would fit nicely on the front page of the *Boston Globe* and over the shoulder of Tom Brokaw on the *Evening News*.

As soon as Kathy walked into the night air she looked straight at me, let her eyes linger a moment, then looked away, giving me license to pretend I didn't know her, license to let her slip through the arms of the law again.

"There's your copycat killer," I said to Rice.

He whipped around. "What? What are you saying?"

"Singleton. You'll find her prints on the gun that killed Hancock and Trembley."

He squinted at me. "How can you know that?"

"Hancock and I were working the case," I said. "She had it solved."

Rice studied me several seconds, then waved to one of the troopers. He pointed at Kathy and grabbed each of his wrists, signaling for her to be cuffed.

I turned and walked away. I looked around the crowded green for North Anderson, but he was nowhere to be found. I climbed into my truck. The media was busy feeding on Kathy's arrest, so I had no trouble making my way off hospital grounds, down Jessup Lane and back to the Lynnway.

As I passed the right-hand turn to the Y, I thought fleetingly of Cynthia—that part of me still wanted to see her, that I ought to be able to forgive her. But I kept driving.

I had just made it home to my Chelsea loft when my body began detoxifying itself, shaking and sweating to reclaim its natural physiology. I lay down on my green velvet comforter and closed my eyes. Within an hour the symptoms of withdrawal had doubled. By midnight I was curled into a ball, my fists tight, my knuckles bloodless, my gut screaming.

The pain grew into something unspeakable, like some rabid beast ripping razor teeth into my flesh and soul at the same time, but I welcomed it, because I knew it was cleansing, and that it would end, and that, eventually, I would be restored.

By 4:00 A.M. my body was battered, my mind a haze. I had slept in ten-minute respites from violent cramps and fits of nausea. And now I could not sleep at all. The image of Trevor Lucas dead at my feet haunted me whenever I closed my eyes.

I stood up quickly, which was a mistake. The room whirled around me so wildly that I lost my balance and fell back to the mattress. I righted myself again, this time very slowly. The room turned wavy, but stayed in one place.

I showered and rubbed myself pink with a towel, but never managed to get dry. The sweat kept coming.

I called a taxi and waited outside in the dark.

A gnarled man seventy or older who had driven through the night told me I was his last delivery, corrected himself by grumbling the word _fare_, then asked where we were going.

"Mass. General Hospital."

"Emergency?"

Now I knew for certain that I looked as sick as I felt. "Main entrance."

We shot through the Sumner Tunnel into Boston, the driver humming a rising and falling tune as I hugged myself to keep from shaking.

I walked through the Mass. General lobby and took the elevator to the thirteenth floor of the

Blake Building. I had to hold up my medical
license at the door to Labor and Delivery to prove
I wasn't there to steal anyone's child.

I walked by the front desk. The ward clerk recognized me from television. "You're Dr. Clevenger," she said in that amazed way people react
when televised and real life intersect.

I nodded. My gut twisted, nearly doubling me
over.

"You're here to see the baby."

"Yes," I managed.

She escorted me down the hallway, stopping at
a wall of windows onto the nursery. A half-dozen
nurses tended to a dozen or more infants, some
lying in bassinets, others cradled into swings that
gently rose toward the window, then fell away.

"That's him," she said, pointing at a bassinet
that held a tiny baby swaddled in a white blanket
with pale blue stripes. His eyes were closed. His
breathing was peaceful. His delicate hand gripped
the edge of the blanket just under his chin.

"Does he have a name?"

"Isaac." Several seconds passed. "I have to get
back to the desk. You can stay as long as you
want."

I thanked her, and she walked away. Then I
stood there, watching Isaac, catching the reflection of my own tired, cut, unshaven face in the
glass from time to time. I shook my head at all the
things that can happen to break a man as he grows

up and away from the pure potential of infancy, all the things that had fractured inside me. And I prayed silently that this infant, born into chaos, might meet with kindness, experience joy and find passion in life.

Every one of us ought to be able to count on that much.

MURDER SUICIDE

Keith Ablow

John Snow is a brilliant inventor who has made millions from his genius in aeronautics. He has everything a man could desire: wealth, family, even a beautiful mistress. But he also has a brain disease, a rare form of epilepsy, that threatens his most valuable possession—his mind. Only one doctor may be able to cure it surgically, but at a terrible cost, one that Snow reveals to no one: Snow will have no memory whatsoever of his past—of its emotional entanglements or its secrets. The night before he is to enter the hospital, he is murdered. Forensic psychiatrist Dr. Frank Clevenger delves into Snow's complex past and tortured relationships to unlock the identity of Snow's killer: Was it the wife who can never forgive what he's done to their child, the son who loathes him, the beautiful mistress who takes pleasure in inflicting emotional cruelty, or the business partner who helped him build his fortune?

"Only Thomas Harris does it more stylishly."
—*Kirkus Reviews* on *Psychopath*

ISBN: 0-312-32389-1

Visit Keith Ablow's Web site at: www.keithablow.com

AVAILABLE WHEREVER BOOKS ARE SOLD
From St. Martin's Press

MS 01/04

Psychopath

KEITH ABLOW

Having achieved celebrity status with the handling of his last case, forensic psychiatrist Dr. Frank Clevenger is approached by the FBI in regards to The Highway Killer, an elusive murderer who has left a trail of twelve bodies in twelve states with no obvious link. But from the opening pages of *Psychopath*, the reader is privy to the killings and knows that the predator is Jonah, a prodigiously talented, and dedicated, psychiatrist who specializes in *locum tenens* work—temporary assignments to hospitals all over the country unable to support a full time psychiatrist. It is the perfect job for a serial killer. In an open letter to *The New York Times*, Jonah taunts and challenges Clevenger to catch him. Now Clevenger must embark on a bizarre kind of public therapy in which his goal is to stop the killings by either apprehending Jonah—or curing him. Using his brilliant mastery of the tools of psychiatry, Clevenger must match wits with a killer who knows all the tricks of the trade.

"Keith Ablow is king of the psychological thriller."
—Dennis Lehane, author of *Mystic River*

"Keith Ablow's setting is the darkest of all—the twists and turns of the human mind."
—Harlan Coben, author of *Gone for Good*

ISBN: 0-312-99605-5

AVAILABLE WHEREVER BOOKS ARE SOLD
FROM ST. MARTIN'S PAPERBACKS

COMPULSION
KEITH ABLOW

Burdened by his own psychological scars, brilliant forensic psychiatrist Dr. Frank Clevenger has weathered the most extreme twists of the human mind. Then he receives a disturbing call from Nantucket's Chief of Police. The five-month-old daughter of prominent billionaire, Darwin Bishop, has been found murdered in her crib. The obvious suspect is Darwin's adopted sociopathic son, Billy. Even Clevenger can't fathom the motive behind the troubled boy's murder of an infant. Falling for Julia is Clevenger's first mistake. Investigating the Bishops' twisted emotional landscape is his second. It's done more than just draw him into the maze of a psychosexual family history. It's trapped him. As his own demons rise to the surface, he must play the ultimate mind game to catch a killer—and make it out alive...

"FASCINATING."
—*The New York Times*

"A FIRST-RATE THRILLER."
—*Washington Post*

"MESMERIZING...TENSE AND SEXY."
—James W. Hall

ISBN: 0-312-98824-9

Visit Keith Ablow's Web site at: www.keithablow.com

AVAILABLE WHEREVER BOOKS ARE SOLD
From St. Martin's Paperbacks

COMP 01/04

DENIAL
KEITH ABLOW

When a young woman is discovered brutally murdered, her body mutilated, forensic psychiatrist Frank Clevenger is shocked to discover that he knows _____ friend of his girlfriend), and tha_____ main suspect, a schizophrenic ho_____ committed the crime. As evidenc_____ ders begins to mount over the _____ Clevenger must race to stop the _____ in the fight of his life against a _____ trademark…

"You can see why Ablow is cor_____
—*Entertainme*_____

"Spellbinding an_____
—Nelson DeMille

"Gripping."
—*People*

ISBN: 0-312-96596-6

**Available wherever books are sold
from St. Martin's Paperbacks**

Visit Keith Ablow's Web site at: www.keithablow.com